Alfred Hitchcock was born in London in 1899. Now the most celebrated master of suspense in motion pictures, he started his career as an assistant layout man in advertising. Soon afterwards, however, he won a job as title writer with Famous-Players–Lasky – now Paramount – and from 1925 onwards his career was meteoric. His television show *Alfred Hitchcock Presents* was enormously successful both here and in America.

Alfred Hitchcock Presents

STORIES TO
STAY AWAKE BY

Book Two

Pan Books London and Sydney

Books One and Two originally published in
one volume as *Alfred Hitchcock Presents
Stories to Stay Awake By*
First published in Great Britain 1971 by
Max Reinhardt Ltd
This edition published 1975 by Pan Books Ltd,
Cavaye Place, London SW10 9PG
© Random House Inc 1971
ISBN 0 330 24607 0

The editor gratefully acknowledges the
invaluable assistance of Harold Q. Masur
in the preparation of this volume

Made and printed in Great Britain by
Richard Clay (The Chaucer Press) Ltd, Bungay, Suffolk

Contents

Acknowledgements

A FELINE FELONY, by Lael J. Littke, is reprinted by permission of Larry Sternig Literary Agency. Copyright © 1967 by Davis Publications Inc. First published in *Ellery Queen's Mystery Magazine*.

THE HOMESICK BUICK, by John D. MacDonald, is reprinted by permission of Max Wilkinson Associates. Copyright 1950 by John D. MacDonald. First published in *Ellery Queen's Mystery Magazine*.

CAMPAIGN FEVER, by Patricia McGerr, is reprinted by permission of Curtis Brown Ltd. Copyright © 1964 by This Week Magazine Inc.

RUN WITH THE WIND, by James McKimmey, is reprinted by permission of A. D. Peters and Company. Copyright © 1970 by James McKimmey. First published in *Alfred Hitchcock's Mystery Magazine*.

SQUEAKIE'S SECOND CASE, by Margaret Manners, is reprinted by permission of the author. First published in *Ellery Queen's Mystery Magazine*.

THE SILENT BUTLER, by Harold Q. Masur, is reprinted by permission of the author.

MCGOWNEY'S MIRACLE, by Margaret Millar, is reprinted by permission of Harold Ober Associates Incorporated. Copyright 1954 by The Hearst Corporation.

TEN MINUTES FROM NOW, by Jack Ritchie, is reprinted by permission of Larry Sternig Literary Agency. Copyright © 1963 by HSD Publications Inc. First published in *Alfred Hitchcock's Mystery Magazine*.

SEE AND TELL, by Mary Linn Roby, is reprinted by permission of the author and her agent, Scott Meredith Literary Agency Inc, 580 Fifth Avenue, New York, NY 10036.

FAIR'S FAIR, by Jane Speed, is reprinted by permission of the author. Copyright © 1966 by Davis Publications Inc. First published in *Ellery Queen's Mystery Magazine*.

THE DOE AND THE GANTLET, by Pat Stadley, is reprinted by permission of Larry Sternig Literary Agency. Copyright © 1957 by Mercury Publications Inc. First published in *Ellery Queen's Mystery Magazine*.

THE LAST DAY OF ALL, by Fay Grissom Stanley, is reprinted by permission of the author.

THE NAIL AND THE ORACLE, by Theodore Sturgeon, is reprinted by permission of Robert P. Mills.

DOCTOR'S ORDERS, by John F. Suter, is reprinted by permission of the author. Copyright © 1969 by Davis Publications Inc (formerly Mercury Publications Inc). First published in *Ellery Queen's Mystery Magazine*.

THE MAN WHO LAUGHS AT LIONS, by Bryce Walton, is reprinted by permission of the author and his agent, Campbell Thompson & McLaughlin Ltd. Copyright © 1964 by Davis Publications Inc. First published in *Ellery Queen's Mystery Magazine*.

THE UNSUSPECTED, by Jay Wilson, is reprinted by permission of Curtis Publishing. Copyright © 1958 by the Saturday Evening Post.

Introduction

In previous anthologies I have often begun my introduction with the words 'Good evening'. In all good conscience I cannot do that now.

I believe that such a greeting would be highly inappropriate. The contents of this volume are designed to give you a bad evening. A very bad evening indeed. And perhaps an even worse night. Not in any sense of dissatisfaction with the product herein. If you are an adventurous soul you have sampled my wares before. It will be a bad evening in the sense of wakefulness and delicious nightmare.

Now, that phrase – delicious nightmare – may sound like a contradiction of terms. Perhaps it is. Then again, perhaps not. A very large segment of the species *anthropos* revels in just such a sensation. I know. For many years, purveying the ingredients of macabre enjoyment has been my livelihood and my pleasure.

You may of course induce an equivalent insomnia by consuming large quantities of pickles, ice cream, caviare and pastrami just before retiring. A quick glance at my silhouette may lead you to assume that this is a method I adopt. On that, I stand mute. In any event, I do not recommend it. The induced nightmare is delicious only in the transitory sense of taste. I can assure you that the after-effect of such over-indulgence is acute discomfort.

On the other hand, the stories in this volume will produce no such effect. They may indeed keep you awake. They may chill you. They may set you to trembling. But you will remember them with pleasure.

I am not certain of the reason for this. They tell me that we are descended from some marauding prehistoric monster. Perhaps so. I am not an anthropologist. But I do know that now, in the twentieth century, if a man wants to stay out of jail, he must satisfy his primitive instincts in a more civilized manner. And to me the most civilized is reading. That is the purpose of this book. So if you are a timid soul, you will find *The Bobbsey Twins* at the library.

If you enjoy tingling excitement, lock the doors, lock the windows, turn the page, and begin.

ALFRED HITCHCOCK

A Feline Felony

LAEL J. LITTKE

Jerome Kotter looked like a cat. However, this did not bring him any undue attention from his schoolmates since almost all of them had an unusual quality or two. Beverly Baumgartner had a laugh like a horse. Bart Hansen was as rotund as an elephant. Carla Seaver's long neck resembled that of a giraffe. And Randy Ramsbottom always smelled remarkably like a dog on a rainy day.

The only person who worried about Jerome's unusual appearance was his father, who quietly set about arming his son to face a world in which he was a bit different. He taught Jerome gentle manners, assuring him that no matter how different he looked he would always get along fine if he acted right. He taught him to recite all the verses of *The Star-Spangled Banner* by heart. He encouraged him to read the Bible. And he taught him to sing the songs from the best-known Gilbert and Sullivan operettas. He felt Jerome was well equipped to face the world.

When Jerome got to high school he became the greatest track star that Quigley High had ever produced, although he had to be careful because the coaches from rival schools cried foul when Jerome resorted to running on all fours.

Altogether, Jerome's school years would have been quite happy – if it hadn't been for Benny Rhoades.

Whereas Jerome was tall, polite, studious, and well groomed with silken fur and sparkling whiskers, Benny was wizened, unkempt, rude, and sly. His face was pinched and pointed and his hair stuck up in uneven wisps. He hated anyone who excelled him in anything. Almost everybody excelled him in everything, and since Jerome surpassed him in the one thing he did do fairly well – running – he hated Jerome most of all. When Jerome took away his title of champion runner of Quigley High, Benny vowed he would get even if it took him the rest of his life.

One of Benny's favourite harassments was to tread on Jerome's tail in study hall, causing him to yeowl and thereby incurring the wrath of the monitor. Benny tweaked Jerome's whiskers and poured honey on his fur. He did everything he could think of to make Jerome's life miserable.

When it came to Benny Rhoades, Jerome found it hard to follow the admonitions of his father – that he should love his enemies and do good even to those who used him spitefully. He looked forward to the day when he would finish school and get away, for he had to admit in his heart that he loathed the odious Benny. It rankled him to think that Benny was the only person who could make him lose his composure and caterwaul in public, thus making people notice that despite his suave manner and intellectual conversation he was a bit different. To keep his temper he took to declaiming *The Star-Spangled Banner* or passages from the Bible. Once he got all the way through the 'begats' in Genesis before he took hold of himself and regained his composure.

Just before Jerome was graduated from college, Benny stole all the fish from Old Man Walker's little fish cart and deposited them in Jerome's car, after which he made an anonymous phone call to the police. The police, who had always regarded Jerome as the embodiment of what they would like all young men to be, preferred to believe his claim of innocence; but then again, looking as he did, it was natural for them to believe that he might have swiped a mess of fish.

People began to whisper about Jerome when he passed on the street. They pointed out that although his manners were perfect, he did have those long swordlike claws, and they certainly wouldn't want to be caught alone with him in an alley on a dark night. And wasn't there a rather feline craftiness in his slanted eyes?

Jerome left town after graduation enveloped in an aura of suspicion and an aroma of rotting fish which he never could dispel completely from his car.

Jerome decided to pursue a career as a writer of advertising copy in New York, reasoning that what with all the strange creatures roaming about in that city no one was apt to notice anything a bit different about him. He was hired at the first place he applied, Bobble, Babble and Armbruster, Inc, on Madison Avenue. Mr Armbruster had been out celebrating his fourteenth wedding anniversary the night before and had imbibed himself into near oblivion trying to forget what devastation those fourteen years had wrought. When Jerome walked into his office he naturally figured him to be related to the ten-foot polka-dot cobra that had pursued him the night before and thought he would fade with the hangover. After ducking behind his desk for a little hair-of-the-dog, he hired Jerome. By the time Mr Armbruster had fully recovered from his celebration, Jerome had proved himself capable at his job and affable with the other employees, so he was allowed to stay. Mr Armbruster naturally put him on the cat-food account.

Before long Jerome fell in love with his secretary, Marie, a shapely blonde, who thought Jerome's sleek fur and golden eyes sexy. He wanted to ask her for a date, but first, in all fairness, he thought he should find out how she felt about him.

'Marie,' he said one day as he finished the day's dictation, 'do you like me as a boss?'

'Oh, yes,' breathed Marie. 'Gee, Mr Kotter, you're the swellest boss I ever had. You're so different.'

Jerome's heart sank. 'Different? In what way, Marie?'

'Well,' said Marie, 'Mr Leach, my old boss, used to pinch me sometimes. And he used to sneak up behind me and kiss me.' She peered coyly at Jerome from under her lashes.

'You're a perfect gentleman, Mr Krotter. You're real different.'

Jerome was enchanted and wasted no further time asking her out to dinner.

For several weeks everything was wonderful. Then, unexpectedly, Benny Rhoades turned up. Jerome looked up from his desk one day to see his nemesis standing in the doorway.

'Man,' said Benny, 'if it ain't Jerome Kotter.' He grinned.

'Benny Rhoades,' exclaimed Jerome. 'What are you doing here?'

'Man, you're the most,' said Benny softly. 'I work in the mail room, man. You're gonna see a lot of me, Jerome.'

Jerome's tail twitched.

'Why did you come here?' he asked. 'Why don't you leave me alone?'

Offended innocence replaced the calculating look on Benny's pasty face.

'Why, man, I ain't done a thing. A man's got to work. And I work here.' He lounged against the door jamb. 'I hear you're a real swingin' cat around here. I wonder how long that's gonna last.'

'Get out,' said Jerome.

'Sure, Mr Kotter, sir. Sure. Think I'll drop by your secretary's desk. Quite a dish, that Marie.'

'You stay away from her.' Jerome could feel the fur around his neck rising. His whiskers bristled.

Benny smiled and glided away like an insidious snake.

From that time on Benny did what he could to torment Jerome. He held up his mail until important clients called the bosses to complain about lack of action on their accounts. He slammed Jerome's tail in doors, usually when some VIP was visiting the office. Worst of all, he vexed Marie by hanging around her desk asking for dates and sometimes sneaked up to nibble at her neck. Marie hated him almost as much as Jerome did.

Jerome didn't know quite what he could do about it without jeopardizing his job, of which he had become very fond. The other people at the agency liked him, although they regarded him as a trifle eccentric since he always insisted on sampling the cat food he wrote about. But then everyone to his own tastes, they said.

Things came to a head one evening when Jerome invited Marie to his apartment for a fish dinner before going out to a show. They were just sitting down to eat when the doorbell rang.

It was Benny.

'Cosy,' he murmured, surveying the scene. He slammed the door shut behind him.

'A real swingin' cat,' he said, sidling into the room. He produced a small pistol from his pocket.

'Are you out of your mind, Benny?' said Jerome. 'What do you think you're doing?'

'I lost my job,' smiled Benny.

'What's that got to do with me?'

'Marie complained that I bothered her. They fired me.' Benny's small eyes glittered. 'I'll repay her for the favour, then I'll take care of you, Jerome. I'll fix it so they'll think you shot her for resisting your charms, and then shot yourself. Everybody knows a big cat like you could go berserk anytime.'

'You're a rat,' said Marie. 'You're a miserable, black-hearted little rat.'

Jerome stepped protectively in front of her.

'Sticks and stones may break my bones but names will never hurt me,' chanted Benny gleefully.

Jerome was looking at Benny thoughtfully. 'A rat,' he said. 'That's what he is. A rat. Funny it never occurred to me before.' His tail twitched nervously.

Benny didn't like the look on Jerome's face. 'Stay away from me, man. I'll shoot.'

Before Benny could aim, Jerome leaped across the room with the swift, fluid motion of a tiger. He knocked Benny to the floor and easily took the gun from him.

'A rat,' repeated Jerome softly.

Benny looked at Jerome's face so close to his own. 'What are you going to do?' he squeaked, his own face pinched and white and his beady eyes terror-stricken. 'What are you going to do?'

Jerome ate him.

It took a long time to get the police sergeant to take the matter seriously. Marie had urged Jerome to forget the whole thing, but Jerome felt he must confess.

'You say you ate this guy Benny?' the sergeant asked for the twentieth time.

'I ate him,' said Jerome.

'He was a rat,' said Marie.

The sergeant shook his head. 'We get all kinds,' he muttered. 'Go home. Sleep it off.' He sighed. 'Self-defence, you say?'

'Benny was going to shoot both of us,' said Marie.

'Where's the body?' asked the sergeant.

Jerome shook his head. 'There is no body. I ate him.'

'He was a rat,' said Marie.

'There's no body,' said the sergeant. 'We sent a coupla men up to your apartment and there's no body and no sign of anybody getting killed. We even called this Benny's family long distance to find out if they knew where he is, but his old man said as far as they are concerned he died at birth. So go home.'

'I ate him,' insisted Jerome.

'So you performed a public service. I got six kids to support, buddy. I don't want to spend the next two years on a head-shrinker's couch for trying to make the Chief believe I got a six-foot cat here who ate a guy. Now go home, you two, before I get mad.'

Jerome remained standing in front of the desk.

'Look,' said the sergeant. 'You ate a guy.'

'A rat,' corrected Marie.

'A rat,' said the sergeant. 'So how do you feel?'

'Terrible,' said Jerome. 'I have a most remarkable case of indigestion.'

'You ate a rat,' said the sergeant. 'Now you've got a belly-ache. That's your punishment. Remember when you ate green apples as a kid?' He sighed. 'Now go home.'

As they turned to leave, Jerome heard the sergeant muttering to himself about not having had a vacation in four years.

Despite his indigestion, Jerome felt marvellous. 'Let the punishment fit the crime,' he said with satisfaction. He took Marie's arm in a courtly fashion and sang softly as they walked along. 'My object all sublime, I shall achieve in time, to let the punishment fit the crime, the punishment fit the crime . . .'

'Gee, Mr Kotter,' said Marie, gazing up at him in admiration. 'You're so different from anyone else I ever went with.'

'Different?' asked Jerome. 'How, Marie?'

'Gee,' said Marie, 'I never went out before with anybody who quoted poetry.'

The Devil-Dog

JACK LONDON

Bâtard was a devil. This was recognized throughout the Northland. 'Hell's Spawn' he was called by many men, but his master, Black Leclère, chose for him the shamename 'Bâtard'.

Now Black Leclère was also a devil, and the twain were well matched. There is a saying that when two devils come together, hell is to pay. This is to be expected, and this certainly was to be expected when Bâtard and Black Leclère came together. The first time they met, Bâtard was a part-grown puppy, lean and hungry, with bitter eyes; and they met with snap and snarl and wicked looks, for Leclère's upper lip had a wolfish way of lifting and showing the white, cruel teeth. And it lifted then, and his eyes glinted viciously as he reached for Bâtard and dragged him out from the squirming litter. It was certain that they divined each other, for on the instant Bâtard had buried his puppy fangs in Leclère's hand, and Leclère, with thumb and finger, was coolly choking his young life out of him.

'*Sacredam*,' the Frenchman said softly, flirting the quick blood from his bitten hand and gazing down on the little puppy choking and gasping in the snow.

Leclère turned to John Hamlin, storekeeper of the Sixty Mile Post. 'Dat fo' w'at Ah lak heem, 'Ow moch, eh, you, *M'sieu*? 'Ow much? Ah buy heem, now – Ah buy heem quick.'

And because he hated him with an exceeding bitter hate Leclère bought Bâtard and gave him his shameful name. And for five years the twain adventured across the Northland, from St Michael's and the Yukon delta to the head reaches of the Pelly and even so far as the Peace River, Athabasca, and the Great Slave. And they acquired a reputation for uncompromising wickedness, the like of which never before attached itself to man and dog.

Bâtard did not know his father – hence his name – but, as John Hamlin knew, his father was a great grey timber wolf. But the mother of Bâtard, as he dimly remembered her, was snarling, bickering, husky, full-fronted, and heavy-chested, with a malign eye, a catlike grip on life, and a genius for trickery and evil. There was neither faith nor trust in her. Her treachery alone could be relied upon, and her wildwood amours attested her general depravity. Much of evil and much of strength were there in these, Bâtard's progenitors, and bone and flesh of their bone and flesh, he had inherited it all. And then came Black Leclère, to lay his heavy hand on the bit of pulsating puppy life, to press and prod and mould till it became a big bristling beast, acute in knavery, overspilling with hate, sinister, malignant and diabolical. With a proper master Bâtard might have made an ordinary, fairly efficient sled-dog. He never got the chance: Leclère but confirmed him in his congenital iniquity.

The history of Bâtard and Leclère is a history of war – of five cruel, relentless years, of which their first meeting is fit summary. To begin with, it was Leclère's fault, for he hated with understanding and intelligence, while the long-legged, ungainly puppy hated only blindly, instinctively, without reason or method. At first there were no refinements of cruelty (these were to come later), but simple beatings and crude brutalities. In one of these Bâtard had an ear injured. He never regained control of the riven muscles, and ever after, the ear drooped limply down to keep keen the memory of his tormentor. And he never forgot.

His puppyhood was a period of foolish rebellion. He was

always worsted, but he fought back because it was his nature to fight back. And he was unconquerable. Yelping shrilly from the pain of lash and club, he nonetheless contrived always to throw in the defiant snarl, the bitter vindictive menace of his soul which fetched without fail more blows and beatings. But his was his mother's tenacious grip on life. Nothing could kill him. He flourished under misfortune, grew fat with famine, and out of his terrible struggle for life developed a preternatural intelligence. His were the stealth and cunning of the husky, his mother, and the fierceness and valour of the wolf, his father.

Possibly it was because of his father that he never wailed. His puppy yelps passed with his lanky legs, so that he became grim and taciturn, quick to strike, slow to warn. He answered curse with snarl, and blow with snap, grinning the while his implacable hatred; but never again, under the extremest agony, did Leclère bring from him the cry of fear nor of pain. This unconquerableness merely fanned Leclère's wrath and stirred him to greater devilries.

Men and dogs looked askance at Bâtard when he drifted into their camps and posts. The men greeted him with feet threateningly lifted for the kick, the dogs with bristling manes and bared fangs. Once a man did kick Bâtard, and Bâtard, with quick wolf snap, closed his jaws like a steel trap on the man's calf and crunched down to the bone. Whereat the man was determined to have his life, only Black Leclère, with ominous eyes and naked hunting-knife, stepped in between. The killing of Bâtard – ah, *sacredam*, that was a pleasure Leclère reserved for himself.

They had become problems to each other. The very breath each drew was a challenge and a menace to the other. Their hate bound them together as love could never bind. Leclère was bent on the coming of the day when Bâtard should wilt in spirit, and cringe and whimper at his feet. And Bâtard – Leclère knew what was in Bâtard's mind, and more than once had read it in Bâtard's eyes. And so clearly had he read it that when Bâtard was at his back he made it a point to glance often over his shoulder.

Men marvelled when Leclère refused large sums of money for the dog. 'Someday you'll kill him and be out his price,' said John Hamlin once, when Bâtard lay panting in the snow where Leclère had kicked him, and no one knew whether his ribs were broken, and no one dared look to see.

'Dat,' said Leclère, dryly, 'dat is my biz'ness, M'sieu'.'

And the men marvelled that Bâtard did not run away. They did not understand. But Leclère understood. To him Bâtard spoke clear and direct. Full well he understood why Bâtard did not run away, and he glanced more often over his shoulder.

When in anger, Bâtard was not nice to look upon, and more than once had he leaped for Leclère's throat, only to be stretched quivering and senseless in the snow by the butt of the ever-ready dogwhip. And so Bâtard learned to bide his time. When he reached his full strength and prime of youth, he thought the time had come. He was broad-chested, power-fully muscled, of far more than ordinary size, and his neck from head to shoulders was a mass of bristling hair – to all appearances a full-blooded wolf. Leclère was lying asleep in his furs. Bâtard crept upon him stealthily, head low to earth and lone ear laid back, with a feline softness of tread. Bâtard breathed gently, very gently and not till he was close did he raise his head. He paused for a moment and looked at the bronzed bull-throat, naked and knotty, swelling to a deep and steady pulse. The slaver dripped down his fangs and slid off his tongue at the sight. Without a sound he sprang on the sleeping man.

Leclère awoke to the fangs in his throat; and, perfect animal that he was, he awoke clear-headed and with full comprehension. He closed on Bâtard's windpipe with both his hands and rolled out of his furs to get his weight uppermost. But thousands of Bâtard's ancestors had clung at the throats of un-numbered moose and caribou and dragged them down, and the wisdom of those ancestors was his. When Leclère's weight came on top of him, he drove his hind legs upward and in, and clawed down chest and abdomen, ripping and tearing through skin and muscle. And when he felt the man's body wince above him and lift, he worried and shook at the man's throat. His team-mates closed around in a snarling circle. Bâtard with failing breath and fading sense, knew that their jaws were hungry for him. But that did not matter – it was the man, the man above him, and he ripped and clawed and shook and worried to the last ounce of his strength. But Leclère choked him with both his hands till Bâtard's chest heaved and writhed for the air denied to him, and his eyes glazed and set, his jaws slowly loosened, and his tongue protruded black and swollen.

'Eh? *Bon*, you devil!' Leclère gurgled, mouth and throat clogged with his own blood, as he shoved the dizzy dog from him.

And then Leclère cursed the other dogs off as they fell upon Bâtard. They drew back into a wider circle, squatting alertly on their haunches and licking their chops, the hair on every neck bristling and erect.

Bâtard recovered quickly. He tottered to his feet and swayed weakly back and forth.

'A-a-ah! You beeg devil!' Leclère spluttered. 'Ah fix you – Ah fix you plentee, by Gar!'

Bâtard, the air biting into his exhausted lungs like wine, flashed full into the man's face, his jaws missing and coming together with a metallic clip. They rolled over and over on the snow, Leclère striking madly with his fists. Then they separated, face to face, and circled back and forth before each other. Leclère could have drawn his knife. His rifle was at his feet. But the beast in him was up and raging. He would do the thing with his hands – and his teeth. Bâtard sprang in. Leclère knocked him over with a blow of the fist, fell upon him, and buried his teeth to the bone in the dog's shoulder. Then Leclère leaped upon the wolf-dog with his feet, and sprang up and down, striving to grind him into the earth. Both Bâtard's hind legs were broken before Leclère stopped for breath.

'A-a-ah! A-a-ah!' Leclère screamed, incapable of speech, shaking his fist, through sheer impotence of throat and larynx.

But Bâtard was indomitable. He lay there in a helpless welter, his lip feebly lifting and writhing to the snarl he had not the strength to utter. Leclère kicked him again, and the tired jaws closed on the ankle, but could not break the skin.

Then Leclère picked up the whip and proceeded almost to cut Bâtard to pieces, at each stroke of the lash crying: 'Dis taim Ah break you! Eh? By Gar, Ah break you!'

In the end, exhausted, fainting from loss of blood, he crumpled and fell by his victim. But when the wolf-dogs closed in to take their vengeance, Leclère with his last consciousness dragged his body over Bâtard's to shield him.

This occurred not far from Sunrise, and the missionary, opening the door to Leclère a few hours later, was surprised to note the absence of Bâtard from the team. Nor did his surprise lessen when Leclère threw back the robes from the sled, gathered Bâtard into his arms and staggered across the threshold. It happened that the surgeon of McQuestion, who was something of a gadabout, was up on a gossip, and between them they proceeded to repair Leclère.

'Merci, non,' he said. 'Do you fix firs' de dog. To die? Non. Eet is not good. Becos' heem Ah mus' yet break. Dat fo' w'at he mus' not die.'

The surgeon called it a marvel, the missionary a miracle, that Leclère pulled through at all; and so weakened was he that in the spring the fever got him, and he went on his back again. Bâtard had been in even worse plight, but his grip on life prevailed, and the bones of his hind legs knit, and his organs righted themselves, during the several weeks he lay strapped to the floor. By the time Leclère, finally convalescent, sallow and shaky, took the sun by the cabin door, Bâtard had reasserted his supremacy among his kind, and brought not only his own team-mates but the missionary's dogs into subjection.

He moved never a muscle, nor twitched a hair, when for the first time Leclère tottered out on the missionary's arm, and sank with infinite caution on to the stool.

'*Bon!*' he said. '*Bon!* De good sun!' And he stretched out his wasted hands and washed them in the warmth.

Then his gaze fell on the dog, and the old light blazed back in his eyes. He touched the missionary lightly on the arm. '*Mon père*, dat is one beeg devil, dat Bâtard. You will bring me one pistol, so, dat Ah drink de sun in peace.'

And thenceforth for many days he sat in the sun before the cabin door. He never dozed, and the pistol lay always across his knees. Bâtard had a way, the first thing each day, of looking for the weapon in its wonted place. At sight of it he would lift his lip faintly in token that he understood, and Leclère would lift his own lip in an answering grin. One day the missionary took note of the trick.

'Bless me!' he said. 'I really believe the brute comprehends.'

Leclère laughed softly. 'Look you, *mon père*. Dat w'at Ah now spik, to dat does he lissen.'

As if in confirmation, Bâtard just perceptibly wriggled his lone ear up to catch the sound.

'Ah say "keel".'

Bâtard growled deep down in his throat, the hair bristled along his neck and every muscle went tense and expectant.

'Ah lift de gun, so, like dat.' And suiting action to word, he sighted the pistol at Bâtard.

Bâtard, with a single leap sideways, landed around the corner of the cabin out of sight.

'Bless me!' the missionary repeated at intervals.

Leclère grinned proudly.

'But why does he not run away?'

The Frenchman's shoulders went up in the racial shrug that means all things from total ignorance to infinite understanding.

'Then why do you not kill him?'

Again the shoulders went up.

'*Mon père*,' he said after a pause, 'de taim is not yet. He is one beeg devil. Some taim Ah break heem, so, an' so, all to leetle bits. Hey? Some taim. *Bon!*'

A day came when Leclère gathered his dogs together and floated down in a bateau to Forty Mile, and on to the Porcupine, where he took a commission from the P.C. Company and went exploring for the better part of a year. After that he poled up the Koyokuk to deserted Arctic City, and later came drifting back, from camp to camp, along the Yukon. And during the long months Bâtard was well lessoned. He learned many tortures, notably the torture of hunger, the torture of thirst, the torture of fire and, worst of all, the torture of music.

Like the rest of his kind, he did not enjoy music. It gave him exquisite anguish, racking him nerve by nerve, and ripping apart every fibre of his being. Leclère, on the other hand, passionately loved music – as passionately as he loved strong drink. And when his soul clamoured for expression, it usually uttered itself in one or the other of the two ways, and more usually in both. And when he had drunk, his brain a-lilt with unsung song and the devil in him aroused and rampant, his soul found its supreme utterance in torturing Bâtard.

'Now we will haf a leetle museek,' he would say. 'Eh? W'at you t'ink, Bâtard?'

It was only an old and battered harmonica, tenderly treasured and patiently repaired; but out of its silver reeds he drew weird vagrant airs. Then Bâtard, dumb of throat, with teeth tight clenched, would back away, inch by inch, to the farthest cabin corner. And Leclère, playing, playing, a stout club tucked under his arm, followed the animal up, inch by inch, step by step, till there was no further retreat.

At first Bâtard would crowd himself into the smallest possible space, grovelling close to the floor; but as the music came nearer and nearer, he was forced to uprear, his back jammed into the logs, his forelegs fanning the air as though to beat off the rippling waves of sound. He still kept his teeth together, but severe muscular contractions attacked his body till he was all aquiver and writhing in silent torment. As he lost control, his jaws spasmodically wrenched apart, and deep throaty vibrations issued forth, too low in the register of sound for human ears to catch. And then, nostrils distended, eyes dilated, hair bristling in helpless rage, arose the long wolf howl. It came with a slurring rush upward, swelling to a great heart-breaking burst of sound, and dying away in sadly cadenced woe – then the next rush upward, octave upon octave; the bursting heart; and the infinite sorrow and misery, fainting, fading, falling, and dying slowly away.

It was fit for hell. And Leclère, with fiendish ken, seemed to divine each particular nerve and heart-string, and with long wails and tremblings and sobbing minors to make it yield up its last shred of grief. It was frightful, and for twenty-four hours after, Bâtard was nervous and unstrung, starting at common sounds, tripping over his own shadow, but, withal, vicious and masterful with his team-mates. But no sign did he show of a breaking spirit. Rather he grew more grim and taciturn, biding his time with an inscrutable patience that began to puzzle and weigh upon Leclère. The dog would lie in the firelight, motionless, for hours, gazing straight before him at Leclère, and hating him with his bitter eyes.

But all bad things come to an end, and so with Black Leclère. On the summer-low water, in a poling boat, he left McDougall for Sunrise. He left McDougall in company with Timothy Brown, and he arrived at Sunrise by himself. Further, it was known that they had quarrelled just previous to pulling out; for the *Lizzie*, a wheezy ten-ton sternwheeler, twenty-four hours behind, beat Leclère in by three days. And when he did get in, it was with a clean-drilled bullet-hole through his shoulder muscle, and a tale of ambush and murder.

A strike had been made at Sunrise, and things had changed considerably. With the infusion of several hundred gold-seekers, a deal of whisky, and half a dozen equipped gamblers, the missionary had seen the page of his years of labour with the Indians wiped clean. He took to his bed, said 'Bless me' several times, and departed to his final accounting in a rough-hewn, oblong box. Whereupon the gamblers moved their roulette and faro tables into the mission house, and the click of chips and clink of glasses went up from dawn till dark and to dawn again.

Now, Timothy Brown was well beloved among these adventurers of the north. The one thing against him was his quick temper and ready fist – a little thing, for which his kind heart and forgiving hand more than atoned. On the other hand, there was nothing to atone for Black Leclère. He was 'black', as more than one remembered deed bore witness, while he was as well hated as the other was beloved. So the men of Sunrise put an antiseptic dressing on his shoulder and hauled him before Judge Lynch.

It was a simple affair. He had quarrelled with Timothy Brown at McDougall. With Timothy Brown he had left McDougall. Without Timothy Brown he had arrived at Sunrise. Considered in the light of his wickedness, the unanimous conclusion was that he had killed Timothy Brown. On the other hand, Leclère acknowledged their facts but challenged their conclusion, and gave his own explanation. Twenty miles out of Sunrise he and Timothy Brown were poling the boat along the rocky shore. From that shore two rifle shots rang out. Timothy Brown pitched out of the boat and went down bubbling red, and that was the last of Timothy Brown. He, Leclère, pitched into the bottom of the boat with a stinging shoulder. He lay very quiet, peeping at the shore. After a time two Indians stuck up their heads and came out to the water's edge, carrying between them a birchbark canoe. As they launched it, Leclère let fly. He potted one, who went over the side after the manner of Timothy Brown. The other dropped into the bottom of the canoe, and then canoe and poling boat went down the stream in a drifting battle. After that they hung up on a split current, and the canoe passed on one side of an island, the poling boat on the other. That was the last of the canoe, and he came on into Sunrise. Yes, from the way the Indian in the canoe jumped, he was sure he had potted him. That was all.

This explanation was not deemed adequate. They gave him ten hours' grace while the *Lizzie* steamed down to investigate. Ten hours later she came wheezing back to Sunrise. There had been nothing to investigate. No evidence had been found to back up his statements. They told him to make his will, for he possessed a fifty-thousand-dollar Sunrise claim, and they were a law-abiding as well as a law-giving breed.

Leclère shrugged his shoulders. 'Bot one t'ing,' he said; 'a leetle, w'at you call, favour – a leetle favour, dat is eet. I gif my feefty t'ousan' dollair to de church. I gif my husky dog, Bâtard, to de devil. De leetle favour? Firs' you hang heem, an' den you hang me. Eet is good, eh?'

Good it was, they agreed, that Hell's Spawn should break trail for his master across the last divide, and the court was adjourned down to the river bank, where a big spruce tree stood by itself. Slackwater Charley put a hangman's knot in the end of a hauling-line, and the noose was slipped over Leclère's head and pulled tight around his neck. His hands were tied behind his back, and he was assisted to the top of a cracker box. Then the running end of the line was passed over an overhanging branch, drawn taut, and made fast. To kick the box out from under would leave him dancing on the air.

'Now for the dog,' said Webster Shaw, sometime mining engineer. 'You'll have to rope him, Slackwater.'

Leclère grinned. Slackwater took a chew of tobacco, rove a running noose, and proceeded leisurely to coil a few turns in his hand. He paused once or twice to brush particularly offensive mosquitoes from his face. Everybody was brushing mosquitoes except Leclère, about whose head a small cloud was visible. Even Bâtard, lying full-stretched on the ground, rubbed the pests away from eyes and mouth with his forepaws.

But while Slackwater waited for Bâtard to lift his head, a

faint call came down the quiet air, and a man was seen waving his arms and running across the flat from Sunrise. It was the storekeeper.

'C-call 'er off, boys,' he panted, as he came in among them.

'Little Sandy and Bernadotte's jes' got in,' he explained with returning breath. 'Landed down below an' come up by the short cut. Got the Beaver with 'em. Picked 'm up in his canoe, stuck in a back channel, with a couple of bullet holes in 'm. Other buck was Klok-Kutz, the one that knocked spots out of his squaw and dusted.'

'Eh? W'at Ah say? Eh?' Leclère cried exultantly. 'Dat de one fo' sure! Ah know. Ah spik true.'

'The thing to do is teach these damned Siwashes a little manners,' spoke Webster Shaw. 'Round in all the bucks and string up the Beaver for an object lesson. That's the programme. Come on and let's see what he's got to say for himself.'

'Heh, *M'sieu*!' Leclère called, as the crowd began to melt away through the twilight in the direction of Sunrise. 'Ah lak ver'moch to see de fon.'

'Oh, we'll turn you loose when we come back,' Webster Shaw shouted over his shoulder. 'In the meantime meditate on your sins and the ways of providence. It will do you good.'

As is the way with men who are accustomed to great hazards, whose nerves are healthy and trained to patience, so it was with Leclère. He settled himself to the long wait – which is to say that he reconciled his mind to it. There was no settling of the body, for the taut rope forced him to stand rigidly erect. The least relaxation of the leg muscles pressed the rough-fibred noose into his neck, while the upright position caused him much pain in his wounded shoulder. He projected his underlip and expelled his breath upward along his face to blow the mosquitoes away from his eyes. But the situation had its compensation. To be snatched from the maw of death was well worth a little bodily suffering, only it was unfortunate that he should miss the hanging of the Beaver.

And so he mused till his eyes chanced to fall upon Bâtard, head between forepaws and stretched on the ground asleep. And then Leclère ceased to muse. He studied the animal closely, striving to sense if the sleep were real or feigned. Bâtard's sides were heaving regularly, but Leclère felt that the breath came and went a shade too quickly; also he felt that there was a vigilance or alertness to every hair that belied sleep. He would have given his Sunrise claim to be assured that the dog was not awake, and once, when one of his joints cracked, he looked quickly and guiltily at Bâtard to see if he roused. He did not rouse then, but a few minutes later he got up slowly and lazily, stretched, and looked carefully about him.

'*Sacredam,*' said Leclère, under his breath.

Assured that no one was in sight or hearing, Bâtard sat down, curled his upper lip almost into a smile, looked up at Leclère, and licked his chops.

Then Bâtard came nearer, the useless ear wobbling, the good ear cocked forward with devilish comprehension. He thrust his head on one side quizzically and advanced with mincing, playful steps. He rubbed his body gently against the box till it shook and shook again. Leclère teetered carefully to maintain his equilibrium.

'Bâtard,' he said calmly, 'look out. Ah keel you.'

Bâtard snarled at the word and shook the box with greater force. Then he upreared, and with his forepaws threw his weight against it higher up. Leclère kicked out with one foot, but the rope bit into his neck and checked so abruptly that it nearly overbalanced him.

'Hi, ya! *Chook! Mush-on!*' he screamed.

Bâtard retreated, for twenty feet or so, with a fiendish levity in his bearing that Leclère could not mistake. He remembered the dog often breaking the scum of ice on the water hole, by lifting up and throwing his weight upon it; and, remembering, he understood what the dog now had in mind. Bâtard faced about and paused. He showed his white teeth in a grin, which Leclère answered; and then he hurled his body through the air, in full charge, straight for the box.

Fifteen minutes later Slackwater Charley and Webster Shaw returning, caught a glimpse of a ghostly pendulum swinging back and forth in the dim light. As they hurriedly drew in closer, they made out the man's inert body, and a live thing that clung to it, and gave it the swaying motion.

'Hi, ya! *Chook!* You Spawn of Hell,' yelled Webster Shaw.

But Bâtard glared at him, and snarled threateningly, without loosing his jaws.

Slackwater Charley got out his revolver, but his hand was shaking as with a chill, and he fumbled.

'Here, you take it,' he said, passing the weapon over.

Webster Shaw laughed shortly, drew a sight between the gleaming eyes, and pressed the trigger. Bâtard's body twitched with the shock, threshed the ground spasmodically for a moment, and went suddenly limp. But his teeth still held fast ...

The Homesick Buick

JOHN D. MacDONALD

To get to Leeman, Texas, you go southwest from Beaumont on Route 90 for approximately thirty miles and then turn right on a two-lane concrete farm road. Five minutes from the time you turn, you will reach Leeman. The main part of town is six lanes wide and five blocks long. If the hand of a careless giant should remove the six gas stations, the two theatres, Willow's hardware store, the Leeman National Bank, the two big air-conditioned five-and-dimes, the Sears' store, four cafés, Rightsinger's dress shop, and the Leeman House, a twenty-room hotel, there would be very little left except the super-market and four assorted drugstores.

On 3 October 1949, a Mr Stanley Woods arrived by bus and carried his suitcase over to the Leeman House. In Leeman there is no social distinction of bus, train, or plane, since Leeman has neither airport facilities nor railroad station.

On all those who were questioned later, Mr Stanley Woods seemed to have made very little impression. They all spoke of kind of a medium-size fella in his thirties, or it might be his forties. No, he wasn't fat, but he wasn't thin either. Blue eyes? Could be brown. Wore a grey suit, I think. Can't remember whether his glasses had rims or not. If they did have, they were probably gold.

But all were agreed that Mr Stanley Woods radiated quiet confidence and the smell of money. According to the cards that were collected here and there, Mr Woods represented the

Groston Precision Tool Company of Atlanta, Georgia. He had deposited in the Leeman National a certified cheque for twelve hundred dollars and the bank had made the routine check of looking up the credit standing of Groston. It was Dun and Bradstreet double-A, but, of course, the company explained later that they had never heard of Mr Stanley Woods. Nor could the fake calling cards be traced. They were of a type of paper and type face which could be duplicated sixty or a hundred times in every big city in the country.

Mr Woods's story, which all agreed on, was that he was 'nosing around to find a good location for a small plant. Decentralization, you know. No, we don't want it right in town.'

He rented Tod Bishner's car during the day. Tod works at the Shell station on the corner of Beaumont and Lone Star Streets and doesn't have any use for his Plymouth sedan during the day. Mr Woods drove around all the roads leading out of town and, of course, real estate prices were jacked to a considerable degree during his stay.

Mr Stanley Woods left Leeman rather suddenly on the morning of 17 October under unusual circumstances.

The first person to note a certain oddness was Miss Trilla Price on the switchboard at the phone company. Her local calls were all right but she couldn't place Charley Anderson's call to Houston, nor, when she tried, could she raise Beaumont. Charley was upset because he wanted to wangle an invitation to go visit his sister over the coming weekend.

That was at five minutes to nine. It was probably at the same time that a car with two men in it parked on Beaumont Street, diagonally across from the bank, and one of the two men lifted the hood and began to fiddle with the electrical system.

Nobody agrees from what direction the Buick came into town. There were a man and a girl in it and they parked near the drugstore. No one seems to know where the third car parked, or even what kind of car it was.

The girl and the man got out of the Buick slowly, just as

Stanley Woods came down the street from the hotel.

In Leeman the bank is open on weekdays from nine until two. And so, at nine o'clock, C. F. Hethridge, who is, or was, the chief teller, raised the green shades on the inside of the bank doors and unlocked the doors. He greeted Mr Woods, who went on over to the high counter at the east wall and began to ponder over his cheque book.

At this point, out on the street, a very peculiar thing happened. One of the two men in the first car strolled casually over and stood beside the Buick. The other man started the motor of the first car, drove down the street, and made a wide U-turn to swing in and park behind the Buick.

The girl and the man had gone over to Bob Kimball's window. Bob is second teller, and the only thing he can remember about the girl is that she was blonde and a little hard-looking around the mouth, and that she wore a great big alligator shoulder-bag. The man with her made no impression on Bob at all, except that Bob thinks the man was on the heavy side.

Old Rod Harrigan, the bank guard, was standing beside the front door, yawning, and picking his teeth with a broken match.

At this point C. F. Hethridge heard the buzzer on the big time-vault and went over and swung the door wide and went in to get the money for the cages. He was out almost immediately, carrying Bob's tray over to him. The girl was saying something about cashing a cheque and Bob had asked her for identification. She had opened the big shoulder-bag as her escort strolled over to the guard. At the same moment the girl pulled out a small vicious-looking revolver and aimed it between Bob's eyes, her escort sapped Old Rod Harrigan with such gusto that it was four that same afternoon before he came out of it enough to talk. And then, of course, he knew nothing.

C. F. Hethridge bolted for the vault, and Bob, wondering whether he should step on the alarm, looked over the girl's shoulder just in time to see Stanley Woods aim carefully and bring Hethridge down with a slug through the head, catching him on the fly, so to speak.

Bob says that things were pretty confusing and that the sight of Hethridge dying so suddenly sort of took the heart out of him. Anyway, there was a third car and it contained three men, two of them equipped with empty black-leather suitcases. They went into the vault, acting as though they had been all through the bank fifty times. They stepped over Hethridge on the way in, and on the way out again.

About the only cash they overlooked was the cash right in front of Bob, in his teller's drawer.

As they all broke for the door, Bob dropped and pressed the alarm button. He said later that he held his hands over his eyes, though what good that would do him, he couldn't say.

Henry Willows is the real hero. He was fuddying around in his hardware store when he heard the alarm. With a reaction-time remarkable in a man close to seventy, he took a little .22 rifle, slapped a clip into it, trotted to his store door, and quickly analysed the situation. He saw Mr Woods, whom he recognized, plus three strangers and a blonde woman coming out of the bank pretty fast. Three cars were lined up, each one with a driver. Two of the men coming out of the bank carried heavy suitcases. Henry levelled on the driver of the lead car, the Buick, and shot him in the left temple, killing him outright. The man slumped over the wheel, his body resting against the horn ring, which, of course, added its blare to the clanging of the bank alarm.

At that point a slug, later identified as having come from a Smith & Wesson Police Positive, smashed a neat hole in Henry's plate-glass store window, radiating cracks in all directions. Henry ducked, and by the time he got ready to take a second shot, the two other cars were gone. The Buick was still there. He saw Bob run out of the bank, and later on he told his wife that he had his finger on the trigger and his sights lined up before it came to him that it was Bob Kimball.

It was agreed that the two cars headed out towards Route 90 and, within two minutes, Hod Abrams and Lefty Quinn had roared out of town in the same direction in the only police car. They were followed by belligerent amateurs, to whom Henry Willows had doled out firearms. But on the edge of town all cars ran into an odd obstacle. The road was liberally sprinkled with metal objects shaped exactly like the jacks that little girls pick up when they bounce a ball, except they were four times normal size and all the points were sharpened. No matter how a tyre hit one, it was certain to be punctured.

The police car swerved to a screaming stop, nearly tipping over. The Stein twins, boys of nineteen, managed to avoid the jacks in their souped-up heap until they were hitting eighty. When they finally hit one, the heap rolled over an estimated ten times, killing the twins outright.

So that made four dead. Hethridge, the Stein twins, and one unidentified bank robber.

Nobody wanted to touch the robber, and he stayed right where he was until the battery almost ran down and the horn squawked into silence. Hod Abrams commandeered a car, and he and Lefty rode back into town and took charge. They couldn't get word out by phone and within a very short time they found that some sharpshooter with a high-powered rifle had gone to work on the towers of local station WLEE and had put the station out of business.

Thus, by the time the Texas Rangers were alerted and ready to set up road blocks, indecision and confusion had permitted an entire hour to pass.

The Houston office of the FBI assigned a detail of men to the case, and from the Washington headquarters two bank-robbery experts were dispatched by plane to Beaumont. Reporters came from Houston and Beaumont and the two national press services, and Leeman found itself on the front pages all over the country because the planning behind the job seemed to fascinate the average Joe. The FBI from Houston was there by noon on the particular Thursday, and the Washington contingent arrived late Friday. Everyone was very confident. There was a corpse and a car to work on.

These would certainly provide the necessary clues to indicate which outfit had pulled the job, even though the method of the robbery did not point to any particular group whose habits were known.

Investigation headquarters were set up in the local police station, and Hod and Lefty, very important in the beginning, had to stand around outside trying to look as though they knew what was going on.

Hethridge, who had been a cold, reserved, unpopular man, had, within twenty-four hours, fifty stories invented about his human kindness and generosity. The Stein twins, heretofore considered to be trash who would be better off in prison, suddenly became proper sons of old Texas.

Special Agent Randolph A. Sternweister who, fifteen years before, had found a law office to be a dull place, was in charge of the case, being the senior of the two experts who had flown down from Washington. He was forty-one years old, a chain smoker, a chubby man with incongruous hollow cheeks and hair of a shade of grey which his wife, Claire, tells him is distinguished.

The corpse was the first clue. Age between thirty and thirty-two. Brown hair, thinning on top. Good teeth, with only four small cavities, two of them filled. Height, five foot eight and a quarter, weight a hundred and forty-eight. No distinguishing scars or tattoos. X-ray plates showed that the right arm had been fractured years before. His clothes were neither new nor old. The suit had been purchased in Chicago. The shirt, underwear, socks and shoes were all national brands, in the medium-price range. In his pockets they found an almost full pack of cigarettes, a battered Zippo lighter, three fives and a one in a cheap, trick billclip, eighty-five cents in change, a book of matches advertising a nationally known laxative, a white bone button, two wooden kitchen matches with blue and white heads, and pencilled map, on cheap notebook paper, of the main drag of Leeman – with no indication as to escape routes. His fingerprint classification was teletyped to the Central

Bureau files, and the answer came back that there was no record of him. It was at this point that fellow workers noted that Mr Sternweister became a shade irritable.

The next search of the corpse was more minute. No specific occupational calluses were found on his hands. The absence of laundry marks indicated that his linen, if it had been sent out, had been cleaned by a neighbourhood laundress. Since Willows had used a .22 hollow-point, the hydraulic pressure on the brain fluids had caused the eyes of Mr X to bulge in a disconcerting fashion. A local undertaker, experienced in the damage caused by the average Texas automobile accident, replaced the bulging eyeballs and smoothed out the expression for a series of pictures which were sent to many points. The Chicago office reported that the clothing store which had sold the suit was large and that the daily traffic was such that no clerk could identify the customer from the picture; nor was the youngish man known to the Chicago police.

Fingernail scrapings were put in a labelled glassine envelope, as well as the dust vacuumed from pants cuffs and other portions of the clothing likely to collect dust. The excellent lab in Houston reported back that the dust and scrapings were negative to the extent that the man could not be tied down to any particular locality.

In the meantime the Buick had been the object of equal scrutiny. The outside was a mass of prints from the citizens of Leeman who had peered morbidly in at the man leaning against the horn ring. The plates were Mississippi licence plates, and in checking with the Bureau of Motor Vehicle Registration, it was found that the plates had been issued for a 1949 Mercury convertible which had been totally destroyed in a head-on collision in June 1949. The motor number and serial number of the Buick were checked against central records and it was discovered that the Buick was one which had disappeared from Chapel Hill, North Carolina, on 5 July 1949. The insurance company, having already replaced the vehicle, was anxious to take possession of the stolen car.

Pictures of Mr X, relayed to Chapel Hill, North Carolina, and to myriad points in Mississippi, drew a large blank. In the meantime a careful dusting of the car had brought out six prints, all different. Two of them turned out to be on record. The first was on record through the cross-classification of Army prints. The man in question was found working in a gas station in Lake Charles, Louisiana. He had a very difficult two hours until a bright police officer had him demonstrate his procedure for brushing out the front of a car. Ex-Sergeant Golden braced his left hand against the dashboard in almost the precise place where the print had been found. He was given a picture of Mr X to study. By that time he was so thoroughly annoyed at the forces of law and order that it was impossible to ascertain whether or not he had ever seen the man in question. But due to the apparent freshness of the paint, it was established – a reasonable assumption – that the gangsters had driven into Texas from the East.

The second print on record was an old print, visible when dust was carefully blown off the braces under the dismantled front seat. It belonged to a garage mechanic in Chapel Hill who once had a small misunderstanding with the forces of law and order and who was able to prove, through the garage work orders, that he had repaired the front-seat mechanism when it had jammed in April 1949.

The samples of road dirt and dust taken from the fender wells and the frame members proved nothing. The dust was proved, spectroscopically, to be from deep in the heart of Texas, and the valid assumption, after checking old weather reports, was that the car had come through some brisk thunderstorms en route.

Butts in the ashtray of the car showed that either two women, or one woman with two brands of lipstick, had ridden recently as a passenger. Both brands of lipstick were of shades which would go with a fair-complexioned blonde, and both brands were available in Woolworth's, Kress's, Kresge's, Walgreen's – in fact, in every chain outfit of any importance.

One large crumb of stale whole-wheat bread was found on the floor mat, and even Sternweister could make little of that, despite the fact that the lab was able to report that the bread had been eaten in conjunction with liverwurst.

Attention was given to the oversized jacks which had so neatly punctured the tyres. An ex-OSS officer reported that similar items had been scattered on enemy roads in Burma during the late war, and after examining the samples, he stated confidently that the OSS merchandise had been better made. A competent machinist looked them over and stated with assurance that they had been made by cutting eight-inch rods into short lengths, grinding them on a wheel, putting them in a jig, and spot-welding them. He said that the maker did not do much of a job on either the grinding or the welding, and that the jig itself was a little out of line. An analysis of the steel showed that it was a Jones & Laughlin product that could be bought in quantity at any wholesaler and in a great many hardware stores.

The auditors, after a careful examination of the situation at the bank, reported that the sum of exactly $94,725 had disappeared. They recommended that the balance remaining in Stanley Woods's account of $982.80 be considered as forfeited, thus reducing the loss to $93,742.20. The good citizens of Leeman preferred to think that Stanley had withdrawn his account.

Every person who had a glimpse of the gang was cross-examined. Sternweister was appalled at the difficulty involved in even establishing how many there had been. Woods, the blonde and the stocky citizen were definite. And then there were two with suitcases – generally agreed upon. Total, so far – five. The big question was whether each car had a driver waiting. Some said no – that the last car in line had been empty. Willows insisted angrily that there had been a driver behind each wheel. Sternweister at last settled for a total of eight, seven of whom escaped.

No one had taken down a single licence number. But it was

positively established that the other two cars had been either two- or four-door sedans in dark blue, black, green, or maroon, and that they had been either Buicks, Nashes, Oldsmobiles, Chryslers, Pontiacs, or Packards – or maybe Hudsons. And one lone woman held out for convertible Cadillacs. For each person that insisted that they had Mississippi registration, there was one equally insistent on Louisiana, Texas, Alabama, New Mexico, and Oklahoma. And one óld lady said that she guessed she knew a California plate when she saw one.

On Saturday morning, nine days after the robbery, Randolph Sternweister paced back and forth in his suite at the hotel which he shared with the number two man from the Washington end, one Buckley Weed. Weed was reading through the transcripts of the testimony of the witnesses, in the vain hope of finding something to which insufficient importance had been given. Weed, though lean, a bit stooped and only thirty-one, had, through osmosis, acquired most of the personal mannerisms of his superior. Sternweister had noticed this and for the past year had been on the verge of mentioning it. As Weed had acquired Sternweister's habit of lighting a cigarette off the last half-inch of the preceding one, any room in which the two of them remained for more than an hour took on the look and smell of any hotel room after a Legion convention.

'Nothing,' Sternweister said. 'Not one censored, unmentionable, unprintable, unspeakable thing! My God, if I ever want to kill anybody, I'll do it in the Pennsy Station at five-fifteen.'

'Yes, at five-fifteen,' said Weed.

'The Bureau has cracked cases when the only thing it had to go on was a human hair or a milligram of dust. My God, we've got a whole automobile that weighs nearly two tons, and a whole corpse! They'll think we're down here learning to rope calves. You know what?'

'What, Ran?'

'I think this was done by a bunch of amateurs. There ought to be a law restricting the practice of crime to professionals. A bunch of wise amateurs. And you can bet your loudest argyles, my boy, that they established identity, hideout, the works, before they knocked off that vault. Right now, blast their souls, they're being seven average citizens in some average community, making no splash with that ninety-four grand. People didn't use to move around so much. Since the war they've been migrating all over the place. Strangers don't stick out like sore thumbs any more. See anything in those transcripts?'

'Nothing.'

'Then stop rattling paper. I can't think. Since a week ago Thursday fifty-one stolen cars have been recovered in the South and Southwest. And we don't know which two, if any, belonged to this mob. We don't even know which route they took away from here. Believe it or not – nobody saw 'em!'

As the two specialists stared bleakly at each other, a young man of fourteen named Pink Dee was sidling inconspicuously through the shadows in the rear of Louie's Garage (Tow car service – open 24 hrs). Pink was considered to have been the least beautiful baby, the most unprepossessing child, in Leeman, and he gave frank promise of growing up to be a rather coarse joke on the entire human race. Born with a milk-blue skin, dead-white hair, little reddish weak eyes, pipe-cleaner bones, narrow forehead, no chin, beaver teeth, a voice like an unoiled hinge, nature had made the usual compensation. His reaction-time was exceptional. Plenty of more rugged and more normal children had found out that Pink Dee could hit you by the time you had the word out of your mouth. The blow came from an outsize, knobbly fist at the end of a long thin arm, and he swung it with all the abandon of a bag of rocks on the end of a rope. The second important item about Pink Dee came to light when the Leeman School System started giving IQs. Pink's was higher than they were willing to admit the first time, as it did not seem proper that the only genius in Leeman should be old Homer Dee's only son. Pink caught on, and the second time he was rated he got it down into the cretin class.

The third rating was ninety-nine and everybody seemed happy with that.

At fourteen Pink was six feet tall and weighed a hundred and twenty pounds. He peered at the world through heavy lenses and maintained, in the back room of his home on Fountain Street, myriad items of apparatus, some made, some purchased. There he investigated certain electrical and magnetic phenomena, having tired of building radios, and carried on a fairly virulent correspondence on the quantum theory with a Cal Tech professor who was under the impression that he was arguing with someone of more mature years.

Dressed in his khakis, the uniform of Texas, Pink moved through the shadows, inserted the key he had filched into the Buick door, and then into the ignition lock. He turned it to the left to activate the electrical gimmicks, and then turned on the car radio. As soon as it warmed up he pushed the selector buttons, carefully noting the dial. When he had the readings he turned it to WLEE to check the accuracy of the dial. When WLEE roared into a farm report, Louie of Louie's Garage (Tow car service – open 24 hrs) appeared and dragged Pink out by the thin scruff of his neck.

'What the hell?' Louie said.

Being unable to think of any adequate explanation, Pink wriggled away and loped out.

Pink's next stop was WLEE, where he was well known. He found the manual he wanted and spent the next twenty minutes leafing through it.

Having been subjected to a certain amount of sarcasm from both Sternweister and Weed, Hod Adams and Lefty Quinn were in no mood for the approach Pink Dee used.

'I demand to see the FBI,' Pink said firmly, the effect spoiled a bit by the fact that his voice change was so recent that the final syllable was a reversion to his childhood squeaky-hinge voice.

'He demands,' Hod said to Lefty.

'Go away, Pink,' Lefty growled, 'before I stomp on your glasses.'

'I am a citizen who wishes to speak to a member of a federal agency,' Pink said with dignity.

'A citizen, maybe. A taxpayer, no. You give me trouble, kid, and I'm going to warm your pants right here in this lobby.'

Maybe the potential indignity did it. Pink darted for the stairs leading up from the lobby. Hod went roaring up the stairs after him and Lefty grabbed the elevator. They both snared him outside Sternweister's suite and found that they had a job on their hands. Pink bucked and contorted like a picnic on which a hornets' nest had just fallen.

The door to the suite opened and both Sternweister and Weed glared out, their mouths open.

'Just ... just a fresh ... kid!' Hod Abrams panted.

'I know where the crooks are!' Pink screamed.

'He's nuts,' Lefty yelled.

'Wait a minute,' Randolph Sternweister ordered sharply. They stopped dragging Pink but still clung to him. 'I admit he doesn't look as though he knew his way home, but you can't tell. You two wait outside. Come in here, young man.'

Pink marched erectly into the suite, selected the most comfortable chair, and sank into it, looking very smug.

'Where are they?'

'Well, I don't exactly—'

'Outside!' Weed said with a thumb motion.

'But I know how to find out.'

'Oh, you know how to find out, eh? Keep talking. I haven't laughed in nine days,' Sternweister said.

'Oh, I had to do a little checking first,' Pink said in a lofty manner. 'I stole the key to the Buick and got into it to test something.'

'Kid, experts have been over that car, half-inch by half-inch.'

'Please don't interrupt me, sir. And don't take that attitude. Because, if it turns out I have something, and I know I have, you're going to look as silly as anything.'

Sternweister flushed and then turned pale. He held hard to the edge of a table. 'Go ahead,' he said thickly.

'I am making an assumption that the people who robbed our bank started out from some hideout and then went back to the same one. I am further assuming that they were in their hideout some time – that is, while they were planning the robbery.'

Weed and Sternweister exchanged glances. 'Go on.'

'So my plan has certain possible flaws based on these assumptions, but at least it uncovers one possible pattern of investigation. I know that the car was stolen from Chapel Hill. That was in the paper. And I know the dead man was in Chicago. So I checked Chicago and Chapel Hill a little while ago.'

'Checked them?'

'At the radio station, of course. Modern car radios are easy to set to new stations by altering the push buttons. The current settings of the push buttons do not conform either to the Chicago or the Chapel Hill areas. There are six stations that the radio in the Buick is set for and ...' Sternweister sat down on the couch as though somebody had clubbed him behind the knees. 'Agh!' he said.

'So all you have to do,' Pink said calmly, 'is to check areas against the push-button settings until you find an area *where all six frequencies are represented by radio stations in the immediate geographical vicinity*. It will take a bit of statistical work, of course, and a map of the country, and a supply of push pins should simplify things, I would imagine. Then, after the area is located, I would take the Buick there, and due to variations in individual sets and receiving conditions, you might be able to narrow it down to within a mile or two. Then by showing the photograph of the dead gangster around at bars and such places ...'

And that was why, on the following Wednesday, a repainted Buick with new plates and containing two agents of the

Bureau roamed through the small towns near Tampa on the West Florida coast, and how they found that the car radio in the repainted Buick brought in Tampa, Clearwater, St Petersburg, Orlando, Winter Haven, and Dunedin on the push buttons with remarkable clarity the closer they came to a little resort town called Tarpon Springs. On Thursday morning at four, the portable floodlights bathed three beach cottages in a white glare, and the metallic voice of the PA system said, 'You are surrounded. Come out with your hands high. You are surrounded.'

The shots, a few moments later, cracked with a thin bitterness against the heavier sighing of the Gulf of Mexico. Mr Stanley Woods, or, as the blonde later stated, Mr Grebbs Fainstock, was shot, with poetic justice, through the head, and that was the end of resistance.

To Pink Dee in Leeman, the president of the Leeman National Bank turned over the envelope containing the reward. It came to a bit less than 6 per cent of the recovered funds, and it was ample to guarantee, at some later date, a Cal Tech degree.

In December the Sternweisters bought a new car. When Claire demanded to know why Randolph insisted on delivery *sans* car radio, his only answer was a hollow laugh.

She feels that he has probably been working too hard.

Campaign Fever

PATRICIA McGERR

Hugh Pierce slumped deeper into the leather chair in Selena's soundproofed den, his teeth clamped hard on the stem of a long-dead pipe. She had, Selena thought, never seen him so irresolute. The incisive manner with which he was accustomed to outline the latest security problem and Section Q's design for solving it had given place to a mood of rare discouragement. Today he had a problem, but no solution. He had come to Selena's house not, as usual, to assign her role in Section Q's plan but – or so it appeared – to seek sanctuary where he could vent his bafflement and frustration.

'Thank the Lord,' he said vehemently, 'foreign intrigue and domestic politics don't often become entangled. I'd rather face a bushful of guerrilla fighters than walk this tightrope of trying to get results without giving aid or comfort to either party.'

The situation, as Hugh described it, involved two totally unrelated future events. In a far-off Red-dominated country a small but zealous underground was preparing an uprising, a last-ditch fight for freedom. The first strike was planned for early Wednesday morning. This was Sunday. And on Tuesday night an American candidate for national office was scheduled to address a giant rally in a Middle Western city whose largest population element was made up of emigrants or descendants of emigrants from that captive country.

'So you're afraid,' Selena suggested, 'that something in his speech will sound like a call to arms.'

'I'm more than afraid,' Hugh answered. 'I guarantee it. It would be humanly impossible for any politician to talk to such a group and not include a ringing promise to set their people free. And no matter how long-ranged and abstract that promise sounds on Tuesday night, when the shooting starts on Wednesday it will be turned into a prediction. We'll never be able to deny convincingly that we had a finger in the revolt.'

'Are you sure we don't?'

'Our agents learned about it only yesterday. We'd stop it if we could. It's ill-timed, poorly staffed, inadequately armed. But the leaders won't listen to argument, they're willing to die for their cause. And that's their right. But if it turns into another bloodbath, like Hungary, and there is any indication that the United States egged them on, well ...' He left the sentence unfinished, spread his hands in graphic illustration of the enormity of the consequences.

'But surely all you need to do is send someone to explain the danger to the candidate and get him to omit all references to liberating the mother country.'

'That won't lift the cloud,' Hugh answered. 'No matter how innocuous his speech, there's bound to be some sentence, some phrase that can – in the light of the next day's events – be given the wrong interpretation. Even if he didn't open his mouth, just sat there on the platform and took a bow, the threat wouldn't disappear. We can't control the other speakers or the audience. A patriotic slogan shouted into a microphone, a banner waved before a television camera could seem like incitement. The very fact that he is with people of that nation on the eve of the outbreak will give everything that happens there a special prominence.'

'Then you'll have to persuade him to stay away.'

'The question is, How? It's not easy to ask a man running for office to stand up several thousand voters. And even assuming his cooperation, his absence might later be made to appear more significant than his presence. He can't cancel out on such short notice without a powerful and credible reason on which no columnist can cast doubt.'

'The obvious excuse is illness.'

'Obvious, but drastic. A man running for office needs to rate high on physical fitness. Send him to bed with the flu and in two hours there'll be a rumour that he's at death's door with an incurable disease.' He rubbed the bowl of his pipe with his thumb, studied it glumly. 'You see what we're up against. Every way we turn there are dagger points.'

'It does look rather hopeless,' Selena agreed. 'But there must be something we can do.' Her eyes took on a distant look, her brows came together in meditation. 'I wonder—'

'Yes?' Hugh leaned forward, tensely alert. 'You've thought of a way?'

'What you just said gave me an idea.' She paused, went on more slowly. 'It could work. Yes, I think it will work. Anyway, it's worth trying.'

'Tell me.' He tapped his pipe decisively on an ashtray's edge. 'I knew this was the right place to do my thinking aloud.'

Early Monday morning Selena stood near the elevators in an office building in the city where the rally was set for the following night. She held a notebook and pencil, wore a badge identifying the magazine for which she was Washington correspondent, the job that served as cover for her counter-espionage work. Arriving workers streamed into the building and, one by one, she approached them.

'We're taking a poll,' she announced. 'Do you mind telling me for whom you intend to vote for President this year?'

After each answer she marked her book and said 'Thank you' and moved on to the next.

By 9.30 the stream had turned to a trickle. She went out to the street, boarded a bus to a shopping centre in a residential area. For another hour she put her question to cart-pushing women in a supermarket. Through the day she rode other buses to other areas, roved through shops and rang doorbells till she had a sampling of opinion at a variety of economic levels. Frequently she passed a poster bearing the candidate's picture and summoning one and all to the Tuesday rally. Each was a forceful reminder of the urgency of her mission.

In late afternoon she repeated her early-morning performance with departing workers at the town's principal factory. And in the evening she wound up her canvass in the lobby of a motion-picture theatre. By the time she retired to her hotel she had a notebook full of statistics proving that the November election would be decided by voters who had not yet made up their minds.

Her first stop on Tuesday was City Hall, where she walked down a long corridor to the Department of Health.

'When I was having breakfast this morning,' she told the medical officer, 'I began to feel – well, not ill exactly, but rather queasy. There's a throbbing in my head and I sort of ache all over. I felt very warm, as if I might be feverish, but now, all of a sudden' – she gave a slight shiver – 'I'm chilly. Oh, I know—' As he was about to speak she anticipated his protest. 'You're wondering why I didn't see a private doctor. I was about to, but then it occurred to me. It may be a false alarm, I certainly hope it is – but it seemed best to come directly here. Because last week I was in South America and in one of the villages where I stayed there were two cases of smallpox.'

'Ah!' The word brought him to instant attention. 'Yes, you were right to come to me without delay. Those symptoms—' He made quick jottings on a pad. 'They may mean you are coming down with a cold. But they can also signal the onset of smallpox. And we have to assume the worst, take every possible precaution. That means putting you in isolation while we make tests. Laboratory confirmation will take about twenty-four hours. In the meantime we'll try to reach all those you've had contact with and set up a quarantine. Can you give me a list of the places you've been, the people you've seen since you arrived in town?'

'I'm afraid that's not possible.' She shook her head. 'I spent all day yesterday talking to strangers, hundreds of them.' Briefly she filled him in on Monday's odyssey.

'Oh, brother!' he exploded. 'You sure managed maximum exposure in minimum time. That ends any hope of protecting the city by keeping a handful of people in their houses. It's hard to believe that one woman could cover so much ground so fast.'

'I'm sorry,' Selena said meekly. 'It's my job.' As she spoke she was deeply conscious of the double meaning.

'What's done is done.' His shrug was philosophical. 'And you showed sense in bringing your story straight to headquarters. Now the first order of business is to arrange to get you into the hospital and get the lab tests under way.' He pressed a buzzer at the side of his desk. 'Then I can concentrate on a programme to prevent an epidemic in case you turn out to be a carrier.'

After the strenuous activities of the previous day, the enforced rest was far from unwelcome. Selena lay in the hospital bed and held to her ear a tiny transistor radio. She closed her eyes, lulled to near slumber by soft music. But she came fully awake and turned up the volume when a man's voice broke in with a local news bulletin. His tone was calm, his words carefully chosen to minimize panic.

'Report of a possible case of smallpox was made today to the local health department. Diagnosis is not positive. Results of tests will not be known until tomorrow morning. If the virus proves to be present, a city-wide vaccination programme will then be set up. In the interim, citizens are advised to avoid crowds, to stay away from large public gatherings. Among the events postponed in response to this warning is a campaign rally this evening at which the main speaker was to be—'

Selena switched off the set, relaxed against the pillow with a sigh of content. Mission accomplished. Tomorrow the laboratory would give her a clean bill of health. She'd be free to leave the hospital and the city. The people would go about their ordinary business. The rally could be re-scheduled for a date that, coming after the anti-Communist rising, would be without international implications. And no one outside of Section Q would ever discover a connection between riots behind the Iron Curtain and a short-lived smallpox scare in America's Middle West.

Run with the Wind

JAMES McKIMMEY

The city was cool with a fine rain, and the boy ran lightly down an alley in a gloomy section where poor houses and tenements rose in the last light of day. He stopped beside a garbage can and lifted the lid swiftly, ruddy face showing cheerfully beneath a ragged cap. His jacket was wet and stained. Faded jeans, broken through at the knees, came far short of the venerable tennis shoes encasing his sockless feet.

He prodded and poked and finally found a heel of bread. His white teeth bit hard, cracking the stale crust; then the bread was gone. He rubbed his jacket sleeve against his mouth, heard a sound of footsteps, and ran on, fleet as a deer's shadow. He cut through other alleys, darted across streets, nipping behind the flow of traffic, his motion springing with early youth.

Then there was the sound of complaining tyres. He looked out on a busy boulevard to see a small cat struck and sent spinning.

'No!' he breathed, then ran out between other cars to lift the now-still body. He came back to the sidewalk and trudged to the entrance of another alley where he sat down with the dead animal in his lap. Tears glistened in his eyes. He sniffed mournfully, drawing his hand across his nose, then sat for a long time blinded by tears. When the large hand touched his shoulder, he jumped.

A tall man with a long nose stared down, his fine, white

hair tangled by the breeze coming up as the rain lessened.

'Your kitten?' the man asked gently, smiling, his voice a soft bass like echoing thunder.

'No.'

'Are you frightened of me?'

'Nobody.'

The man nodded, touching the thick woollen sweater covering his broad torso. 'A fine way to be. Dead?'

'Run over.'

'Shame.' His hand was still on the boy's shoulder. The boy twisted out from under its pressure, half crouched, ready for flight. 'You picked it up from the street?' The man's words were easily shaped, bearing the accent of education.

'Yes,' the boy said dully.

'Very good of you. I don't suppose it would be any use to look for its owner, would it? It has no collar and tag.'

'Nobody owns a cat,' the boy said defiantly.

'Quite true. But what's to be done with it? Do you live nearby?'

The boy was silent, holding the cat, poised for escape.

'Well, you see,' the man said, 'he should have a nice burial, shouldn't he? I mean, that would be the very least one could do, wouldn't it? For what was probably a very nice cat?'

'I'll find a place,' the boy said.

'I'll tell you, my kind friend. I have a small cottage no more than three blocks from here. Behind the cottage is a very nice fenced yard. It would be my very great pleasure to offer that as a final resting place for this animal. What do you think of that?'

The boy looked up at him warily, blue eyes ageless and without trust.

'Let's just take him over there.' The man smiled and moved away, long legs swinging. He did not look back; when he had gone a dozen steps, the boy stood up and followed.

The man stopped before a small frame cottage, its time-battered front softened by the dimming light. He unlocked the door and turned to the boy. 'Just bring him in,' he said, then stepped inside.

The boy stared at the door as he might a set trap.

'It's quite all right. The least we can do.'

The boy came forward slowly and followed the man into a small living-room littered with books, magazines, newspapers and strewn clothing.

'Move something and sit down,' the man said cheerfully. He looked at the boy with deeply set grey eyes beneath thick white eyebrows. The boy pushed aside newspapers and sat down on the edge of a sofa tautly, holding the dead cat in his lap. The man moved into a small adjoining kitchen, saying, 'We'll take care of this, don't you worry.'

There was the sound of a door opening and closing. The man reappeared carrying a cardboard box.

'We'll put him in this, you see. Carefully. That's the way. There's dignity even in death, you know. Now – so. I'll just put the poor creature out on the back porch and bury him most properly in the morning.'

'I can help,' the boy said.

'No need. You've already done enough. I admire you, my young friend, for your extraordinary compassion.'

'My what?'

'Your good feeling towards that cat,' he offered in explanation.

The boy looked at the door.

'No need to rush off,' the man said pleasantly. 'Have you had dinner?'

The boy's eyes widened a fraction.

The man moved into the small kitchen, saying, 'I think we can find something here.' He brought a can of spaghetti from a shelf, opened it and poured its contents into an old saucepan. He removed a half loaf of French bread from a cupboard and cut it in slices. He found a cloth and dusted the round kitchen table, then placed two chipped plates and aged silverware on its surface. The spaghetti began to bubble in the pan on the stove. He turned to see the boy standing at the edge of the kitchen, staring at the stove. 'Sit down, my boy. Hardly a feast, but something against the night anyway.' He got a bottle of red wine and a glass from the cupboard and sat down opposite the boy. 'I don't think it would be proper to offer you any of this, but I trust you don't mind my taking a few drops for myself?'

The boy sat wordlessly, staring from the man to the stove.

The man filled the glass and said, smiling, 'Here's to – ah, I don't think we've exchanged names, have we? Mine is Mr Wiggins. Mr Alfred Q. Wiggins. And yours?'

'Mickey,' the boy said, almost inaudibly.

'A nice name. I like that. And do you have a last name, Mickey?'

'No,' the boy said softly.

'Then I'll just call you Mickey X. Is that acceptable to you, sir?'

'Is it what?'

'Is it all right if I call you Mickey X?'

'I don't care.'

'Very good. And I'll drink to your good health.' The boy was looking at the stove again. The man got up to remove the steaming spaghetti from the burner, the aroma of the sauce flavouring the air. The boy bent forward against the table, watching the progress of the pan towards his plate. His hands appeared on the surface of the table, clenching in anticipation. Using a spoon, the man pushed a quantity of the spaghetti on to the boy's plate. Finally he scraped all of it out. 'Fact of the matter,' he said, 'I really would prefer just a bit of this bread with the wine, nothing more. You go at it, as they say.'

The boy lifted the plate with one hand, clutched a knife in the other and scooped the spaghetti into his mouth, chewing and swallowing furiously. When the man had settled himself in his chair, the spaghetti was gone. The boy reached for the bread and stuffed one piece after another into his mouth. The man swiftly took a slice for himself and leaned back, sipping the wine, looking at the boy in admiration. When the bread was gone, the boy slid his chair back. 'I've got to go.'

'Where, my boy?'

'I've got to.'

'It really isn't polite, of course, to eat and run, as it were. Why don't you relax, my good friend? Am I going to hurt you?'

Nervously, the boy remained in his chair, looking at the man defensively.

'Mickey X,' the man said softly. 'Where do you live, my boy?'

'I don't have to stay here.'

'Of course you don't. I merely thought it might be pleasant to have someone with whom to chat while I enjoy this modest wine. Do you have anything against talking with me?'

'I don't have to.'

'Absolutely not. Where do you live, my small friend?'

'Alleys, mostly. Alleys are dark, at night. They're safe.'

The man looked at the boy with fresh interest. 'Safe from what?'

'From being caught.'

'And why would someone want to catch you?'

'Because I don't want to be caught. That's the way it goes.'

The man nodded and sipped the wine carefully. 'That is a certain truth, isn't it? You don't want to be caught. And so, naturally, someone would like to catch you.'

'*You're* not going to.'

'I have no intention of it. I like you as you are. Free. As the wind, I would suspect.'

The boy nodded positively.

'No family?'

'Orphan.'

'I see. Well, I'm sorry about that.'

'I'm not. I never knew anything else.'

'Then, of course, you wouldn't be sorry, would you? You have no home at all?'

'Three years ago I was at a home. Lots of us. I ran away.'

'And you've been on your own ever since? Living off your wits, so to speak, all of that time?'

'I don't need anybody.'

The man shook his head. 'Quite an incredible boy all around. Let's see now, how old would you be?'

'I don't know.'

'Seven, eight – possibly ten? It's hard to guess, isn't it?'

'I don't care how old I am.'

'Naturally not. All that matters is that you're free, is that it?'

'They'll never catch me.'

'Somehow, my boy, I have no doubt of that. I think I understand something else too: your feeling for the cat. You're quite alike, really. You said it yourself – nobody owns a cat. And nobody owns Mickey X either, does he? We feel very deeply, when we can see ourselves in something or someone else; then when tragedy happens to that something or someone, we feel most sympathetic to it. In this case, the poor cat, now lying dead on my back porch. The cat ran free, didn't he? As you run free.'

The boy stared at the man, now obviously awed by his philosophical examination of himself. 'Are *you* free?'

The man laughed softly. 'I'm afraid not.'

The boy looked about, tensing. 'Don't you live alone?'

'Quite true. Free in that fashion. But, you see, we're opposites, you and I. Do you understand?'

'No.'

The man sipped the last wine in his glass, then poured more. 'Well, I believe you are a totally free body, beholden to nothing or to no one. But I am a captive, a prisoner.'

'Of what?'

'My brain.'

'Your *brain*?'

'Torment of my life. I have quite an exceptional brain, my young friend. No fault of my own, certainly. It simply is; has been, all of my life. That is my burden. I'm locked in the discipline of my brain, forced to carry out all of its desires. It is my master and always will be, until I might reach senility, or the sudden extinguishing of the flame, as our poor cat so recently experienced. Do you understand that?'

'No,' the boy said.

'I'm simply trying to explain that you are north and I am south. You are east and I am west. And, I suppose, because the grass always appears so much greener on the other lawn, that's why I admire you so deeply. You are like the cat prowling the alleys, running with the wind; obligated to no one and to nothing, with no master anywhere.'

The boy blinked slowly, as if trying to comprehend.

'You like cats, do you?' the man asked.

'Yes.'

'Manx, Persian, Angora, those of inestimable blood mixtures, any of them – it doesn't matter, does it?'

'So they're cats.'

'Of course,' the man nodded.

'I'm leaving.'

'Well, if you must. But I've enjoyed this chat immensely.'

'You'll bury him, won't you?'

'You can count on it.'

The boy was on his feet. The man got up to follow him to the door.

'You take care of yourself, Mickey X, as I'm sure you're capable of doing. You're not going to forget Mr Wiggins, are you?'

The boy looked at him suspiciously.

'What I'm saying is that one doesn't make a good friend every day.'

'I don't have any friends,' the boy said defiantly.

'Yes, I see – one of the pleasures a boy in your particular circumstances can't afford, I suspect. But remember, my boy, I admire your freedom. You have nothing to fear from me. I also admire your concern for that poor cat. If you should – and mind you, I hope all cats prowling freely on the streets tonight will be safe for ever – but if you should find another such poor animal, you just bring him to Mr Wiggins. That is quite a nice backyard I have, a much better resting place than most poor animals will ever receive.'

The boy stared at him with his ageless eyes. 'You're trying to trick me into coming back.'

'Trick you! Why would I?'

The boy stared at him a moment longer, then went out the door swiftly.

Mr Wiggins smiled at the closed door, then returned to the kitchen where he finished the wine in his glass. Finally he stepped out to the small back porch and lifted the box containing the cat. Humming softly, he walked with it back through the house, along a short hallway, then opened the door of a darkened room. He reached knowingly through the blackness and switched on a bright light centred in a flat reflector hanging over a shining metal table. Still humming he lifted the cat from the box and placed it on the metal table in the harsh light. He surveyed the dead animal for a few moments, then his hand dropped and came back up with a scalpel. 'So,' he said gently, and the scalpel flashed.

Three days later, in the pale glow of sunset, the boy appeared at Mr Wiggins's yard door, holding the limp body of a very large yellow cat.

'Oh, my heavens,' Mr Wiggins said sympathetically. 'The poor fellow.'

'It was a she,' the boy said.

'Ah – well, even so, a dreadful shame. Freeway?'

The boy nodded solemnly.

'Freeways. Progress. But it would be very hard to explain that to a cat, wouldn't it? Should he understand?'

'Can we bury her?'

'Just bring her right through the house, Mickey X. Come right along.' The boy followed the man through the house to the porch. 'Now you put her in that box, and I'll see that she's properly attended to in the morning.'

'Can't I help now?'

'You leave the matter up to Mr Wiggins, my boy. Work such as that can be done in the lonely morning hours. But I would so much rather enjoy your visit now, even on this tragic note, by offering you a bit of dinner.'

The boy's eyes brightened. 'You sure you buried the other one?'

'Of course.'

'Where?'

'Let's step outside.' The man motioned towards a plot of recently turned earth. 'A very nice spot, wouldn't you say?'

'There isn't anything to mark it.'

The man nodded seriously. 'That's true, isn't it? Well, now.' He looked across the yard at a collection of rocks near the gate leading to the alley behind. 'Of course.' He walked over and got a rock and placed it carefully over the grave. 'That should do nicely, shouldn't it? And I'll bet you might have got up an appetite running with the wind today, as you do. Let's see what we can find.'

The boy sat waiting for a can of macaroni to be heated. After the man had dished it, the food was gone in a twinkling. The man smiled, sat down with his wine, and looked at the boy fondly.

'Very good of you to bring that poor creature for its proper burial. You have a large heart, my boy.'

Now the boy appeared less nervous. 'What do you do?'

'For a living?'

The boy nodded.

'Oh, I've done several things.'

'Like?'

'I was a lawyer.'

'You?'

'Surprises you, does it? But it's quite true. My brain, you see, driving me always. Yes, I was quite a good lawyer. Quite a famous lawyer, as a matter of fact.'

The boy looked at him in disbelief. Mr Wiggins smiled.

'You don't believe that?'

'You don't have to lie to me. I mean, I don't have any friends, but if I did ...'

'I could be one of them?'

The boy looked down at his plate self-consciously.

'That's nice to hear,' the man said gently. 'But I'm not lying. You see, I wouldn't have any reason, would I? Yes, a successful and famous lawyer. Then, because I have this most disastrously curious brain, I was driven into finance. A challenge, and I met it, my boy; made quite a fortune. Gave much advice. Then lost interest, gave away most of the money.' He shrugged. 'I kept enough to live in this fashion. But you don't believe me, do you?'

The boy rubbed his nose, silently.

'Well, you stop at a library sometime, when you have a moment. I think you'll find that Mr Alfred Q. Wiggins is telling you the truth. There are substantial references.' The man sighed and sipped his wine. 'Law, finance; have to keep going, make full use of that which God gave me. Exploring, exploring. Why? Why does the world go 'round. My only value in this universe is, I suppose, taking on the new challenge, testing it, defeating it, giving it my measure of contribution. It's something, isn't it, my boy?'

'I don't know.'

'There always must be something, a reason. But you, now—' He shook his head regretfully. 'Must be there somewhere. It must be.'

'I've got to go.'

'Yes. But I'm glad you came back, Mickey X. You never need fear Mr Wiggins. It was awfully good of you to think of that poor cat. She'll be well taken care of, you can be sure. And if you find another—'

'Goodbye, Mr Wiggins.'

The man smiled warmly. 'Goodbye.'

When the boy had gone, Mr Wiggins finished his final glass,

then stood up and moved briskly to the back porch. Moments later, he opened the door to the darkened room.

In twilight, the man stood beside the boy in the small yard and gazed at five stones, each set a foot apart from the other. He had dropped his hand absently on the boy's shoulder; but the boy made no effort to slip away.

'I can help with this one,' the boy said.

'Enough for you to be so kind as to pick up these poor creatures and carry them here. You leave the digging to Mr Wiggins. I'll take care of the new one first thing in the morning. Now let's see about dinner for you.'

When the contents of a can had been devoured by the boy, the man leaned back in his chair, touching his glass of wine. The boy stared back at him, saying, 'I went to the library.'

'Oh. You mean about checking the truth of what I told you?'

The boy nodded. 'I can't read, but I asked a woman. She looked it up – about you. It's true, isn't it? She said you were famous as a lawyer, then as an econo—'

'Economist?' Mr Wiggins nodded agreeably.

'She said she didn't know what had become of you. I didn't tell her. I shouldn't have, should I?'

'I think you did the right thing entirely. Past days should be forgotten, except to bring forth knowledge gained.' Mr Wiggins nodded again. 'So now you know the truth about me.'

'Could I become a famous lawyer, Mr Wiggins?'

Mr Wiggins smiled sadly. 'Ah, my boy, I wish I could answer that positively. I wish I could say it might come true. But one makes his choice, you see. And you've made yours.'

'Why can't I be?'

'It requires schooling, for one thing. Quite a lot. Then you've got to deal with people, constantly. You say you can't read.'

'No,' the boy said, obviously regretful about the fact for the first time in his life.

'And people – you've escaped from them rather well all along, haven't you?'

'I don't know anybody – except you.'

'Yes, and I feel honoured about that, Mickey X. But, you see, you'd have to give up this life of yours, go to school first, catch up, get ahead of it. Years and years, and people – you'd have to accept people – dozens, hundreds. Would you like that?'

'No,' the boy said definitely.

'Well, there it is. To run with the wind, Mickey X, you have to sacrifice other things.' The man sipped his wine thoughtfully. 'And where will it lead?' He shrugged. 'I'm afraid, my boy, the age is against you – or you are against the age. This is the age of purpose, you see? At least it gives the illusion of it. Everyone is seeking purpose, direction, meaning – whether or not he finds it. Perhaps nothing will amount to anything, finally, but we have to think it will – most of us, anyway. Law, Economy, Science, whatever it might be, there must be a contribution left behind, something for others to use as a rung on the ladder, in order to climb steadily.'

'Why?' the boy asked.

'Why, indeed? Because this is the way of man, most men; but not your way. Your way is to breathe, live, darting about, like a freedom-loving cat, the animal you love so dearly; never to be restricted, never to be imprisoned, never to be caught.'

'No, *sir*.'

The man nodded. 'And so it is. A remarkable young man you are. All out of step with things, and yet a very bright light. Don't you worry about becoming a lawyer, an economist, anything at all. You must have a meaning, my good friend, somewhere in the pattern of things. That must be. And be glad you're not bound and tied to that which controls me.' He leaned back, furrows cutting deeply around his eyes. 'Would that I could be as you are, or could have been. But first it was the law. Then the matter of finance. And now – something that has obsessed me all along.'

'Did what?'

'Been in my brain, deeply, so that I knew I could never escape it – science, my friend, most specifically medical science. There all the time, and no escaping it; so I must do what I must, to leave behind what I can. No time left now for the formal education for that. But, you see, I don't need it. Not really ...' He straightened finally. 'Enough of that. I am what I am. You are what you are.'

The boy was silent for a time, then he said, 'Mr Wiggins, I'm glad we met.'

'So am I, Mickey X.'

The afternoon was fading, the sky turning grey with the last sunlight; a chill was in the air, and there was the sound of cars moving on the freeway beyond. Mr Wiggins stood in his yard and counted twenty-two stones placed in careful rows. Finally he went inside to his kitchen, passing an empty cardboard box. He looked at a clock above the old stove, then at the unopened can on the table. He sat down and drummed his long fingers against the table, looking at the wine bottle. Finally, he got up and put on his thick sweater, tugging up the collar, and went outside.

Cars hummed by infrequently along the neighbourhood avenue, and he walked along, looking. He turned into an alley and went its length, then came out and moved down another avenue. Nearing the freeway, he watched lights flaring as cars whipped along its surface. The air was cold against his face now, and he kept his hands shoved deeply into his trouser pockets.

There was a sudden sound of tyres skidding, and he heard a boyish exclamation of dismay. Hurrying, he approached an off-ramp to see the boy darting towards the unmistakable form lying inert.

'Mickey?' he called.

As the boy lifted the fallen cat, other headlights flared as a car cut down the ramp, swiftly. Again tyres shrieked against the pavement.

'Mickey X!' the man screamed.

There was a thumping sound. The boy spun sideways. The car slowed, momentarily, its driver looking back, then it whipped on.

Mr Wiggins moved quickly, scrambling on to the ramp to lift the slight figure into his arms, then dodged off just as new lights shone and another car sped down the ramp. He carried the boy through dark shadows, off the avenue, into an alley, where he examined the still form in the dim light of a street-lamp beyond.

'My boy?' he said softly.

There was no reply.

Slowly then, wearily, he walked through the alleys, keeping to the darkness, until he reached the small cottage. He carried the boy inside and paused in the living-room with its litter. He whispered, 'Like a freedom-loving cat.' He nodded slowly. 'Yes.'

He carried the boy to the darkened room where his hand reached through blackness and switched on the bright light centred in the flat reflector hanging over the shining metal table.

Squeakie's Second Case

MARGARET MANNERS

I should have realized that things would begin to happen when Squeakie announced that she was taking a course in journalism. She broke the news to me in her own fashion, something like this:

'I think a wife should understand her husband's work, don't you, darling?'

'Yes,' I said, leaving myself wide open.

'And then, dear, I'll be able to help you. Your stuff is excellent, but newspaper work is stultifying.'

I dropped the book I was trying to read. I realized that this was a serious moment. 'Newspaper writing is a profession,' I said, 'an interesting profession, and not stultifying unless one harbours the delusion that one is a Pulitzer-prize novelist.'

'Oh,' she said softly, 'I couldn't feel that way about you, dear. But your writing *is* full of clichés. "Harbours a delusion", for instance.'

'Of course it is,' I said. 'I cultivate them carefully.' I refrained from remarking that Squeakie uses clichés too, but that she quotes them incorrectly which gives them a peculiar freshness. Rather like finding an avocado on an apple tree.

'After all,' she said, 'I *have* the woman's angle. That can only be helpful.'

'What are you talking about, sweetheart?' I said warily.

She smiled benevolently. 'My course. Professor Van Cornfeldt's course, Journalism as the New American Literature.'

'Good God!' I said. 'When did this happen?'

'It's a surprise for you, darling. And now I'm ready to handle one of your assignments.'

'One of *my* assignments? Squeakie!'

'Yes,' pridefully. 'Drink your coffee, dear, it will get cold. One with a feminine slant. You know, something I can get my teeth into!'

Being married to Squeakie is a full-time job. Her name is Desdemona really, but I do my best to forget it. Her father was a gentleman of the old school, a chronic quoter of Shakespeare. Squeakie takes after him. Not that that makes things so difficult. A little Shakespeare is a wonderful thing. It's just that sometimes I feel like the guy who was riding the tiger; he couldn't dismount. Well, for days I kept her at bay. Once I stayed out with the boys till four in the morning, because I didn't want to face it.

'Harris,' I kept telling her, 'would certainly know. Besides he's paying for my copy, not yours. And then your style, dear, it's different!'

'Harris,' she said, 'might like the difference.'

I tried to appeal to a better nature that wasn't there. 'Imagine, darling, what your style would be, full of Shakespearean quotes and all!'

'That,' she said smugly, 'is my idea. Freshen the journalistic jargon!'

Was it any wonder that I gave in when Harris presented me with the perfect (as I thought) way out? He wanted me to interview Ruth Denver Bradley, the popular novelist. It wasn't my sort of beat, and anyway I don't like lady authoresses. I had it all doped out. I'd make Squeakie happy by letting her interview the lady. Then I'd take her stuff and rewrite it, killing two birds with one stone.

If Squeakie didn't like it I could say the office had edited her piece. Naturally we couldn't do anything about that because I was supposed to have written it. There was always a chance that such a shocking experience might kill Squeakie's germinating talent in the first flower of youth. But I doubted it.

The night before the interview Squeakie talked about Ruth Denver Bradley and nothing else. She read the paragraph in *Who's Who* until I could have recited it. She informed me that she had been reading Ruth Denver Bradley's latest serial in *Modern Magazine*, and wasn't that lucky? She told me that it was a wonderful psychological novel, and favoured me with a synopsis.

'It's about a man who wants to marry but won't because something terrible happened to him when he was a child. There's something queer about his parents too. His father died from a fall one day, and that was a great shock to him. His mother isn't dead, but he acts as if she is, never mentions her. Oh, it's very mysterious. He's on the threshold of a political career ... David, which doctor is the one that Ruth Denver Bradley is married to?'

'He's a psychiatrist,' I said. 'Dr Robert Bradley.'

'She's a remarkable woman,' Squeakie said enviously. 'I wonder where she gets her material. Her stuff is so authentic.'

'Did Professor Van Cornfeldt teach you to say that?' I asked.

'Don't be jealous, darling. She's an amazing person – an invalid, you know. Never goes out. Rheumatic heart. Her life is a triumph of mind over matter.'

'Speaking of clichés!' I said.

I never did get to rewrite the interview because Squeakie never gave it to me. She simply sent it in to Harris with my name on top – and he liked it! Said he hadn't realized I was so versatile.

It was two weeks later, on my day off. The phone rang. I picked up the receiver and sure enough it was Harris.

'Ruth Denver Bradley killed in domestic accident!' Harris shouted. He always talks in headlines. 'Call her editor, David.

Get the story. See the bereaved husband. Give us the picture of the famous invalid at home, and death lurking on the staircase.'

'What happened?' I said.

Harris dropped the rhetoric and went to work. 'Tall, private house with a big stair well in the centre. She fell from the top all the way down. There's an invalid's elevator, a lift without a shaft, rigged up in the stair well for the convenience of the sick wife. But the lady was timid about it, and didn't use it very often. Obliging husband takes top floor for office, even though inconvenient for a doctor. His wife used downstairs floor. This morning she went up to see him and fell over – dizzy spell – bad heart— Look, do I have to tell you your business? Get busy!'

Squeakie was shocked by the news. 'All the same,' she said, 'I don't know how she could have fallen over, David. She wasn't tall, and those banisters are high.'

The phone rang again.

Harris was in a state. 'Listen, Meadow, the police say it wasn't an accident. The angle is suicide. Did you notice any melancholy when you interviewed the lady?'

'I don't think so,' I said, 'but it doesn't always show.'

But Squeakie wouldn't have suicide. 'It's ridiculous, darling. She didn't kill herself. I know. I talked to her. Do you think I wouldn't know? David, it was *murder*!'

The phone rang. 'Here we go again,' I said. I felt as if the top of my head would come off any minute. 'Go away,' I said to the mouthpiece, 'I don't like you.'

'Likewise,' said Harris, 'but there are things above our personal feelings. Louis Kingdon, editor of *Modern Magazine* called us up just now. He insists that it isn't suicide. He's going to raise the roof if the police accept that as the answer. Also he's saying some very nasty things about Ruth Bradley's husband. I think they're putting your friend Lieutenant Gregory Sawyer on the case. For God's sake, get over there. It's disgusting the way I keep getting you on the phone. If you were any sort of newspaper man you'd be there now.'

'The editor,' I told Squeakie, 'also feels it couldn't have been suicide. All right for the editor. He ought to know. But you! ... If this were the seventeenth century they'd burn you in the village square!'

She had the sense to keep quiet.

The first thing we saw when we entered the Bradley house was a square of heavy black fabric lying in a bulky heap on the tiled floor of the hall. We couldn't see the poor twisted body underneath it, but the grotesque impersonal shape of death was a terrible thing. It was a strange way for a woman to lie dead in her own house.

A few of the lads from downtown were hanging around. Doc Evans had evidently looked at the body and they were waiting to have it taken away. Lieutenant Gregory Sawyer looked pleased to see us, or maybe I should say to see Squeakie.

Before I could even pass the time of day with anyone, Squeakie went straight to the heart of the problem. 'It wasn't suicide,' she said, by way of answering Gregory's greeting. 'I talked with her two weeks ago.'

Gregory was a little taken aback, so I explained about the interview.

'I wondered when it would come to that, David,' he said. 'Be careful or they'll be calling you Mrs Meadow's husband.' He smiled fatuously at Squeakie and took us upstairs to show us the place from which Ruth Denver Bradley had fallen.

The house was impressively proportioned with very high ceilings. We walked slowly up the long flight of magnificent marble stairs which seemed to coil around the huge banistered oval of the stair well. Unfortunately the purity of classic line was marred by the heavy cables which ran from floor to roof. We reached the top landing and I looked down and saw the little lift cage crouching at the bottom. Beside it the black cloth spread like a stain on the tiled floor.

I asked Gregory where the cage had been when she fell.

'Just where it is now,' he said, 'at the bottom.'

'But I thought she rode up in it.'

'She did, but . . .'

'But the nurse must have gone down in it again,' Squeakie said. 'Of course! The nurse left her patient upstairs and went down in the lift cage. Then the patient fell. Since the cage was still downstairs the nurse must have been downstairs too. There's an alibi for you, Gregory. But where is the nurse? Have you questioned her? She's a pretty little thing. I saw her, you know, when I interviewed Mrs Bradley. Gregory, why did the nurse go downstairs after she had taken Mrs Bradley up?'

Gregory looked at me over Squeakie's head.

I shrugged. 'She does it by remote control,' I said. 'But the opinions expressed are not necessarily those of the management.'

He led us along the top landing. 'This is where she fell. The gate in the banisters was closed – but not bolted. You can see that it couldn't have been an accident.'

He was right. It was obvious that Mrs Bradley must have fallen through the gate which had been cut into the banisters to allow passage from the lift to the landing. The banisters *were* too high for anyone to have fallen over accidentally, and one couldn't very well fall through the gate unless one wanted to. It opened *inward* on the landing. There was a spring-closing so that if anyone stepped through it and forgot to bolt the gate there would be no dangerous gap. You could lean against it all you wanted to, and, bolted or not, it would never swing out. It had to be opened deliberately by the victim herself, or by someone else. Murder or . . .

'It might have been suicide,' I said.

Squeakie turned on me more in sorrow than in anger. 'But didn't I tell you that it wasn't suicide, David? Where is the nurse, Gregory?'

He shook his head. 'Gone, Squeakie – just like that! According to the maid who was cleaning silver in the pantry, the nurse, Katherine Dawson, came down in the lift to get her patient's shawl. She went out through the rear of the house and vanished. We haven't found her yet. But Haley is out looking.'

'Why did she run away?' Squeakie asked, and then went on dreamily, 'Ruth Denver Bradley hated her nurse. I saw that when I interviewed her. She kept smiling and saying little things in a nasty way. I think she wanted the girl to lose control of herself.'

'You ought to tell us things like that,' Gregory said gently. 'Any helpful word would be humbly appreciated by the police department.'

'That's sweet of you, Gregory. Where was Ruth Denver Bradley's husband when it happened?'

Gregory pointed to a door almost opposite the little gate. 'Dr Bradley was right in there, in his office. He was waiting for a patient to come for analysis.'

I measured the distance with my eye. 'Two or three steps would have been enough,' I said. 'Open the gate, push your wife through it, go back into the office ...'

'And the patient?' Squeakie asked, interrupting me without apology.

'It's a confusing case,' Gregory said sadly. 'Haley, bless his heart, calls it "distinguished". He's very proud of it. You see, the doctor's patient is none other than Harvey Thompson. And, of course, he doesn't want publicity, David. I gather he's been seeing the doctor for nerves. Probably brought on by his last campaign.'

'Harvey Thompson! The name is familiar,' Squeakie said.

'It ought to be,' I told her. 'You'll be voting him into office next time round if I know anything about women voters. He'll be the next candidate for comptroller. He's the power behind the clean-government campaign. What company you keep, Lieutenant!'

'Yes,' Gregory said. 'The guy exposes corruption wherever he finds it. I wonder if Haley's been stealing any candy bars lately. Anyway, Thompson just got in on this one. He was, if you can believe it, looking at his feet as he climbed the stairs to the doctor's office. He didn't see anything until Ruth Denver Bradley shrieked as she fell past him.'

'But he must have seen the nurse come down in the lift cage,' Squeakie said.

'He did. The cage came down with the nurse in it just as he began walking up. He had no idea that there was anyone waiting on the top landing.'

Squeakie's brow furrowed. 'But if she was going to see her husband in the office, why did Mrs Bradley wait on the landing? She was a sick woman. Why didn't she go into his office and sit down. The nurse could have brought the shawl to her there. Was she afraid that the nurse wouldn't come back?'

Gregory looked at her closely. 'I don't know,' he said. 'Dr Bradley took his wife's death pretty well, considering the circumstances. But when we told him the nurse was missing he nearly passed out. Look, I've got to go down and talk to all of them now. If you two want to hang around, I guess I won't have to notice you too much.'

We had barely reached the hall below when the front door opened and a gust of cold air carried a booming voice to us. 'Got her,' it said. 'I've got the nurse, Lieutenant. She's no bigger than a kitten, and is she scared! She says she forgot. Maybe it's amnesia.'

'Gosh!' Gregory said, very much pleased. 'Haley's done it again. Now we'll find out a few things.'

Sergeant Haley, better known in police circles as the Comet, stood there red-faced and proud. If he'd been holding the girl in his teeth he couldn't have looked more like a well-trained retriever bringing in the kill. Before I could say hello to him, the door of the living-room opened and a man came into the hall.

He was wearing a small brown beard and carried himself with a self-conscious air of assurance that some actors and doctors occasionally affect when dealing with other poor mortals. At the moment, however, his assurance seemed the worse for wear. It was evident that Dr Bradley had been badly shaken. He didn't look at us but at his wife's nurse. We looked at her too. She stood staring stupidly, pathetic as a frightened schoolgirl. Her navy topcoat hung from slender shoulders, and her hair was a mass of wind-ruffled curls.

'Katherine,' the doctor said, 'why did you go away? I've been so worried.'

The girl's eyes opened wider and wider until her whole face seemed to be lost and only eyes were left. They were so horrified I wanted to put my hands over them. I realized that it wasn't the doctor she was looking at but the form under the black fabric.

'My God!' she whispered. 'Who?'

'The doctor's wife is dead, Miss Dawson.' That was all Squeakie said, but it had a violent effect. The tired white face of the nurse seemed to float over her shoulders, and the enormous eyes lost focus.

'Oh,' she said softly, 'she killed herself. How cruel!' Then she swayed and Haley caught her as she fell.

Dr Bradley knelt anxiously beside the girl he called Katherine. He spoke only once, and then it was to Gregory. 'She didn't know,' he said. 'Can't you see she didn't even know?'

'Yes, I see.' Gregory's voice was as deliberate as an accusation.

Gregory chose to use the dead woman's study for his investigation, and Squeakie was there to take notes. Shorthand is the pretext Squeakie uses to intrude on the secret conversations of the police. As is usual with volunteer workers she didn't seem to be taking her work too seriously. Her principal interest was the dead woman's desk and bookcase. She made a thorough search of everything, but it was the bookshelves which seemed to fascinate her.

We were waiting for Haley to bring Louis Kingdon, the editor, in. Gregory thought we ought to do him first because he was in such a fury.

Suddenly Squeakie turned from her anxious perusal of book titles. 'They're so noncommittal,' she said sadly.

'Nonsense,' I said. For here I might be expected to shine. After all, I was a writer too, of sorts. 'They're craft books,' I explained. 'Dictionaries, reference books ... What would you expect in a writer's study?'

'Why – ideas, inspiration, something ...' Squeakie stopped and shook her head.

'You get those from life,' I said patiently. 'From going and seeing, hearing and doing.'

'But,' Squeakie said, 'she didn't go. She stayed right in this house.'

Louis Kingdon came into the room, and Gregory motioned us to keep quiet. He was a heavy man with powerful well-kept hands and a thick mane of brown hair. He had a way with women, courteous and bland, as if they were skittish horses. Squeakie looked as if she liked him. It interests me to see the men that Squeakie admires. They almost never look like me.

'Ruth Bradley didn't kill herself.' Kingdon spoke first. 'There are things going on in this house, Lieutenant. I think she was pushed over. It's the only answer. She certainly did not commit suicide.'

'You seem very sure,' Gregory spoke quietly.

'Of course, I'm sure. She had three instalments of the novel we're running still unwritten. Do you think any author would kill herself with a third of a book to write?'

'Isn't that unusual?' Gregory asked. 'I mean, don't you buy these things complete? Awful risk, isn't it?'

'Well, in a way,' Kingdon said. 'We don't do it often, but she worked better that way. We always had a full synopsis of the story. We knew we could have it finished if ... she wasn't a well woman,' he added lamely. 'But she'd been an invalid for years, there was no reason to suspect that anything would happen. You see, she was one of those writers who don't finish things unless the pressure is on. If I'd waited for a completed manuscript I'd have waited for ever.'

'You have the synopsis in your office?' Squeakie was standing in front of an open file she had been rummaging in. There was a gleam in her eye that I didn't like.

'No,' Kingdon said. 'I haven't. She kept it here.'

'And how were the various instalments sent to you? By mail?' I didn't get the drift of Squeakie's questions at all. Neither did Gregory but he sat there trying hard to look as if he did.

Kingdon smiled graciously. 'As a matter of fact, young lady, I usually called for them myself. That's why I came here today.' He frowned angrily.

'The nurse and the maid both say there was a manuscript waiting for me on the hall table in a manila envelope. It's not there now. I wish you'd try to find it for me.'

Gregory glared at him, then said, 'You think Ruth Bradley was murdered. Why?'

The editor looked satisfied at last. This was the question he had obviously been waiting for. 'Less than a week ago,' he said, 'Ruth telephoned me and asked me to come to see her. She sounded almost hysterical. I came immediately. She told me that she had discovered that her husband and her nurse, Katherine Dawson, were in love with each other. She hadn't said anything to either of them. But she said she couldn't go on pretending any longer. She was going to have her revenge. She was going to discharge the nurse, but she loved her husband and there would be *no* question of a divorce.'

Kingdon paused dramatically.

Gregory rose. 'Thanks,' he said dryly. 'I'll keep that in mind. You can go. We'll call you if we need you.'

Kingdon shook his head. 'I'd like to stay and look for that manuscript,' he said.

The maid, Mary, came in next. She was pretty and malicious, and evidently didn't like Miss Dawson. She told her story with many suggestive glances.

'I was polishing the fish slice when Mrs Bradley and Miss Dawson left the study together. I saw them both get into the lift cage. I looked special because I was surprised. Mrs Bradley never liked to use the elevator unless she had to. But before Katherine Dawson followed Mrs Bradley into the elevator I saw her – Katherine Dawson – deliberately lean over and *drop the shawl she was carrying on one of the hall chairs*.'

Gregory nodded, looking solemn as an owl. 'That's extremely important, Mary. What else can you tell us?'

'Well, I heard the noise of the lift going up, and then I heard it coming down again. I thought maybe Mrs Bradley had missed her shawl and was sending Dawson back for it. But I couldn't understand Dawson having dropped it like that, on purpose. Sure enough, I saw Dawson get out of the lift and pick up the shawl, but instead of taking it up she walked out through the hall to the rear of the house.'

'Haven't you forgotten something, Mary?' Squeakie said. 'Didn't you open the front door for someone?'

'I did not.' Mary sounded very sure of herself.

'But what about Mr Thompson?'

'Oh, him? When there's office hours for the doctor the door is left open. The patients walk in. I did see Mr Thompson for just a second. It was just before Dawson came down. After she went to the back of the house, I heard the rear door slam. I didn't see her again till just now when the sergeant brought her back.'

'You saw Mr Thompson start up the stairs, and then Miss Dawson came down in the lift and went towards the rear of the house? Is that right, Mary?' Gregory spoke carefully.

'That's right, sir. A minute or two later I heard the scream and saw Mrs Bradley's body hit the ... Oh, Sergeant, it was terrible! That poor, poor woman!' Mary turned to Haley and began to sniffle in her handkerchief.

Squeakie stuck her head out of the closet she was poking in to ask if Mary had seen the manuscript on the hall table that morning. Yes, Mary had seen it. Was it there later when Mrs Bradley fell? Mary looked puzzled and decided she couldn't remember. Squeakie sighed and stuck her head back in the closet.

Gregory told Mary how helpful she had been, and she went out still sniffling.

'Can I escort Mr Thompson in now, Lieutenant?' Haley asked in tones that would have been suitable for a church.

'Yes, you can escort him in now, Sergeant,' Gregory answered just as gravely. Haley marched out carrying his head as carefully as if the slightest breeze would blow it off his shoulders.

'Haley likes a distinguished case to be properly handled,' Gregory said.

'Heavens! Look what I've found! It was in an envelope under some papers.' With all the flourish of a magician bringing a rabbit out of the hat, Squeakie held out her hand to us. On it there was a tiny key.

'So what?' I said. 'Everybody has an old key or two knocking around in desk drawers. It doesn't mean a thing.'

Squeakie put her head on one side and fixed one bright eye on the key. She looked like a sparrow about to pounce on a juicy worm. 'Well,' she said vaguely, 'suppose it's the "*key of villainous secrets*"!'

'What's that?' demanded Gregory.

'A key of villainous secrets? It's a line from *Othello*.'

'Oh,' said Gregory. 'Is that all the reward of so much searching, Squeakie?'

It was a rhetorical question, but Squeakie saw fit to answer it with a provocative I-know-something-I-won't-tell shake of the head.

I translated for him. 'She says no. In other words she did find something else, but she wants to be coaxed.'

Gregory brought his hand down on the desk in a slap that made the lamp wobble. 'Don't withhold evidence,' he thundered. 'What did you find?'

'Well! If you're going to be nasty about it. I found the

synopsis to Ruth Denver Bradley's novel.'

Gregory tried not to look disappointed. 'Better turn it over to Kingdon.'

Squeakie gave him a winning smile. 'Not right away, Gregory. We can leave it where it is for a while. You see, I've been following the serial in *Modern Magazine* and later on I'd like to read the synopsis and see how the story ends.'

'Good Lord!' I said.

Fortunately at this moment Harvey Thompson came in. He was a tall, thin man, slightly grey at the temples and had the worried air of the reformer. He looked the part of the righteous man, the enemy of corruption, but I had to admit he lived up to it. A man who made it his business to uncover ugly scandals couldn't be too careful. Thompson neither smoked nor drank. It was rumoured that he had recently been courting a young society girl, but his behaviour on this was, as the saying goes, above reproach.

'Sit down, Mr Thompson,' Gregory spoke carefully. 'Nasty for you to have been here just at that moment. You had an appointment with the doctor, I presume?'

Harvey Thompson nodded. 'I had an appointment,' he said. 'You must forgive me if I seem a little shaky. It was pretty dreadful. She fell right past me, you know?'

'Have you any opinion at all about the case?' Gregory asked.

Thompson smiled thinly. 'I'm not qualified to have one,' he said graciously, 'but being human, of course I have. I think it was suicide. The woman was ill. Probably she was depressed. When the nurse left her alone at the top of the stairs the impulse came to her. She was fascinated by the idea of falling ...'

'Bosh,' Squeakie said rudely. 'She wasn't that type, Mr Thompson. She'd have been more likely to kill someone else than herself.'

'Oh,' Mr Thompson said, 'I may very well be wrong. I didn't know Mrs Bradley. Just seen her once or twice walking around with her cane and shawl. Such a pity for a young woman to be an invalid. Must have been hard on her husband.'

'Excuse me,' Squeakie said, rising and moving towards the door. 'I'll go and tell Mr Kingdon that I've found the synopsis. Isn't it lucky?' she said smiling at Thompson. 'I found the synopsis of Mrs Bradley's serial in *Modern Magazine* right here in this room.'

The door closed quietly and she was gone.

'Hmmmm,' Gregory said, 'I think I'll go and see Miss Dawson.' He opened the door and indicated that Harvey Thompson could go out first. 'If you'd like to leave, Mr Thompson, I think ...'

'Thank you, Lieutenant. But I'll wait for a few words with the doctor. There may be something I can do. I shouldn't like him to think I ran off.'

When we crossed the hall I saw that the body had been removed, and that made me think of fingerprints. But Haley said only those of the nurse and Mrs Bradley had been found on the gate.

We found Miss Dawson in the library. She was very nervous. Her fists were clenched in her lap until the knuckles showed white. She didn't look at us as she talked.

'Mrs Bradley wanted to go up to talk to her husband. She didn't say why. I went with her, but when we reached the top I discovered I'd left her shawl downstairs. It's very important that Mrs Bradley be protected from chill. Any change in temperature is ...' she stopped short, stricken. 'I mean, was bad for her. I went down to get the shawl but I couldn't find it anywhere. I looked and looked. I thought that Mrs Bradley had probably gone into the doctor's office and was talking to him there, so I just kept on looking.' She paused apologetically as if ashamed to offer us a feeble excuse.

'I haven't been well these last few days, overtired or something. Suddenly I felt dizzy and ill. I slipped into a coat that I keep in the rear of the house and went out through the back door to take a walk around the block. I must have been feeling worse than I thought, because I forgot where I was and wandered around in a daze. I didn't know what the sergeant wanted when he found me.' Her eyes filled with tears. 'It never occurred to me that Mrs Bradley would kill herself. I feel guilty. I shouldn't have left her.'

'You didn't tell that quite right, Miss Dawson,' Gregory said softly. 'You didn't have to look for that shawl. It was on the hall chair where you had deliberately dropped it. Mary saw you pick it up when you went to the rear of the house.'

The girl moaned and bent forward as if to protect herself from a blow. 'I haven't been well,' she said brokenly. 'I forget things.'

'It won't do, Miss Dawson. You knew something was going to happen up there on the landing. At the last minute you lost your nerve and dropped the shawl so that you'd have an excuse to get away before it did happen. You see, we know about you and the doctor.'

The girl covered her face with her hands.

'Leave her alone!' Dr Bradley had opened the door and was standing on the threshold. I wondered how much he had heard.

'You can see the girl is near collapse. She didn't know. I didn't know. There was no plan. Do you think I murdered my wife? Why, I didn't even know she was coming upstairs to see me! Stop badgering Miss Dawson – she can't bear any more.'

That was pretty evident to all of us. But Gregory was a policeman, and this was a queer case. 'Who was responsible for your wife's death? You had a motive. Miss Dawson ran away. She evidently knew something was going to happen. I'm sorry but I may have to do quite a bit of badgering, as you call it.'

'All right, I'll tell you,' the doctor said. He came into the room and Squeakie slipped in after him. How much had *she* heard?

'Robert, please!' Katherine Dawson was trembling.

'Why not?' the doctor said bitterly. 'It's just a matter of

washing a little dirty linen in front of others. After all, people have done it before me all my life. I've listened to all the sins of humanity. Now I must talk about my own. Don't be afraid, my dear.'

Katherine Dawson stared at him in amazement. 'But, Robert, I . . .'

'Don't be silly, Katherine. Reticence is all very well, but not if one is charged with murder because of it. Lieutenant, my wife was a sick woman, physically and spiritually. You noticed I do not say mentally. She was a thwarted woman. "Hell hath no fury . . ." I didn't scorn her,' he added, 'but I no longer loved her. I gave her cause for misery, but I tried not to show it. I had no idea she knew about Katherine and me.'

'She told Mr Kingdon about it,' said Squeakie, 'and he thinks your wife was murdered.'

'Murdered!' Dr Bradley shouted. 'But she wasn't murdered! That's what I want to tell you. Kingdon can say what he likes but I know human nature. Human nature is my business. My wife killed herself, and no unwritten story could have stopped her. Her motive was the cruellest, the ugliest one that exists. Spite! She did it to punish us, to make us feel responsible for her death. She was bringing Katherine up to my office to make a scene that would humiliate us both. Katherine couldn't bear to go through such a scene in front of me. That was why she dropped the shawl and came down in the elevator. Ruth couldn't follow her down the stairs. My wife stood there thwarted. Her prey had run away. She was beside herself. The strain on her heart must have been terrible. Perhaps she felt she might never recover from the effects of her rage. In any case, she knew what it would do to our lives if she were found dead. She threw herself down. It's the only way it could have been. Before God, I didn't push her. I didn't even know she was there.'

He said it sincerely, impressively, but somehow it wasn't satisfactory. Katherine Dawson, on the other hand, was suddenly radiant. It was clear that she had thought him guilty of his wife's death. It was equally clear that she believed his story, whether we did or not.

'Tell me, Doctor,' Squeakie said suddenly, 'did you read your wife's stories?'

'No,' he said, 'I did not. I have never been particularly fond of popular fiction. Perhaps I should have taken more interest in Ruth's career,' he added apologetically, 'but I was terribly busy myself and somehow . . .' his voice trailed away.

'I wish,' Squeakie said, 'that you would read one now. There's a current issue of *Modern Magazine* in the living-room. Read an instalment of your wife's story. It will take your mind off yourself. And you'll understand your wife better.'

'All right,' the doctor said, 'you ask in a way that makes it impossible for me to refuse. But I want to say that I think you are inexcusably impertinent.'

Squeakie smiled at him without rancour. 'You'll feel better later,' she said smugly. 'To understand me is to pardon all.' She turned her back on him and stood looking down at the fireplace.

'The hitch,' I said, 'lies in understanding her. It can't be done.'

As the doctor and Miss Dawson left, Squeakie suddenly dropped to her knees. 'Gregory, something has been burned in this fireplace. I wonder when.'

Gregory was grubbing in the fireplace. 'I'll have Haley's skin for this,' he said. 'Paper ash, quite a lot of it! And completely burned.'

We went after Mary, who seemed much pleased by so much attention from the police. Yes, she *had* smelled something burning. It was while Dr Bradley was calling the police. She had rushed out to the kitchen to see if there was anything on the stove, but there hadn't been, so she decided it was just the incinerator smoking.

We thanked her and asked Mr Kingdon. Evidently the missing manuscript still had Mr Kingdon worried; he was quite snappy. How did we expect him to smell anything burning when he wasn't in the house until after the doctor's telephone call?

We tried Mr Thompson, who was standing uncomfortably in the hall, looking as if he didn't want to stay and didn't want to go. He hadn't smelled anything, but he had been so upset. There might have been such an odour and he would not have noticed it.

'Look,' Squeakie said suddenly, as if she were about to do us a great favour. 'You carry on down here, Gregory, and I'll go up and see if I can find what this key fits.'

'Wait,' Gregory said. But Squeakie had already stepped into the lift cage. We stood and watched its crawling ascent to the top floor.

'Maybe she wants us to see that nobody follows her. She shouldn't be doing that, David.'

'Are you a policeman or a mouse?' I said. 'Why don't you stop her?'

Gregory changed the subject quickly. 'Do you think the doctor killed his wife?'

'I don't know,' I said. 'But I bet Squeakie doesn't. She doesn't like her suspects obvious. It wouldn't surprise me if she tried to pin it on Kingdon. He seems awfully eager to have us arrest Bradley.'

'But Kingdon wasn't in the house at the time of her death!' Gregory protested.

'That's probably what'll make Squeakie suspect him,' I said. 'And don't worry, she'll find a way to put him in the house if she needs him there.'

'Bradley's suicide theory looks all right. It *could* have happened that way.'

'Maybe,' I said. 'But when these professional students of the human mind are out, they are way out. I agree with Kingdon that she wouldn't have left the story unfinished. And what *did* happen to that missing instalment, Gregory? Is Squeakie looking for it?'

'I think Squeakie found it,' he said. 'That's what was

burned in the fireplace. But who did it? And why?'

The living-room door was thrown open and Dr Bradley came out. He was holding a copy of *Modern Magazine* in his hands and his voice shook when he spoke.

'My wife,' he said unsteadily, 'my wife! This story ... Lieutenant, I don't ... Good God!'

A woman had screamed somewhere upstairs. We stood there transfixed, and suddenly moved all at once. 'It's Squeakie,' I said. 'Hurry! It's Squeakie!'

The lift was at the top, so I started to run up the stairs. Gregory was right behind me. But it was the bulky Haley who passed us and reached the top first. 'Coming, Mrs Meadow!' he yelled, as he knocked me out of the way. 'We'll get him!'

We followed him into the doctor's office. Squeakie was standing in the middle of the room. She looked just as she always does, except that one of her shoes was missing. She stood there, one shoe on and one shoe off, looking at us, calm and self-possessed. Haley was red in the face and puffing like a locomotive. Everybody looked like the devil except Squeakie.

At that moment Dr Bradley came in. Squeakie limped over to him with the uneven gait caused by the shoeless foot. She picked up his hand and dropped the little key into it. 'I found that in your wife's study,' she said.

'Darling,' I said, 'what happened?'

Bradley stared at the little key in horror. 'But I had only one,' he said. 'How did she get it?' He pulled a little chain out of his vest pocket and showed us another key just like it.

'At first,' Squeakie said, 'I thought you had killed her. You were the only one with a motive. But there was *another* motive. I didn't see it immediately. It was so *unusual*. Even stranger than your suicide theory, Doctor. It was a motive as fantastic as something distorted in a dream.'

'Squeakie,' I said wildly, 'why did you scream?'

'There was a mouse, I think,' she said. 'Hurry, let's go, Gregory.'

'Jeepers!' Haley said, 'you didn't scream on account of a

mouse did you, Mrs Meadow?'

'No, I didn't scream on account of it.'

'What *did* you do on account of it?' I asked.

'I threw my shoe at it.' She pointed to the far corner of the room. I went and retrieved her shoe.

'Where are we going?' Gregory asked her. He sounded rather tired.

'To get the murderer,' she said.

He clutched his hair. 'Where would the murderer be, Squeakie?'

'If we hurry we'll find him in Ruth Denver Bradley's study. He'll be in an awful dither. He's looking for the synopsis of her novel, and I hid it behind the bookcase!'

We tiptoed down the stairs. Squeakie said we shouldn't use the lift because it would make a noise.

When we reached the study door we all heard the faint sounds of someone moving around inside.

'Careful, Lieutenant,' Haley said importantly. He opened the door and slipped into the study. Gregory went in after him. The rest of us had to peer through the half-opened door. But the angle of the door made it impossible for us to see who was in the room. The faces of Gregory and Haley were registering emotion, but not revealing information. Then they both turned and looked at Squeakie in pained surprise, as if she had dropped a red-hot rivet in their laps.

To my amazement Dr Bradley spoke. He couldn't see any more of the person in the room than we could – but he said: 'Arrest him, Lieutenant. He killed my wife.'

They brought Harvey Thompson out quietly. There was a look about him that I can't describe, a look of having come to the end of a long road and being glad it was over. Patient and doctor looked at each other, and the patient's eyes fell.

'I am very sorry,' he said. 'She must have been a remarkable woman. Doctor, I am sorry.'

Dr Bradley stared at the man before him. 'I understand,' he said at last. 'But the tragedy is greater than you suppose. There was no need to kill my wife, Mr Thompson. No one in this world would ever have known, no one would have recognized you. It is a waste of both your lives.'

The man who fought corruption in high places bowed his head and they took him away.

Afterwards we had a quiet session in the library and Squeakie told us all about it.

'Gregory,' Squeakie said, 'was looking for clues to support the motive of the husband in love with his wife's nurse. It was a good, orthodox motive. But I said to myself, Suppose he didn't kill her? You see?'

There was a pause while Squeakie sat there purring.

Gregory looked at me. 'I'll bite my tongue off before I'll ask her,' I said.

'OK,' he said, 'but the whole police department is losing face.' He turned to Squeakie. 'Where did you get by *supposing* he didn't kill her, Squeakie?'

'Well, then, I had to look for another motive. When I found one I had another suspect at the end of it. You see, I had to have a clue that led me to a motive.'

'The missing manuscript?' I asked.

Squeakie beamed on me. 'That was it, David. At first the manuscript seemed to point to Mr Kingdon. After all, what would a politician *who had never met his doctor's wife* have to do with her manuscript? *And why would a man kill a woman he didn't even know?*'

She went on, fixing us with a glittering eye, 'What was in the missing manuscript?'

'I'll bite,' I said.

'Remember, David, I told you about the story? It was the story of a man whose life was cruelly warped in his childhood. His father fell downstairs and was killed. Everyone thought it was an accident and the man was buried. There was a great deal of sympathy for the beautiful young widow and her little son. The mother wears mourning and shows great sorrow. But the child is horrified by her grief. He knows that she killed his father. He saw her push her husband to his death. The boy grows up, haunted by the knowledge of his mother's crime, fearing its discovery.

'In an effort to compensate for his tainted heritage he lives a goody-goody life, never indulging in any of the normal amusements of the young male. The self-righteous puritan flourishes. His zeal for reforming leads him into politics where he is successful. After years of a careful bachelor existence he falls in love and wishes to marry. Very sensibly, he consults a psychiatrist, and in seeking his cure, tells the doctor his life story.

'You remember, David, I wondered where Ruth Denver Bradley got the material for her plots? Now do you see? She had a key made to her husband's case records. The *key of villainous secrets* indeed! She found a wealth of material there. Strangely enough, she didn't even know the name of the man whose story she stole. The case histories used numbers instead of names.

'But one day the man who is struggling with his past picks up a copy of a magazine and begins a serial that seems terribly familiar. He looks at the author's name and is horrified to see that it is written by the wife of his own doctor. He tells himself it is only a coincidence. But when the next instalment appears he knows it is true. His shameful story is being offered to the public. He feels sure that as the story progresses it will reveal his identity. He sees his career ruined, his marriage shattered. He, the incorruptible politician, will be branded as the son of a murderess!'

Squeakie paused for breath.

'Hold on,' Gregory said, 'how did he know that the manuscript wasn't already completed and in the editor's hands?'

Louis Kingdon answered him. 'I told him,' he said. 'I knew Thompson. Made it a point to be cordial whenever I met him. I ran into him one day when I was leaving Ruth's house with a manuscript. I chatted about it, among other things.'

'Well,' Squeakie said, snatching the narrative away from Kingdon, 'when Thompson came into the house today he saw the instalment lying on the hall table and took it. He probably hid it inside his coat. He had intended to see Ruth Denver Bradley, I think, to ask her to change the end of the story completely. He saw the nurse leave Mrs Bradley alone. He ran up the stairs, spoke to her. He remembered his father's death. He opened the gate quietly and pushed her through it. Then he turned and ran downstairs. When Dr Bradley came out of his office it looked as if Harvey Thompson was just coming *up* the steps. While Dr Bradley was calling the police, Thompson burned the manuscript in the fireplace. It didn't occur to him that there would be a synopsis.

'I hadn't any proof,' Squeakie added. 'I had to get Dr Bradley to read the story so that he would see what his wife had done. Even so, it would have been hard to prove if Thompson had denied it. That's why I told him that I had found the synopsis. Then I went upstairs and screamed so that you'd all come up there. I wanted him to have an opportunity to get into the study to look for it, so that we could find him there.'

I was very weary when I took my wife home. 'You complicated this story,' I said. 'You really ought to write it.'

She smiled at me.

'Was there really a mouse upstairs, Squeakie?' I said.

'Darling, why do you think I threw my shoe?'

But that wasn't an answer, was it? I think that mouse was a red herring.

The Silent Butler

HAROLD Q. MASUR

Dr Rollo Butler was not a handsome man. He was slight in stature, myopic, with a large mottled nose, a small prim mouth and a retiring chin. Middle age had thickened the paunch around his middle and removed most of the hair on top. He was vague, unassuming and slightly abstracted.

All these unprepossessing features, however, did not preclude other endowments. He was a noted internist, highly regarded, with an active practice and a position on the staff of a leading hospital. He was a bachelor, somewhat shy; nevertheless he had an eye for feminine architecture – the nurse who greeted me was extraordinarily decorative.

'Good afternoon, Mr Jordan,' she said. 'I expect the doctor shortly. Will you wait?'

'Of course,' I said, and sat down to contemplate the view.

The pages of a magazine rustled and I became aware of additional scenery. She was ensconced in a chair, reading a copy of *Vogue*, her legs crossed. They were excellent legs, long and silken, with slender ankles, shapely calves, and delicately dimpled knees. My gaze wandered appreciatively upward along the tall, svelte, provocatively assembled figure and finally reached the face. Here I received a bit of a shock. She was not young. Neither was she past the deadline. There was considerable mileage left in both face and body. About forty, I judged, with artfully applied make-up, a bold and vivid mouth, eyes cool and incurious.

I had risen and walked over to a window that looked out at East End Avenue. It was precisely four o'clock when I saw the doctor arrive in a cab. Some construction work at the side of the road prevented the cab from making a U turn, so it deposited him on the far corner.

He headed diagonally towards the building entrance and was halfway across when the automobile roared into sight. It was drizzling lightly and the doctor had turned up his collar. I saw what happened and I was powerless to stop it. The car was rocketing north at breakneck speed. I knew it was inevitable and I saw the whole thing in a sudden, shocking flash.

In that one brief instant before the accident I saw Dr Butler's face, his appalled expression, his rigidly stretched mouth. I did not hear him scream, nor did I hear any blast of the car's horn.

I watched in horror.

I saw the shattering impact and I saw the doctor sail high like a limp rag doll and I saw him bounce on the pavement alongside the kerb. The car faltered slightly and then it high-balled on, careening wildly around the corner, heading west and out of sight.

For a moment longer I was rooted to the floor. Then I plunged for the door. The nurse jumped and the brunette patient half-rose from her chair with a stifled gasp.

When I reached the street I knew at once there was nothing anyone could do. That fine brain crammed with special knowledge was no longer functioning.

Two inquisitors from the detective squad kept me in the doctor's office for questioning. Apparently I was the only witness. Neither the nurse nor the patient had seen a thing, the rain had emptied the streets, and so the boys concentrated on me. De Castro was a tall, rangy specimen with an angular face and ravenous eyes. Hahn was heavy, shambling and disarmingly benevolent, a man with a habit of fingering his left earlobe while he talked. De Castro I had never met; Hahn knew me. He glanced at his partner with a bland smile.

'You ever get in trouble, this is your boy. Quick on the trigger, brainy, knows the law, knows a few loopholes, knows some of the brass down at Headquarters.' He turned back to me. 'We got an epidemic in this city, Counsellor. Hit-and-run drivers, must be catching. Tell us about the car.'

'Buick,' I said. 'A 1956 four-door sedan, light blue, white-walled tyres in front and black in rear on left side – which is all I saw – plus a slight dent in the fender on the same side.'

'Not bad,' De Castro grunted.

'See?' Hahn told him. 'What did I tell you? An eye for details too. Big help to us. Let's get the ball rolling right now.' He looked at me hopefully as he reached for the phone. 'Didn't happen to catch the licence number, did you, Counsellor?' I shook my head and he put a report through to Communications, demanding an immediate broadcast. Then he sat back and regarded me with long-faced deliberation. 'How long have you known the victim?'

'About five years.'

'Were you here this afternoon on a professional visit?'

'I'm not sick, if that's what you mean,' I said.

'Why, then?'

'A matter of instruction. I'm trying a negligence case next week. Client of mine was injured and I needed some background. The defence will put a couple of specialists on the stand I'll have to cross-examine and Doctor Butler was coaching me on the medical aspects. That's part of a lawyer's job. In court he has to know almost as much as the experts.'

'Was Butler going to testify?'

'No, sir. In this case his opinion probably wouldn't carry much weight.'

De Castro frowned. 'Why not?'

'Because the defence would claim bias. He's the plaintiff's uncle.'

'What's the name?'

'Ellen Bryant. Matter of fact, he referred this case to my

office, told his niece to retain me.'

'Let's get back to the Buick. You say the driver didn't stop for a look at his victim.'

'No, sir. If anything he increased his speed.'

'Panic,' Hahn said. 'Lost his head.'

'Let's get on with it,' De Castro said. 'Any description of the driver, Jordan?'

'All I caught was a blur. He was rolling too fast and the windshield wipers were going.'

'This bird we'll nail,' Hahn said. 'We got a prominent victim, and the Commissioner will probably assign fifty men to the case.'

'He's dead right now,' De Castro said.

There was no further information I could give them. Both men rose and thanked me for my assistance. I was sitting in Dr Rollo Butler's chair when they left. I looked around at all the trappings of his profession – the examination table, X-ray machine, sterilizer, blood-pressure gauge and a lot of other equipment I couldn't identify.

The door opened and the nurse appeared. Nancy Cook, nurse-receptionist. Oval face, olive-tinted, with delicate nostrils and a full mouth. Her usual smile had vanished; now she was subdued and distressed. My eyes followed her movements with appreciation. More than once I had considered trying to ripen our acquaintance into something deeper, but had always swallowed the impulse.

She held out a folder. 'I thought you might want this, Mr Jordan.'

'What is it?'

'Some notes the doctor dictated. About his niece Ellen Bryant, about her case. Medical facts he thought you might need. He gave them to me last night and I typed them this morning.'

I brightened a little. 'You're very kind.'

'Not at all.' She hesitated, looking troubled. 'I – I wonder if you'd make a suggestion.'

'About what?'

'Well, you were the doctor's lawyer. I hardly know what to do now that he ... that he's ...'

'No problem,' I said. 'Stay on the job until we get his estate organized. There must be plenty of work. Put his records in order and start cancelling appointments. Who handled his patients when he took a vacation?'

'Dr Butler never took a vacation.'

'They can shift for themselves. There's no shortage of doctors in this town.'

She nodded gravely. 'You're quite right. There is a tremendous amount of work. I'll start this evening.'

Loyal, I thought, conscientious too, and lovely – a dwindling commodity in the employment market. So I made a prompt decision. 'You can't work without nourishment. May I take you to dinner?'

There was no manufactured surprise. She merely glanced down at her uniform. 'Like this?'

'On you it's elegant.'

'I really have no appetite.'

'Neither do I. But we both need a drink. And we can force ourselves. Do us good. I'll get you back early.'

She nodded and retired to touch up her face. We found a small oasis in the neighbourhood and settled for a booth in the rear. Alcohol always helps to cement a friendship, and two Sidecars apiece had us talking freely. She was a warm, responsive and knowledgeable companion. We dined sparingly and departed reluctantly. I took her back to the office and headed for home.

By ten o'clock I was studying the notes she had prepared, memorizing the names of various bones, muscles and tendons.

My client, Ellen Bryant, had been injured by a fall. Liability was conclusive and I'd been haggling with the insurance company for almost two years. The court dockets in New York are jammed, but now the case was coming to trial. I fully expected the defence to make an acceptable offer after we selected a jury, but in any event I had to be prepared.

I found it hard to concentrate. My brain kept wandering, reviving pictures of the accident, the rag-doll figure flopping brokenly through the air, bouncing on the pavement, lying motionless in a puddle of water.

The doorbell rang.

I rose, shuffled through the foyer and opened up. It was Ellen Bryant, standing small and forlorn, her raincape dripping. She was under considerable strain, holding her face together with a visible effort. She was a petite girl with tawny hair and wistful eyes.

I held the door wide and pulled her in.

She stood for a moment in the living-room, facing me, her throat working. I said, 'What is it, Ellen?' and then the clutch slipped. Her eyes welled up with moisture. I moved in and put my arms around her.

'Let it go,' I said. 'You're entitled. He was your only blood relative.'

She wept silently. After a while the convulsions subsided. She backed away and looked at me through tear-stained eyes. She swallowed twice before getting wired for sound. 'It's not Uncle Rollo,' she said. 'I was all broken up when they told me and I cried. But he's gone now and there's nothing we can do about it. It's Mark I'm worried about. My husband.'

'What about Mark?'

'They arrested him.'

'Who? Why?'

'Two policemen. They say it was Mark's car that killed Uncle Rollo. They say he did it deliberately.' A shiver ran through her. 'They took him away two hours ago.'

'What kind of car does Mark drive?'

'A Buick.'

'Light blue?'

'Yes.'

'A 1956 model?'

'Yes.'

'White-walled tyres in front, black in rear?'

'Yes.'

The boy was in trouble, deep trouble. 'All right,' I said, 'what else happened?'

'They asked Mark if he knew Dr Rollo Butler and he said yes, the doctor was my uncle. Then they asked him where he'd been at four o'clock. He said he was in the office, working. They were sceptical. And then they asked me if I knew how to drive. I told them no, I never learned. They put handcuffs on Mark and took him away. I wanted to go along, but they wouldn't let me. I was frightened, I tried to phone you, nobody answered. I just couldn't sit around the apartment, so I came over here.' Her chin went out of control for a moment, but she pressed her lips together and looked at me beseechingly. 'Please, Mr Jordan, I—'

The phone rang and I reached and got a vaguely familiar voice in my ear. 'Counsellor?'

'Speaking.'

'Detective Hahn. Got a little job of identification for you. Can you come down here at once?'

'Where?'

'Station house at Forty-ninth.'

'In about twenty minutes,' I said. I hung up and took Ellen's arm. 'Come along. Maybe I can arrange for you to see Mark.'

She was silent in the taxi, her fingers laced tightly together, staring straight ahead. I eased some of the tension by getting her to talk about Butler. As a boy the doctor had been shy and diffident. So he found refuge in books. Here was a field in which he could compete, in which he could excel. His muscles remained flabby but his brain toughened. He was an honours student at college and made a brilliant record in medical school. But the childhood trauma of rejection and his un-attractiveness to girls had left him with few social graces. He was a lonely man, lost in his work.

'Did you see him often?' I asked.

'He'd come to dinner about once a month.'

'How did he get along with Mark?'

She hesitated, nibbling her lip. 'Well ... they didn't have much in common.'

'And you?'

'We were very fond of each other.'

I knew that to be true. I had drawn the doctor's will and he'd made Ellen his sole legatee. I could not estimate the size of his estate, but it must have been substantial. Ellen had suddenly become a rich girl.

She plucked at my sleeve. 'Mark has no motive. Why would they think that he ...'

I hated to disillusion her, but she had a right to know. And it would come out soon enough. I explained about the will, about her inheritance, and she shrank away, knuckles plugged against her mouth. She sat, shaking her head, disbelieving.

The local precinct on Forty-ninth Street had a pair of green lights on each side of the entrance door. It was a forlorn structure that also accommodated the offices of Homicide East. We climbed a flight of stairs and entered an anteroom where a police stenographer busy at a typewriter was being watched by a large, impressive gent seated in a hard-backed chair against the wall. He stood instantly at the sight of Ellen and advanced, quick concern etched across his face.

'Mrs Bryant,' he said. 'This is terrible, a dreadful mistake. I'm sure everything is going to be all right.' He patted her hand in a paternal gesture. 'I phoned your apartment as soon as I heard, but you were gone. I thought you might want me to call my attorney.'

'Thank you, Mr Korvin. You're very kind, but it won't be necessary. This is Scott Jordan, our lawyer. Scott, I'd like you to meet Charles Korvin, Mark's employer.'

Korvin was a man in his middle forties. He had rugged, flat-cheeked features. He was muscular, solid and self-assured. I knew that he was a building contractor operating in the suburbs, with a sales office located in New York where Mark Bryant was employed.

'Heard of you, Jordan. Delighted to meet you. I think Mark is in good hands, Ellen.'

I nodded at the compliment. But was curious, wondering how he'd got there so soon. 'Did Mark ask them to call you, Mr Korvin?'

He shook his head. 'Mark told them he'd been at the office all afternoon, that he hadn't left until six. They wanted to check with me.'

An effective alibi, I thought, if substantiated. 'And what did you tell them?'

He shrugged expressively. 'I wasn't there myself. I had left about three for the Architect's Exhibit to look at some new building materials.'

Hahn appeared at the door. 'There you are, Counsellor. Come in. Everybody else stay put.'

Mark Bryant was sitting on the edge of a chair. His hands were clamped over his knees, white-knuckled. He looked stunned and lethargic.

'Hello, Mark,' I said.

He attempted a smile that only distorted his mouth. De Castro, towering over him, said, 'Can you identify him, Jordan?'

'Sure,' I said. 'He's Mark Bryant.'

'That's not what I mean. Can you identify him as the man driving the Buick when Butler was killed?'

'No. I thought I made that clear. I barely saw the driver's face at the time of the accident.'

Mark turned his worry-kneaded face pathetically towards mine and gave it a negative shake. 'It wasn't me. Honest, Mr Jordan—'

'Quiet!' snapped De Castro.

'Are you quite sure it was his car?' I asked.

'Positive. The description fits and the lab boys dug a piece of fabric out of a broken headlight that matches Butler's coat.'

Mark's head came up and his voice rose on a thin edge of hysteria. 'They're framing me. I want a lawyer.'

'You have a lawyer,' I said. 'Me. Your wife just asked me to represent you, Mark.'

'Now, wait a minute,' Hahn said mildly. 'Aren't you putting yourself in a peculiar predicament, Counsellor? You're the only eyewitness we have and the State is going to use you as its star witness. How the hell are you going to appear against the defendant and represent him at the same time?'

He was right, of course. It was highly unorthodox. But my testimony would be limited to the identification of a specific vehicle, not its driver. And then a sudden thought exploded in my head. If Mark's car had been stolen from its parking place, it would not have returned to the same location. Parking spots are at a premium in New York and that particular site probably would have been taken. 'Did you find your car where you left it?' I asked him.

'Yes. It was in a parking lot. They brought it to me when I presented the ticket.'

'Did you notice a broken headlight?'

'No. The attendant backed it out and I didn't look at the front of the car, not until I got home, and then I wasn't sure when it happened.'

'How about Mr Korvin's secretary? Wasn't she with you all afternoon?'

He shook his head miserably. 'She's been out a couple of days with the flu. That's why I had to stick around the office.'

De Castro said, 'Hard up for money, are you, Bryant?'

There was a show of spirit. 'No. I have a pretty good job.'

'But if your wife inherited a bundle from the doctor's estate, that would help, wouldn't it?'

'I – I wouldn't kill a man for money.'

'We've got a case against you, boy. Means, motive and opportunity. Why not come clean? Save everybody a lot of trouble.'

'All right, Mark,' I said. 'You've told them your side of the story. From now on, clam up. You've lost the use of your tongue. Just sit tight.'

'You're a big help,' De Castro said.

'What did you expect? He's my client. And now, gentlemen, if you'll excuse me, I have some work to do.'

The work included a visit on the following morning to the parking lot used by Mark Bryant. Nobody recalled the Buick, or remembered when it had arrived or left. Several hundred cars were in and out all the time.

The work also included a visit to Dr Butler's office. Nancy Cook was busy on the phone, but she gave me a welcoming smile, her eyes warm. 'How's it going?' I asked when she hung up.

'Not bad. I've cancelled most of the appointments and arranged with another doctor to handle the more urgent cases.'

'Good. Let's go into the other room. I want to ask you some questions and we'll be more comfortable there.'

We got settled in the consulting room and she sat back, regarding me expectantly.

'Look, Nan,' I said, 'you spent a lot of time with the doctor and you probably knew him better than anybody else.'

She nodded soberly. 'I imagine that's true.'

'Was there anything in his private life I ought to know about? Any special friends?'

'The Korvins seemed rather close to him these last six months. I know he entered a business deal with them.'

'What kind of deal?'

'He bought stock in Mr Korvin's real-estate business.'

'For how much?'

'Fifty thousand dollars.'

I whistled softly. 'You sure?'

'I remember seeing a cancelled cheque among his bank statements, and then he mentioned something about it. There were stock certificates, too. I believe they're still in his desk. He never seemed able to get to his safe-deposit box.'

'How did he meet the Korvins?'

'They're both patients of his. As a matter of fact, the woman you saw here yesterday at the time of the accident was Leila Korvin – Charles Korvin's wife.'

I rapped my forehead. 'Of course. I'm not functioning properly. What's wrong with her?'

'Nothing. Hypochondriac mostly. He's the sick one.'

'The husband?' I was surprised. 'He looks healthy as a rhinoceros.'

'Looks are deceiving. The man has a heart condition.' She swung about towards a filing cabinet, flipping through for a card and started to read. 'Patient complains of pain beneath the breastbone, from shoulder to fingertips of left arm. Colouring poor, rapid heartbeat, short of breath.' She looked up and said, 'Typical angina symptoms.'

I considered it for a moment. 'Seems odd. If Korvin's that ill, how come the doctor invested money in his business?'

'I don't know,' she said, and smiled enigmatically, 'unless Mrs Korvin talked him into it.'

I looked at her reproachfully. 'Now, Nan, you're holding back. Come clean, please. Was there anything between those two?'

'I'm not positive. After all, Leila Korvin was an exceedingly attractive woman and Dr Butler was ...'

'Ill-favoured, to put it kindly,' I said. 'An unlikely combination, that pair. What gave you the idea?'

'Well, for one thing, she came here too often, and I know the doctor invited her out for dinner several times.'

'No real harm in that, is there? The gesture of a family friend, perhaps, when her husband had to work late.'

She shrugged expressively. 'Chalk it up to feminine intuition, Scott. Women have a feeling for such things. Besides, I saw the way he looked at her – not professionally at all.' She paused, her eyelids wrinkling into a slight frown. 'Except for one incident.'

'Yes?'

'They had an argument last week. I remember it because

Doctor Butler seldom raised his voice. It was brief and his words were indistinct through the closed door, but he sounded furious. And when she called for the appointment yesterday, he was very reserved.'

I sat back and mulled it over, trying to give these new tidings some meaning. Finally I spoke. 'Where is that stock certificate?'

She came around to the front of the desk, pulled open a drawer and produced an envelope, sliding it over. Scrawled across the face were two words: KORVIN CONTRACTING. The flap was unsealed. Inside I found two items. First, a cancelled cheque in the sum of fifty thousand dollars made out to Charles Korvin. Second, a certificate of stock for twenty-five shares. The stock was registered in the name of Leila Korvin, with no endorsement on the back. So they had set an evaluation on the stock of two thousand dollars per share. Not bad.

I deliberated for a moment and then stood up. 'Dinner tonight, Nan?'

'Love it.'

I leaned towards her and got a silken cheek to kiss.

The Criminal Courthouse on Foley Square. As attorney for the accused, I had the privilege of visiting with Mark Bryant in the counsel room. When they brought him down, I saw that he had endured a sleepless night.

Mark's face was gaunt and bleak. His body was heavy, sagging with gloom. I handed him a pack of cigarettes and he acknowledged the gift listlessly.

'Don't let go, Mark,' I said. 'Get a grip on yourself or you won't be any good to me at all. I need your help.'

'What can I do?' he said. 'They won't even grant bail.'

'You can answer questions. Sit down. Try to relax.' I got him deposited and looked at the haunted face. 'First,' I said, 'you can tell me about the Korvin Construction Company. How is it doing?'

His throat worked soundlessly. Then he moistened his lips.

'I – I lied about that to the detective. Business hasn't been good. Creditors were breathing down our back. I hadn't been paid in two weeks.'

'Did Dr Butler ever question you about the firm?'

'No.'

'Did you know that he had invested some money in the business?'

His eyes widened. 'No,' he said, 'I didn't know that.'

'It's true. Was Korvin trying to raise money elsewhere?'

'All the time. He was always playing golf with prospective backers or handball at his athletic club with bank officials. He never stopped punching.'

'How well do you know Mrs Korvin?'

'They took us to dinner a number of times.'

'They seem to get along all right?'

'She loved him and he loved her. Anybody could see that. She wouldn't even look at another man.'

'Tell me about yesterday. You were alone in the office all day?'

'Only in the afternoon.'

'What, specifically, is your job?'

'I help to estimate construction costs. I buy materials and arrange for shipment. When we have a project going, I do a little supervising.'

'Can the business survive?'

'I don't know,' he said.

Talking to me like this seemed to restore him; it started the vital juices flowing again. At least he knew that someone was working for him. He asked if he could see Ellen and I promised to arrange it. When they took him away, his shoulders were a little straighter and he even managed a kind of lopsided smile.

The Korvins lived in one of those solid antiques on Riverside Drive. Leila Korvin answered the doorbell. She was dressed in a gold-lamé hostess gown, her dark hair pulled tightly into twin buns at the back of her shapely head. Surprise animated her face, and then one inquiring eyebrow arched high.

'May I come in?' I asked.

She remembered her manners. 'Certainly, Mr Jordan.'

The living-room was elegant and had a spectacular view of the Hudson River. The neighbourhood was no longer fashionable, but rooms this size were not obtainable in newer buildings.

'Charles,' she called. 'We have a visitor.'

Korvin appeared, knotting the belt of his robe. He recognized me at once and advanced with a cordial handshake. He offered me a drink, bourbon, rye, Scotch, anything. I shook my head. He offered me a cigar. Also refused. He offered me a chair, which I accepted.

'Have you seen Mark?' he asked.

'Left him a short while ago.'

'How is he?'

'Shaken, bewildered, frightened.'

'Well, naturally. Quite understandable. Who wouldn't be in his predicament? But he's innocent, of course, absolutely innocent. Can you do anything for him?'

'I'm trying.'

'Can I help?' he asked.

'Yes, if you really mean it.'

'Of course I do. How?'

'By accompanying me to the office of some competent physician for a check-up.'

Korvin's chin jumped. He beetled his eyes in puzzlement and stabbed a quick look at his wife. A sudden stillness had come over the two of them. Korvin spoke in a slow, measured voice. 'I'm afraid I don't understand. Just what are you driving at, Jordan?'

'The solution,' I said, 'to a mystifying phenomenon. How a man with a serious heart condition can afford to play golf and handball.'

'This is all over my head.'

'Is it, Korvin? I saw your medical card at Dr Butler's office.

You called on him because of an ailment. All the major coronary symptoms. And he was an ethical man. He must have prescribed rest, a bit of mild golf perhaps, but not handball. Never. Too strenuous. It would be suicidal and you don't strike me as the kind of man who would destroy himself. And undoubtedly he prescribed medication, digitalis, nitroglycerin pills, heparin. Can you prove through any pharmacist that you bought such drugs? I doubt it.'

'If Butler made such a diagnosis, he was in error.'

'Rollo Butler? With his background, his reputation, his experience? I'm afraid not.'

'A man is entitled to one mistake.'

'Not this kind. You complained of severe pains beneath the breastbone.'

'Indigestion, I told him that.'

'There were other symptoms, Korvin. A fast heart rate. Oh, sure, it can be faked by Benzedrine or Dexedrine, by rapidly climbing stairs or a quick sprint around the block, which would also account for your poor colouring at the time.'

A pulse was throbbing under the tightly drawn skin of his temples. 'Why would I do a thing like that?'

'To make him believe you weren't long for this world.'

'But why? Why?' Korvin was priming me, desperately trying to find out if I really knew.

'So there would be hope for him. Romantic hope. A commodity that had never entered his barren life. He was a homely man in a world that puts a premium on beauty. He was lonely, he was vulnerable and your wife baited him. She enticed him with blandishments and promises, the first attractive woman who ever encouraged him, and the poor, unhappy sucker fell for it. He was a pushover.'

Korvin laughed shortly, an ugly sound manufactured through distorted lips. 'You think my wife would ever leave me for Butler?'

'Never,' I said. 'Not even if you were dead. He meant nothing to her, nothing at all except money. Which you needed desperately. And she soft-soaped him into making a loan. Fifty thousand dollars. I saw the cancelled cheque.'

'It was not a loan. We sold him stock.'

'I saw the stock certificate too. Registered in your wife's name, not Butler's, so I drew the only possible inference. You borrowed the money and gave that certificate as collateral.'

'We sold it, I tell you.' His voice, through clenched teeth, was hoarse.

'Worse still,' I said evenly. 'Then you're guilty of fraud and misrepresentation. Selling stock at two thousand dollars a share in a bankrupt corporation. A felony in this state. Punishable by imprisonment. Take it either way you like. But after you got the money, any promises your wife made never materialized.'

'I made no promises,' Leila Korvin said harshly.

'I say you did. And Butler sensed the change, the sudden coolness and indifference. He threw it up to you and there was a heated argument.'

'That's a lie!'

'I have proof. His nurse heard you quarrelling.' And then I really did lie. 'She eavesdropped and heard enough to testify in court.'

'Testify to what, for God's sake!' Korvin had raised his voice.

'To the fact that you cheated him, played him for a patsy, took his money, faked a heart attack, so that your wife could make promises she never meant to keep. And when he learned the truth, when he threatened to see the DA, to file a complaint against you for fraud, you got scared, panicky. You might be forced to make restitution. You might even go to jail. So there was only one way out. Butler had to be silenced.'

The strain was showing. Korvin stood rigid, his face damp and yellow under the tan.

I said, 'Your wife called the office to make an appointment, so you knew when he'd be returning from the hospital. You filched the parking-lot ticket from Mark's coat pocket and the car keys, and you drove up East End Avenue. Then you parked close by and waited for him. You saw him leave the taxi and start to cross the street and you sent the car hurtling and finished him off. All premeditated. No spur-of-the-moment decision. And you had the perfect fall guy in Mark. His car, nobody in the office to give him an alibi, and a sizeable inheritance to his wife as a solid motive. Everything working for you. Everything except the truth and the fact that you're an amateur.'

Leila Korvin was trembling, her skin as white as paper, and she put her hands out to steady herself against a chair. Korvin made one last effort. He tried to pull himself together, tried for a semblance of composure, but he was disintegrating fast.

I said, 'They'll check your alibi for those critical hours. They have the facilities, the men, the money, the time. They'll turn up someone who saw you in Mark's car. They'll find your fingerprints there, too. And perhaps a thread from the lining of your pocket on the keys. You'd be amazed what those lab boys can do. And the money, Korvin, the fifty thousand dollars, plus the threat of fraud and Butler's quarrel with your wife. You're finished, Korvin – *kaput*.'

His colour was bad and he seemed to shrink in size, cringing against his own bones. He looked dreadfully ill, sufficiently demoralized to confess. I felt no compassion as I walked to the phone and called Homicide East.

McGowney's Miracle

MARGARET MILLAR

When I finally found him, it was by accident. He was waiting for a cable car on Powell Street, a dignified little man about sixty, in a black topcoat and a grey fedora. He stood apart from the crowd, aloof but friendly, his hands clasped just below his chest, like a minister about to bless a batch of heathen. I knew he wasn't a minister.

A sheet of fog hung over San Francisco, blurring the lights and muffling the clang of the cable cars.

I stepped up behind McGowney and said, 'Good evening.'

There was no recognition in his eyes, no hesitation in his voice. 'Why, good evening, sir.' He turned with a little smile. 'It is kind of you to greet a stranger so pleasantly.'

For a moment, I was almost ready to believe I'd made a mistake. There are on record many cases of perfect doubles, and what's more, I hadn't seen McGowney since the beginning of July. But there was one important thing McGowney couldn't conceal: his voice still carried the throaty accents of the funeral parlour.

He tipped his hat and began walking briskly up Powell Street towards the hill, his topcoat flapping around his skinny legs like broken wings.

In the middle of the block, he turned to see if I was following him. I was. He walked on, shaking his head from side to side as if genuinely puzzled by my interest in him. At the next corner, he stopped in front of a department store and waited for me, leaning against the window, his hands in his pockets.

When I approached, he looked up at me, frowning. 'I don't know why you're following me, young man, but—'

'Why don't you ask me, McGowney?'

But he didn't ask. He just repeated his own name, 'McGowney', in a surprised voice, as if he hadn't heard it for a long time.

I said, 'I'm Eric Meecham, Mrs Keating's lawyer. We've met before.'

'I've met a great many people. Some I recall, some I do not.'

'I'm sure you recall Mrs Keating. You conducted her funeral last July.'

'Of course, of course. A great lady, a very great lady. Her demise saddened the hearts of all who had the privilege of her acquaintance, all who tasted the sweetness of her smile—'

'Come off it, McGowney. Mrs Keating was a sharp-tongued virago without a friend in this world.'

He turned away from me, but I could see the reflection of his face in the window, strained and anxious.

'You're a long way from home, McGowney.'

'This is my home now.'

'You left Arbana very suddenly.'

'To me it was not sudden. I had been planning to leave for twenty years, and when the time came, I left. It was summer then, but all I could think of was the winter coming on and everything dying. I had had enough of death.'

'Mrs Keating was your last – client?'

'She was.'

'Her coffin was exhumed last week.'

A cable car charged up the hill like a drunken rocking horse, its sides bulging with passengers. Without warning, McGowney darted out into the street and sprinted up the hill after the car. In spite of his age, he could have made it, but the car was so crowded there wasn't a single space for him to get a hand-hold. He stopped running and stood motionless in the centre of the street, staring after the car as it plunged and reared up the hill. Oblivious to the honks and shouts of motorists, he walked slowly back to the kerb where I was waiting.

'You can't run away, McGowney.'

He glanced at me wearily, without speaking. Then he took out a half-soiled handkerchief and wiped the moisture from his forehead.

'The exhumation can't be much of a surprise to you,' I said. 'You wrote me the anonymous letter suggesting it. It was postmarked Berkeley. That's why I'm here in this area.'

'I wrote you no letter,' he said.

'The information it contained could have come only from you.'

'No. Somebody else knew as much about it as I did.'

'Who?'

'My – wife.'

'Your wife!' It was the most unexpected answer he could have given me. Mrs McGowney had died, along with her only daughter, in the flu epidemic after World War I. The story is the kind that still goes the rounds in a town like Arbana, even after thirty-five years: McGowney, unemployed after his discharge from the Army, had had no funds to pay for the double funeral, and when the undertaker offered him an apprenticeship to work off the debt, McGowney accepted. It was common knowledge that after his wife's death he never so much as looked at another woman, except, of course, in the line of duty.

I said, 'So you've married again.'

'Yes.'

'When?'

'Six months ago.'

'Right after you left Arbana.'

'Yes.'

'You didn't lose much time starting a new life for yourself.'

'I couldn't afford to. I'm not young.'

'Did you marry a local woman?'

'Yes.'

I didn't realize until later that he had taken 'local' to mean Arbana, not San Francisco as I had intended.

I said, 'You think your wife wrote me that anonymous letter?'

'Yes.'

The street lights went on, and I realized it was getting late and cold. McGowney pulled up his coat collar and put on a pair of ill-fitting white cotton gloves. I had seen him wearing gloves like that before; they were as much a part of his professional equipment as his throaty voice and his vast store of sentimental aphorisms.

He caught me staring at the gloves and said, with a trace of apology, 'Money is a little tight these days. My wife is knitting me a pair of woollen gloves for my birthday.'

'You're not working?'

'No.'

'It shouldn't be hard for a man of your experience to find a job in your particular field.' I was pretty sure he hadn't even applied for one. During the past few days, I had contacted nearly every mortician within the Bay area; McGowney had not been to any of them.

'I don't want a job in my particular field,' McGowney said.

'It's the only thing you're trained for.'

'Yes. But I no longer believe in death.'

He spoke with simple earnestness, as if he had said, I no longer play blackjack, or I no longer eat salted peanuts.

Death, blackjack, or salted peanuts – I was not prepared to argue with McGowney about any of them, so I said, 'My car's in the garage at the Canterbury Hotel. We'll walk over and get it, and I'll drive you home.'

We started towards Sutter Street. The stream of shoppers had been augmented by a flow of white-collar workers, but all the people and the noise and the confusion left McGowney untouched. He moved sedately along beside me, smiling a little to himself, like a man who has developed the faculty of walking out on the world from time to time and going to live on some remote and happy island of his own. I wondered where McGowney's island was and who lived there with him. I knew only one thing for sure: on McGowney's island there was no death.

He said suddenly, 'It must have been very difficult.'

'What was?'

'The exhumation. The ground gets so hard back East in the wintertime. I presume you didn't attend, Mr Meecham?'

'You presume wrong.'

'My, that's no place for an amateur.'

For my money, it was no place for anyone. The cemetery had been white with snow that had fallen during the night. Dawn had been breaking, if you could call that meagre, grudging light a dawn. The simple granite headstone had read, *Eleanor Regina Keating, 3 October 1890 – 30 June 1953. A blessed one from us is gone, a voice we loved is still.*

The blessed one had been gone, all right. Two hours later, when the coffin was pulled up and opened, the smell that rose from it was not the smell of death, but the smell of newspapers rotted with dampness and stones grey-greened with mildew.

I said, 'You know what we found, don't you, McGowney?'

'Naturally. I directed the funeral.'

'You accept sole responsibility for burying an empty coffin?'

'Not sole responsibility, no.'

'Who was in with you? And why?'

He merely shook his head.

As we waited for a traffic light, I studied McGowney's face, trying to estimate the degree of his sanity. There seemed to be no logic behind his actions. Mrs Keating had died quite unmysteriously of a heart attack and had been buried, according to her instructions to me, in a closed coffin. The doctor who had signed the death certificate was indisputably honest. He had happened to be in Mrs Keating's house at the time, attending to her older daughter, Mary, who had had a cold. He had examined Mrs Keating, pronounced her dead, and sent for McGowney. Two days later I had escorted Mary, still sniffling (whether from grief or the same cold, I don't know), to the funeral. McGowney, as usual, said and did all the correct things.

Except one. He neglected to put Mrs Keating's body in the coffin.

Time had passed. No one had particularly mourned Mrs Keating. She had been an unhappy woman, mentally and morally superior to her husband, who had been killed during a drinking spree in New Orleans, and to her two daughters, who resembled their father. I had been Mrs Keating's lawyer for three years. I had enjoyed talking to her; she had had a quick mind and a sharp sense of humour. But as in the case of many wealthy people who have been cheated of the privilege of work and the satisfactions it brings, she had been a bored and lonely woman who carried despair on her shoulder like a pet parakeet and fed it from time to time on scraps from her bitter memories.

Right after Mrs Keating's funeral, McGowney had sold his business and left town. No one in Arbana had connected the two events until the anonymous letter arrived from Berkeley shortly before Mrs Keating's will was awaiting admission into probate. The letter, addressed to me, had suggested the exhumation and stated the will must be declared invalid since there was no proof of death. I could think of no reason why McGowney's new wife wrote the letter, unless she had tired of him and had chosen a roundabout method of getting rid of him.

The traffic light changed, and McGowney and I crossed the street and waited under the hotel marquee while the doorman sent for my car. I didn't look at McGowney, but I could feel him watching me intently.

'You think I'm mad, eh, Meecham?'

It wasn't a question I was prepared to answer. I tried to look non-committal.

'I don't pretend to be entirely normal, Meecham. Do you?'

'I try.'

McGowney's hand, in its ill-fitting glove, reached over and touched my arm, and I forced myself not to slap it away. It perched on my coat sleeve like a wounded pigeon. 'But suppose you had an abnormal experience.'

'Like you?'

'Like me. It was a shock, a great shock, even though I had always had the feeling that someday it would happen. I was on the watch for it every time I had a new case. It was always in my mind. You might even say I *willed* it.'

Two trickles of sweat oozed down behind my ears into my collar. 'What did you will, McGowney?'

'I willed her to live again.'

I became aware the doorman was signalling to me. My car was at the kerb with the engine running.

I climbed in behind the wheel, and McGowney followed me into the car with obvious reluctance, as if he was already regretting what he'd told me.

'You don't believe me,' he said as we pulled away from the kerb.

'I'm a lawyer. I deal in facts.'

'A fact is what happens, isn't it?'

'Close enough.'

'Well, this happened.'

'She came back to life?'

'Yes.'

'By the power of your will alone?'

He stirred restlessly in the seat beside me. 'I gave her oxygen and adrenalin.'

'Have you done this with other clients of yours?'

'Many times, yes.'

'Is this procedure usual among members of your profession?'

'For me it was usual,' McGowney said earnestly. 'I've always wanted to be a doctor. I was in the Medical Corps during the war, and I picked up a little knowledge here and there.'

'Enough to perform miracles?'

'It was not my knowledge that brought her back to life. It was my will. She had lost the will to live, but I had enough for both of us.'

If it is true that only a thin line separates sanity and madness, McGowney crossed and recrossed that line a dozen times within an hour, jumping over it and back again, like a child skipping rope.

'You understand now, Meecham? She had lost all desire. I saw it happening to her. We never spoke – I doubt she even knew my name – but for years I watched her pass my office on her morning walk. I saw the change come over her, the dullness of her eyes and the way she walked. I knew she was going to die. One day when she was passing by, I went out to tell her, to warn her. But when she saw me, she ran. I think she realized what I was going to say.'

He was telling the truth, according to his lights. Mrs Keating had mentioned the incident to me last spring. I recalled her words: 'A funny thing occurred this morning, Meecham. As I was walking past the undertaking parlour, that odd little man rushed out and almost scared the life out of me ...'

In view of what subsequently happened, this was a giant among ironies. As we drove towards the Bay Bridge and Berkeley, McGowney told me his story.

It was midday at the end of June, and the little back room McGowney used as a lab was hot and humid after a morning rain.

Mrs Keating woke up as if from a long and troubled sleep. Her hands twitched, her mouth moved in distress, a pulse began to beat in her temple. Tears squeezed out from between her closed lids and slithered past the tips of her ears into the folds of her hair.

McGowney bent over her, quivering with excitement. 'Mrs Keating! Mrs Keating! You are alive!'

'Oh – God.'

'A miracle has just happened!'

'Leave me alone. I'm tired.'

'You are alive, you are *alive*!'

Slowly she opened her eyes and looked up at him. 'You officious little wretch, what have you done?'

McGowney stepped back, stunned and shaken. 'But – but you are alive. It's happened. My miracle has happened.'

'Alive. Miracle.' She mouthed the words as if they were lumps of alum. 'You meddling idiot.'

'I— But I—'

'Pour me a glass of water. My throat is parched.'

He was trembling so violently he could hardly get the water out of the cooler. This was his miracle. He had hoped and waited for it all his life, and now it had exploded in his face like an April-fool cigar.

He gave her the water and sat down heavily in a chair, watching her while she drank very slowly, as if in her short recess from life her muscles had already begun to forget their function.

'Why did you do it?' Mrs Keating crushed the paper cup in her fist as if it were McGowney himself. 'Who asked you for a miracle, anyway?'

'But I— Well, the fact is—'

'The fact is, you're a blooming meddler, that's what the fact is, McGowney.'

'Yes, ma'am.'

'Now what are you going to do?'

'Well, I – I hadn't thought.'

'Then you'd better start right now.'

'Yes, ma'am.' He stared down at the floor, his head hot with misery, his limbs cold with disappointment. 'First, I had better call the doctor.'

'You'll call no one, McGowney.'

'But your family – they'll want to know right away that—'

'They are not going to know.'

'But—'

'No one is going to know, McGowney. No one at all. Is that clear?'

'Yes.'

'Now sit down and be quiet and let me think.'

He sat down and was quiet. He had no desire to move or to speak. Never had he felt so futile and depressed.

'I suppose,' Mrs Keating said grimly, 'you expect me to be grateful to you.'

McGowney shook his head.

'If you do, you must be crazy.' She paused and looked at him thoughtfully.

'You *are* a little crazy, aren't you, McGowney?'

'There are those who think so,' he said, with some truth. 'I don't agree.'

'You wouldn't.'

'Can't afford to, ma'am.'

The windows of the room were closed and no street sounds penetrated the heavy frosted glass, but from the corridor outside the door came the sudden tap of footsteps on tile.

McGowney bolted across the room and locked the door and stood against it.

'Mr McGowney? You in there?'

McGowney looked at Mrs Keating. Her face had turned chalky, and she had one hand clasped to her throat.

'Mr McGowney?'

'Yes, Jim.'

'You're wanted on the telephone.'

'I – can't come right now, Jim. Take a message.'

'She wants to talk to you personally. It's the Keating girl, about the time and cost of the funeral arrangements.'

'Tell her I'll call her back later.'

'All right.' There was a pause. 'You feeling okay, Mr McGowney?'

'Yes.'

'You sound kind of funny.'

'I'm fine, Jim. Absolutely first-rate.'

'Okay. Just thought I'd ask.'

The footsteps tapped back down the tile corridor.

'Mary loses no time.' Mrs Keating spoke through dry, stiff lips. 'She wants me safely underground so she can marry her electrician. Well, your duty is clear, McGowney.'

'What is it?'

'Put me there.'

McGowney stood propped against the door like a wooden soldier. 'You mean, b-b-bury you?'

'Me, or a reasonable facsimile.'

'That I couldn't do, Mrs Keating. It wouldn't be ethical.'

'It's every bit as ethical as performing unsolicited miracles.'

'You don't understand the problems.'

'Such as?'

'For one thing, your family and friends. They'll want to see you lying in— What I mean is, it's customary to put the body on view.'

'I can handle that part of it all right.'

'How?'

'Get me a pen and some paper.'

McGowney didn't argue, because he knew he was at fault. It was his miracle; he'd have to take the consequences.

Mrs Keating predated the letter by three weeks, and wrote the following:

To whom it may concern, not that it should concern anybody except myself:

I am giving these instructions to Mr McGowney concerning my funeral arrangements. Inasmuch as I have valued privacy during my life, I want no intrusion on it after my death. I am instructing Mr McGowney to close my coffin immediately and to see it stays closed, in spite of any mawkish pleas from my survivors.

Eleanor Regina Keating

She folded the paper twice and handed it to McGowney.

'You are to show this to Mary and Joan and to Mr Meecham, my lawyer.' She paused, looking very pleased with herself. 'Well. This is getting to be quite exciting, eh, McGowney?'

'Quite,' McGowney said listlessly.

'As a matter of fact, it's given me an appetite. I don't suppose there's a kitchen connected with this place?'

'No.'

'Then you'd better get me something from the corner drugstore. A couple of tuna-salad sandwiches, on wheat, with plenty of coffee. Lunch,' she added with a satiric little smile, 'will have to be on you. I forgot my handbag.'

'Money,' McGowney said. '*Money*.'

'What about it?'

'What will happen to your money?'

'I made a will some time ago.'

'But *you*, what will you live on?'

'Perhaps,' Mrs Keating said dryly, 'you'd better perform another miracle.'

When he returned from the drugstore with her lunch, Mrs Keating ate and drank with obvious enjoyment. She offered McGowney a part of the second sandwich, but he was too disheartened to eat. His miracle, which had started out as a great golden bubble, had turned into an iron ball chained to his leg.

Somehow he got through the day. Leaving Mrs Keating in the lab with some old magazines and a bag of apples, McGowney went about his business. He talked to Mary and Joan Keating in person and to Meecham on the telephone. He gave his assistant, Jim Wagner, the rest of the afternoon off, and when Jim had gone, he filled Mrs Keating's coffin (the de luxe white-and-bronze model Mary had chosen out of the catalogue) with rocks packed in newspapers, until it was precisely the right weight.

McGowney was a small man, unaccustomed to physical exertion, and by the time he had finished, his body was throbbing with weariness.

It was at this point Mary Keating telephoned to say she and Joan had been thinking the matter over, and since Mrs Keating had always inclined towards thrift, it was decided she would never rest at ease in such an ostentatious affair as the white and bronze. The plain grey would be far more appropriate, as well as cheaper.

'You should,' McGowney said coldly, 'have let me know sooner.'

'We just decided a second ago.'

'It's too late to change now.'

'I don't see why.'

'There are – certain technicalities.'

'Well, really, Mr McGowney. If you're not willing to put yourself out a little, maybe we should take our business somewhere else.'

'No! You can't do that— I mean, it wouldn't be proper, Miss Keating.'

'It's a free country.'

'Wait a minute. Suppose I give you a special price on the white and bronze?'

'How special?'

'Say, twenty-five per cent off?'

There was a whispered conference at the other end of the line, and then Mary said, 'It's still a lot of money.'

'Thirty-five?'

'Well, that seems more *like* it,' Mary said, and hung up.

The door of McGowney's office opened, and Mrs Keating crossed the room, wearing a grim little smile.

McGowney looked at her helplessly. 'You shouldn't be out here, ma'am. You'd better go back and—'

'I heard the telephone ring, and I thought it might be Mary.'

'It wasn't.'

'Yes, it was, McGowney. I heard every word.'

'Well,' McGowney cleared his throat. 'Well. You shouldn't have listened.'

'Oh, I'm not surprised. Or hurt. You needn't be sorry for me. I haven't felt so good in years. You know why?'

'No, ma'am.'

'Because I don't have to go home. I'm free. Free as a bird.' She reached over and touched his coat sleeve. 'I don't have to go home, do I?'

'I guess not.'

'You'll never tell anyone?'

'No.'

'You're a very good man, McGowney.'

'I have never thought I wasn't,' McGowney said simply.

When darkness fell, McGowney got his car out of the garage and brought it around to the ambulance entrance behind his office.

'You'd better hide in the back seat,' he said, 'until we get out of town.'

'Where are we going?'

'I thought I'd drive you into Detroit, and from there you can catch a bus or a train.'

'To where?'

'To anywhere. You're as free as a bird.'

She got into the back seat, shivering in spite of the mildness of the night, and McGowney covered her with a blanket.

'McGowney.'

'Yes, ma'am?'

'I felt freer when I was locked in your little lab.'

'You're a bit frightened now, that's all. Freedom is a mighty big thing.'

He turned the car towards the highway. Half an hour later, when the city's lights had disappeared, he stopped the car, and Mrs Keating got into the front seat with the blanket wrapped around her shoulders, Indian style. In the gleam of oncoming headlights, her face looked a little troubled. McGowney felt duty bound to cheer her up, since he was responsible for her being there in the first place.

'There are,' he said firmly, 'wonderful places to be seen.'

'Are there?'

'California, that's the spot I'd pick. Flowers all year round, never an end to them.' He hesitated. 'I've saved a bit throughout the years. I always thought someday I'd sell the business and retire to California.'

'What's to prevent you?'

'I couldn't face the idea, of, well, of being alone out there without friends or a family of some kind. Have you ever been to California?'

'I spent a couple of summers in San Francisco.'

'Did you like it?'

'Very much.'

'I'd like it, too, I'm sure of that.' He cleared his throat. 'Being alone, though, that I wouldn't like. Are you warm enough?'

'Yes, thanks.'

'Birds – well, birds don't have such a happy time of it that I can see.'

'No?'

'All that freedom and not knowing what to do with it except fly around. A life like that couldn't suit a mature woman like yourself, Mrs Keating.'

'Perhaps not.'

'What I mean is—'

'I know what you mean, McGowney.'

'You – you do?'

'Of course.'

McGowney flushed. 'It's – well, it's very unexpected, isn't it?'

'Not to me.'

'But I never thought of it until half an hour ago.'

'I did. Women are more foresighted in these matters.'

McGowney was silent a moment. 'This hasn't been a very romantic proposal. I ought to say something a bit on the sentimental side.'

'Go ahead.'

He gripped the steering wheel hard. 'I think I love you, ma'am.'

'You didn't have to say that,' she replied sharply. 'I'm not a foolish young girl to be taken in by words. At my age, I don't expect love. I don't want to—'

'But you are loved,' McGowney declared.

'I don't believe it.'

'Eventually you will.'

'Is this another of your miracles, McGowney?'

'This is the important one.'

It was the first time in Mrs Keating's life she had been told she was loved. She sat beside McGowney in awed silence, her hands folded on her lap, like a little girl in Sunday School.

McGowney left her at a hotel in Detroit and went home to hold her funeral.

Two weeks later they were married by a justice of the peace in a little town outside Chicago. On the long and leisurely trip west in McGowney's car, neither of them talked much about the past or worried about the future. McGowney had sold his business, but he'd been in too much of a hurry to wait for a decent price, and so his funds were limited. But he never mentioned this to his bride.

By the time they reached San Francisco, they had gone through quite a lot of McGowney's capital. A large portion of the remainder went towards the purchase of the little house in Berkeley.

By late fall, they were almost broke, and McGowney got a job as a shoe clerk in a department store. A week later, along with his first pay cheque, he received his notice of dismissal.

That night at dinner he told Eleanor about it, pretending it was all a joke, and inventing a couple of anecdotes to make her laugh.

She listened, grave and unamused. 'So that's what you've been doing all week. Selling shoes.'

'Yes.'

'You didn't tell me we needed money that badly.'

'We'll be all right. I can easily get another job.'

'Doing what?'

'What I've always done.'

She reached across the table and touched his hand. 'You don't want to be a mortician again.'

'I don't mind.'

'You always hated it.'

'I *don't mind*, I tell you.'

She rose decisively.

'Eleanor, what are you going to do?'

'Write a letter,' she said with a sigh.

'Eleanor, don't do anything drastic.'

'We have had a lot of happiness. It couldn't last for ever. Don't be greedy.'

The meaning of her words pierced McGowney's brain. 'You're going to let someone know you're alive?'

'No. I couldn't face that, not just yet. I'm merely going to show them I'm not dead so they can't divide up my estate.'

'But why?'

'As my husband, you're entitled to a share of it if anything happens to me.'

'Nothing will ever happen to you. We agreed about that, didn't we?'

'Yes, McGowney. We agreed.'

'We no longer believe in death.'

'I will address the letter to Meecham,' she said.

'So she wrote the letter.' McGowney's voice was weary. 'For my sake. You know the rest, Meecham.'

'Not quite,' I said.

'What else do you want to know?'

'The ending.'

'The ending.' McGowney stirred in the seat beside me and let out his breath in a sigh. 'I don't believe in endings.'

I turned right at the next traffic light, as McGowney directed. A sign on the lamp-post said LINDEN AVENUE.

Three blocks south was a small green-and-white house, its eaves dripping with fog.

I parked my car in front of it and got out, pleasantly excited at the idea of seeing Mrs Keating again. McGowney sat motionless, staring straight ahead of him, until I opened the car door.

'Come on, McGowney.'

'Eh? Oh. All right. All right.'

He stepped out on the sidewalk so awkwardly he almost fell. I took his arm. 'Is anything wrong?'

'No.'

We went up the porch steps.

'There are no lights on,' McGowney said. 'Eleanor must be at the store. Or over at the neighbour's. We have some very nice neighbours.'

The front door was not locked. We went inside, and McGowney turned on the lights in the hall and the sitting-room to the right.

The woman I had known as Mrs Keating was sitting in a wing chair in front of the fireplace, her head bent forward as if she were in deep thought. Her knitting had fallen on the floor, and I saw it was a half-finished glove in bright colours. McGowney's birthday present.

In silence, McGowney reached down and picked up the glove and put it on a table. Then he touched his wife gently on the forehead. I knew from the way his hand flinched that her skin was as cold as the ashes in the grate.

I said, 'I'll get a doctor.'

'No.'

'She's dead?'

He didn't bother to answer. He was looking down at his wife with a coaxing expression. 'Eleanor dear, you must wake up. We have a visitor.'

'McGowney, for God's sake—'

'I think you'd better leave now, Mr Meecham,' he said in a firm, clear voice. 'I have work to do.'

He took off his coat and rolled up his sleeves.

Ten Minutes from Now

JACK RITCHIE

The box I carried was approximately nine by nine by nine, and it was wrapped securely in common brown paper.

I entered the huge lobby of the City Hall and strode rapidly towards the elevators. I noticed several policemen scattered throughout the crowd, several of whom seemed to take more than a passing interest in what I carried – or perhaps it was my beard which attracted their attention. However none of them attempted to intercept me.

The elevator took me to the third floor. In the corridor I walked by several more policemen, one of whom rubbed his jaw and frowned as I passed.

I opened the door to the mayor's reception room. Except for a single young man at a desk at the far end, it was unoccupied.

His eyes flicked uneasily to the box I carried. 'May I help you?'

'You may. I would like to see the mayor immediately.'

His tongue ran over apparently dry lips. 'Do you have an appointment?'

'I would have mentioned it if I did.' I glanced at my watch. 'It is absolutely imperative that I see him at once.'

'Just one moment,' he said quickly. He darted through a door behind him and I thought I heard the click of a Yale lock.

There followed approximately four minutes of silence and then the door from the corridor edged open cautiously.

A tall man in a plain blue suit hesitated in the doorway. Behind him a number of uniformed police officers craned their necks.

He glanced at the box, then at me, and seemed to gauge the situation. Then he motioned the officers behind him to retreat. He sidled into the room alone and closed the door. 'Did you want to see Mayor Pettibone?'

'Are *you* Mayor Pettibone?'

'No,' he said swiftly. 'I'm Lieutenant Wymar.' He manufactured a smile. 'Why do you want to see the mayor?'

'That is plainly my business.'

There was an uneasy silence and then I thought that his ears suddenly flared, radar-like, in reception of a sound. He pointed to the box I held in my hands. 'Is that thing *ticking*?'

It was.

The box almost slipped from my lap, but I managed to retrieve it before it hit the floor. When I looked up, I saw that the lieutenant's eyes were clamped shut and he seemed to be waiting tensely for something to happen.

His eyes finally opened and he exhaled. 'What's in that box?'

'That is *also* my business.' I consulted my watch again. 'I must see the mayor within the next *ten* minutes. Not one second later.'

He seemed to brighten a little. 'Ten minutes?' He took several steps forward. 'The mayor is busy right now. Couldn't you come back later?'

'No.' I put the box down on the bench beside me. 'If I don't see the mayor immediately, I am tempted to blast my way into his office.'

What occurred next was lightning fast. Wymar's hands seized my package and he flung open the corridor door. 'Quick! Somebody get a bucket of water! This thing's timed to go off in less than ten minutes.'

I followed on his heels. 'See here, what's the meaning of this?'

He ignored me. 'Damn it, doesn't *anybody* have a bucket of water?'

I glimpsed half a dozen policemen dashing about. One of them wrenched open a door which proved to be a janitor's closet. It contained various cleaning materials and a deep sink. He immediately plugged the sink and opened both faucets wide. 'Over here, Lieutenant!'

Wymar thrust the package into the sink and in a few moments it was completely immersed in water.

I watched the air bubbles rising from the submerged package and sighed. 'I *do* hope it's waterproof.'

Wymar's eyes widened. '*Waterproof?* I never thought of that.' He waved a hand. 'Everybody back! The bomb may go off any minute.'

I found myself automatically involved in a retreat to the end of the corridor.

'Somebody phone the bomb squad,' Wymar ordered.

A very young policeman saluted. 'Yes, sir. What's the number?'

Wymar turned purple. However, he immediately pointed to a sergeant. 'Murphy, get the bomb squad.'

The sergeant departed and Lieutenant Wymar's attention returned to me. I was rather forcibly escorted into an empty room down on the second floor.

Two policemen remained to guard me while Wymar departed, presumably to superintend evacuation activities. He returned fifteen minutes later, looking considerably relieved. 'The bomb boys are here.'

And then he removed a sheet of paper from an envelope and thrust it before my eyes. '*You* wrote this, didn't you?'

He would not let me touch the paper, and so I had to squint as I read the typewritten words.

Mayor Pettibone:

Your actions on the Veterans' Memorial development were arbitrary and clearly not in the public interest. Since there seems to be no legal means of removing you from office immediately, I intend to blow you to kingdom come.

The Avenger

I shook my head. 'Elite type. I prefer Pica. Much easier to read.'

He scowled. 'Did you or did you not write this note?'

'My dear sir, if I intended to blow up the mayor, would I forewarn him?'

'Maybe,' Wymar said. 'Some bombers are nuts.'

I smiled. 'Are my fingerprints on the note?'

Evidently there weren't any fingerprints on the note, except possibly the mayor's, because Wymar did not answer the question. 'What's your name?'

'James B. Bellington,' I said.

He began writing in a notebook. 'James C. Bellington.'

I corrected him. 'James B. Bellington. As in bomb.'

'And your address?'

'I have a room in the Medford Hotel. A miserable place, but it is all I can afford at the present time.'

'Did you lose any money when the Veterans' Memorial development was switched from the east to the north side?' He paused.

I patted a stray hair of my beard. 'I refuse to say another word until I've seen my lawyer.'

At that moment one of the men who was evidently a member of the bomb squad entered the room. He was encased in pads and he carried my soggy package. He levered up his mesh face mask and spoke. 'We checked it out, Lieutenant.'

'Well?' Wymar demanded.

The padded gentleman shrugged. 'An alarm clock. That's all. Just a cheap alarm clock.'

'Of course an alarm clock,' I seconded testily. 'What did you expect? A bomb?'

Wymar spoke in a slightly strangled voice. 'Do you still want to see Mayor Pettibone?'

'Not at the moment. I'm afraid the mood has left me.' I smiled slightly. 'You *do* protect the mayor very well, don't you? A thing like that is nice to know. Anyone wishing to blow him to bits would have to be very clever about it, wouldn't he?'

Lieutenant Wymar's eyes narrowed slightly as he studied me. I rose. 'Good afternoon, gentlemen.'

Wymar remembered something. 'Don't forget your alarm clock.'

I shrugged. 'I'm afraid it is ruined. You may keep it for exhibition in the police museum.' I smiled again. 'Tell Mayor Pettibone that I shall return. Perhaps this after ...' I stopped, waved amicably, and departed.

In the lobby downstairs I purchased a five-pack of panatellas. I lit one of them and continued out into the street.

At the corner news-stand, I stopped and glared at the garish magazines exhibited, especially those which apparently appealed most to people with damp palms. After a while I snorted. 'Rubbish. Absolute rubbish.'

The news-stand attendant, an elderly man in a frayed overcoat girdled with a change maker, sighed. 'Look, mister, if you wanta copy just stick it under your coat and give me the money. I won't tell nobody.'

'Sir,' I said stiffly, 'I would not be caught dead with any one of these miserable rags. They should be banned from sale.'

He favoured the sky with a weary appeal. 'Why don't you just go to the library and borrow yourself a solid book? Like medical. I'm just a poor man engaged in private enterprise.'

I pointed my walking stick at the base of the stand. 'One bomb placed right there could blow your messy literature sky-high.' I took two savage puffs of my cigar and strode away without looking back.

A block further, as I waited for a light to change, I glanced back. A tall man in a trench coat appeared to be conferring with the attendant. They both looked my way and the attendant shrugged.

The light changed and I crossed the street. I entered a large dime store and purchased a cheap alarm clock. Downstairs, in the hardware department, I bought two dry cells and five feet of No 20 telephone wire. Running down the aisle on my way back to the stairs, I passed the man in the trench coat. He seemed to be supremely absorbed in a display of café curtains.

Out on the street, I lit a fresh cigar. The weather was rather damp, but it was the type of day I prefer. It stimulates the blood.

I walked smartly for several blocks when it began to drizzle. At the Metropolitan Museum of Art, I hesitated. I glanced at the façade. Horrible taste, I thought. How much dynamite would it require to destroy a monstrosity such as that?

I tossed away my cigar and ascended the flight of stairs to the entrance. Inside, I wandered about and eventually reached a small gallery at the rear of the building.

For one of conservative tastes, the exhibit was truly one to raise the hackles – an indiscriminate mixture of Utrillos, Picassos and Modiglianis. I scowled and sharply rapped my walking stick on the brass rail. 'Tripe. Complete tripe.'

One of the uniformed guards appeared at my elbow. 'Don't do that, mister. You're denting the brass rail.'

I indicated one of the paintings. 'This appears to me to be nothing more than a badly wounded piece of canvas.'

He seemed to agree. 'You can't blame them boys too much, though. The invention of the camera must of hit them pretty hard. Like automation and you got to learn a new trade.'

'They should be burned,' I said firmly. 'Every last one of them. Or better yet, blown to bits. To shreds.'

'Mister,' the guard said, 'if you got to point, do it with your finger. Not the cane. I got to account for any holes in them pictures.'

I spent the next fifteen minutes amid the mental security of the Dutch masters.

When I returned to the street, it had stopped raining. At the first corner I noticed the man in the trench coat descending the steps of the museum. Apparently he had been in the building while I had been there.

I rubbed my beard.

Now I entered a succession of stores, departing immediately via side and rear entrances. Eventually I established beyond doubt that I was no longer followed.

In the neighbourhood of my hotel, I purchased a quarter pound of butter, a quart of milk, a loaf of bread, some cold cuts, and a five-pound bag of sugar.

As I entered the Medford, I noticed the man in the trench coat in a lobby chair reading a newspaper.

In my room, I constructed a sandwich and reread last night's newspaper, principally the article dealing with the Veterans' Memorial Centre. It was to be an ambitious project encompassing several acres and consisting of a number of buildings. The anticipated site had been a stretch of semi-tenements near the lake front. As a matter of fact it had been so well anticipated that there had been brisk selling and buying by a number of individuals and the value of the properties had suddenly skyrocketed.

Yesterday, however, the city council, mostly as the result of pressure from Mayor Pettibone, had decided to switch the site to a more northerly – and cheaper – location. Needless to say, a number of holders of the originally planned site had lost their shirts.

My phone rang and Geoffrey Mipple was on the line.

Geoffrey and I were room-mates at College and have since preserved our fast friendship. On any number of subjects we are of a like mind.

'James?'

'Yes,' I said.

'Did you go to the mayor's office?'

'Yes.'

'What happened?'

'Just about what I anticipated.'

'Are you going back this afternoon?'

'I believe so.' I took a bite of my sandwich. 'You're not calling from your room, are you?'

'No. A telephone booth.'

'Good.' I hung up, finished my glass of milk, and then went to the closet. I removed an empty cubic box from the top shelf and went to work.

At two that afternoon, I reached for the phone and got the desk clerk. 'Could you tell me how long the City Hall is open today?' I asked.

'Is that Mr Bellington?'

'Yes.'

There was an appreciable pause. Perhaps he was conferring with someone. He returned to the phone. 'The City Hall is open twenty-four hours a day. However, almost all the offices close at five. Is there anyone in particular you wanted to see?'

'Yes. There is.' I looked at my watch. 'Would you please have a taxi waiting for me in approximately twenty minutes?'

I smoked two inches of my cigar and then put on my coat. I carried my cubic box when I left the room.

The desk clerk's eyes seemed both curious and wary as he glanced at my package. 'Your taxi is waiting, sir.'

A single taxi stood at the kerb. I entered, gave my destination, and as we pulled away, so did another taxi about a half a block behind us.

At the City Hall, I noticed a peculiar vehicle parked near one of the side entrances. It was quite metallically sturdy and its rear consisted of a huge wickerwork cage.

The lobby was incredibly crowded and one had the impression of a defence alert with everyone evacuated to the main floor. At the elevators a number of policemen seemed to be turning back anyone who wished to ascend.

I expected similar treatment, and yet a path cleared before me and I found myself in the elevator alone with the operator. At the third floor he quickly opened the door and when he descended alone I had the impression that it was at high speed.

The corridor before me was completely empty and my foot-falls echoed and re-echoed. When I opened the door to the mayor's reception room, I once again found the nervous young man alone at the desk.

'I would like to see the mayor,' I said. 'Within the next ten minutes.'

'Yes, sir,' he said hastily. 'Of course. Would you please take a seat over there?' He pointed to a leather upholstered davenport.

I sat down and placed the box carefully beside me.

The receptionist cleared his throat. 'Would you do me a small favour, sir?'

'Perhaps.'

He got up. 'I have to move this bookcase from *here* over to *there*. Would you lend me a hand? Or rather, *two* hands?'

I sighed. 'Very well.' I left my box and grasped one end of the bookcase. 'Ready?'

At that precise moment, the corridor door burst open, and Lieutenant Wymar, followed by a bevy of policemen, stormed into the room. Two well-padded gentlemen in masks appeared in their wake.

One of the masked men spoke. 'Everybody out of the room. And don't touch the box.' He turned to Lieutenant Wymar. 'We'll roll in our machine and X-ray the package just where it is.'

Again very shortly I found myself in a room far removed from the mayor's office, with Lieutenant Wymar glowering over me. 'You've got a one-track mind, haven't you?'

'One-track mind?'

'That's right. You threatened to blow up a news-stand.'

I blinked. 'Sir, never in my life would I ...'

He raised a hand. 'Don't bother to deny it. We had you followed when you left here yesterday. And you also threatened to blow up the Metropolitan Museum of Art.'

'Only the modern paintings,' I corrected. 'Have you seen that pathetic Utrillo in which he attempts ...'

The door opened and one of the padded technicians entered. 'It's definitely a bomb, Lieutenant. We can make out the dry cells, the wiring, the alarm clock, and the powder charge.'

I spent four hours in jail before Lieutenant Wymar saw me again, and when he did, he appeared as frustrated as a lip reader at a ventriloquist's convention. With him was an intentionally informal young man wearing a crew cut, a tweed jacket, and a smile of professional wisdom.

Lieutenant Wymar seemed to have difficulty restraining an urge to throttle me. 'The powder charge wasn't a powder charge.'

I smiled. 'Really.'

His hands opened and closed. 'It was just a bag of sugar.'

I nodded. 'If only you'd *asked* me.'

Wymar turned abruptly to his companion. 'All right, Doc. He's all yours.'

When the doctor and I were alone, he offered me a cigar from a new five-pack. It was my brand and he had evidently done research.

He lit the cigar for me. 'My name is Dr Barton. Dr Sam Barton. Just call me Sam.'

'Why?'

He blew out the match. 'Do you often have this compulsion to blow up things? People?'

'Doesn't everybody?'

He smiled tolerantly. 'Did you lose heavily in the Veterans' Memorial operation?'

I said nothing.

'And do you blame Mayor Pettibone? Well, do you or don't you?'

'I believe I'm catching a cold,' I said.

He smiled conspiratorily. 'You were just *testing* their defences, weren't you?'

I sneezed.

He almost patted me on the knee. 'Yes. *Testing*. The first

time, just an alarm clock. Then the alarm clock and the mechanism, but not the powder charge. And you will keep taking boxes with you until the police get ... how shall we say? ... *tired*? Until they no longer bother ... and then one day ...' He seemed to search for the next word.

'*Pow?*'

He nodded. '*Pow.*' And now for half a minute he became thoughtful. 'But the mechanism of the bomb would have to be different from what it is now, wouldn't it? After all, if you merely set the clock for a certain time, there would be no guarantee that you would be *with* Mayor Pettibone precisely at the time that the bomb is due to go off.'

'You have an incisive mind.'

He flushed slightly. 'I was always rather good at logic in school. Straight A's.' He leaned forward. 'You would have to have something on the *outside* of the package. Something like a *doorbell push button*? And when you *pressed* the button, the bomb would go off.'

I savoured my cigar. 'Open circuit? Closed circuit?'

He rubbed his chin. 'With an open circuit, when you pressed the push button, the circuit would *close* ... then current would begin to *flow* ... and the bomb ...' He stopped and shook his head slowly. 'No. That wouldn't really do, you know.'

'It wouldn't?'

'No. You see when you are carrying this package, couldn't the police put a bullet through your head?'

'That seems reasonable to me.'

He nodded. 'And don't you see, the sudden termination of your life might not even leave you with sufficient reflex to *push* the button.'

'That *is* a problem.'

'And so we come to the *closed*-circuit system of wiring. In this case the current is already flowing through the circuit, but the bomb does not explode because the contact device is held magnetically immobilized by the current. However, when the push button is *released*, remagnetization ensues, the contact device is released and ...'

I supplied the word again. *'Pow?'*

'Precisely.' He smiled at his triumph of electromagnetic reasoning. 'In other words, if the police shot you through the head, it would actually serve no constructive purpose. Your finger would merely release its pressure on the push button and the bomb would go off anyway.'

'By George,' I said admiringly, 'I believe you have it.'

He frowned thoughtfully. 'You haven't bought a push button yet, have you?'

'No. But if I ever do, you will be the first to know.'

He was pleased at the precedence. 'Now remember, when you *do* buy a push button, *don't* use it until you talk to me first.' He took a card with his name and office address from his pocket. 'In the meantime, would you care to come to see me? On Thursday at ten AM.'

'Just for a visit?'

'Of course,' he said reassuringly.

'Then I am not to be kept in jail?'

'Of course not. You are free to go.'

'Why?'

'Well ... actually the police have nothing on which to hold you. Not even disorderly conduct ... since it appears that it was actually the police who were disorderly. And since your package wasn't really ... on closer examination ... *rigged* as a bomb ...'

'And there is no law against peacefully carrying a conglomeration of objects in a package?'

He nodded. 'And besides, it's the District Attorney's private suspicion that this may turn out to be some scheme whereby you get to sue the city.' He studied me earnestly. 'Will you?'

'I hadn't planned on it.'

He seemed relieved. 'Good. And besides, I prefer my own theory ... that you were *testing*.'

Twenty minutes later I found myself free on the streets.

After walking a block, I once again observed that the man in the trench coat was dogging my footsteps.

It was evening now and I found it not at all difficult to lose him. When I had satisfied myself of that accomplishment, I returned to the lighted downtown section and entered a dime store.

I purchased a push button.

I did not return to my own hotel room. Instead I registered at Geoffrey's hotel and then went to his room.

Geoffrey is a thin, pipe-smoking man. 'Are you going back tomorrow?'

'Yes,' I said. 'I've purchased the push button.'

'Well ... good luck. I hope it goes off this time.'

'Thank you. It should.'

I did not sleep well that night. I had a number of catastrophe dreams, the most vivid of which being the disintegration of the Metropolitan Museum of Art in one tremendous explosion.

In the morning, I returned to Geoffrey's room and we constructed my third and final cubic package.

At ten o'clock, I phoned Dr Barton. 'Doctor, I just bought a push button.'

He was disturbed. 'You have? So soon? But you haven't had a session with me yet.'

'I called to bid you goodbye. I do not believe that we shall meet in this world again.'

'Now, wait a minute,' he said desperately. 'What are you going to do?'

'I am going to see Mayor Pettibone. This morning I shall not fail.'

'Where are you now? At your hotel?'

'No.' I hung up.

I sat down and read the morning paper while I smoked a full cigar. Then I went downstairs with my cubic box and directed the first taxi driver to take me to the City Hall.

However, one block before my destination, I ordered him to

pull to the kerb. I paid my fare and stepped out on to the side-walk. I carried the package in front of me, one thumb firmly depressing the push button affixed to its top.

I surveyed the panorama before me.

The avenue ahead was innocent of all vehicles and pedes-trians. The side streets had been roped off and uniformed policemen were stationed at intervals to see that none of the spectators – and there appeared to be *thousands* – trespassed into the clearing. In effect, a wide path led directly to the entrance of the City Hall.

To one side I spied Lieutenant Wymar and Dr Barton. The latter, as a matter of fact, seemed to be hiding behind a lamp post.

With all those thousands of eyes staring at me, I suddenly experienced a new and strange sensation.

Stage fright.

I took two tentative steps towards the City Hall, then I turned abruptly and walked away.

For some moments there was silence behind me, and then Lieutenant Wymar shouted. 'Hey, wait a minute!'

I walked faster.

When I glanced back, I saw him, Dr Barton, and a host of police officers in pursuit.

I broke into a trot.

Hundreds of pedestrians seemed to join the procession be-hind me.

I dashed down the block, glanced back again, paused for a breath, and quickly darted up the stairs of the Metropolitan Museum of Art. The swarming mass turned in my direction and I dashed into the building.

I puffed badly as I trotted through the Dutch masters. Be-hind me the roar of the chase clung like adhesive. My heart thumped with the exertion as I quickly traversed an exhibition of Roman sculpture. The relentless pursuit continued.

Eventually only one corridor remained ahead of me. I

staggered past two startled guards into the exhibition of modern art. At the far end of the gallery I came face to face with a blank wall. I turned and faced the far door.

The pack surged through the doorway, Lieutenant Wymar and Dr Barton acting as point.

I held up my free hand and shouted with evident hysteria. 'Stop! Everybody *stop*! One more step and I shall release this push button!'

Lieutenant Wymar and his army skidded to a halt – possibly leaving heel marks on the marble floor.

I took several breaths before I managed to speak again. 'Lieutenant Wymar, I have decided to give up trying to see Mayor Pettibone. Apparently he is completely inaccessible.'

That was pleasant information for the lieutenant. 'Well, now you're showing some sense.' He took a quick, eager step forward.

'*Halt!*' I shouted, my voice verily ricocheting off the walls. 'One more step and I shall release this button.'

Lieutenant Wymar froze.

I again raised my voice for an announcement. 'In exactly ten minutes, I shall release this push button. I would do so at this exact instant, except for the simple fact that I have a desire to regain my breath before making such a momentous decision.'

Dr Barton cleared his throat uneasily. 'If we could just talk to you for . . .'

'On the other hand,' I said, 'waiting to regain one's breath at a time like this is frivolous . . . procrastinating . . . perhaps I should . . .'

Dr Barton spoke quickly. 'No. No. By all means, regain your breath.'

Lieutenant Wymar turned to an aide at his side. 'Just how much damage could that box do if it went off?'

His assistant frowned thoughtfully. 'It's hard to say, Lieutenant. With some of these new combinations, he might be able to blow up the whole building.'

I looked at my watch. 'In *nine* minutes I shall release the button.'

The lieutenant made a swift decision. 'Clear the building. Hop to it.' He then spoke to Dr Barton. 'You stay here and try to talk him out of it.'

Dr Barton seemed unhappy. 'I really don't think I could do anything in a case like this, Lieutenant. We need somebody with a little more experience in this particular field.' He looked at me hopefully. 'A priest? A minister? A rabbi?'

'Eight minutes,' I said.

Dr Barton immediately joined the general retreat.

Through the doorway I saw that my pursuers had at least temporarily halted in the sculpture department. I smiled grimly and advanced. The retreat recommenced immediately.

A new and unique emotion took possession of me.

The feeling of power.

I found myself chuckling as now I pursued them through the Early American primitives, through a lane of lithographs, and pell mell down the hall of prize-winning junior high school watercolours. When they reached the front door they were fairly tumbling over each other.

I laughed triumphantly and then dashed about the building rooting out any brave souls who might have chosen to remain. I discovered two – though not brave – crouching beneath their desks in the administrative department. I sent them fleeing out the back door into the gathering crowd.

When I returned to the front windows, I saw Lieutenant Wymar, Dr Barton and a number of people who appeared to be officials gathered in conference at a safe distance from the building.

I watched them for five minutes. Ten. Twelve.

And then I went to one of the front doors, opened it, and stepped out.

A strong murmur rose from the crowd – possibly at the prospect of witnessing some poor soul blowing himself to bits

– but I noticed that none of the civilized spectators departed permanently. They merely retreated, attempting in the process to preserve their line of sight.

I gazed at the assemblage for fully one minute.

And then I removed my thumb from the push button.

Nothing – of course – happened.

I quickly removed the wrapping from my box and extracted the alarm clock and the wire. I held them up for all to see. Then I upended the box, signifying that it was now indeed empty.

I put the entire mess into a convenient trash box nearby. I did not want to be arrested for litter-bugging.

I was immediately – *immediately* – surrounded by a large number of angry men – of whom Lieutenant Wymar seemed typical. His face was definitely mottled and he communicated in something of a strangled manner. 'Just what kind of practical joke is this?'

I glared. 'It is no practical joke. I merely wanted to see Mayor Pettibone, but apparently that is a capital crime in this city.'

'Now, wait a minute!' he roared. 'So maybe there wasn't any bomb in the box, but ...'

'Of *course* there was no bomb in the box,' I snapped. 'There never has been and there never will be.'

'But the clock ... the wire ... the push button ...'

'Is there a *law* against wires? Push buttons? Experimenting with timing devices happens to be my hobby.' I wagged a finger under his nose. 'The Civil Liberties Union shall hear about this. I shall sue. For a million dollars.'

'Mister,' Wymar announced wearily, '*you're* going to jail.'

I showed my teeth. 'Really? On what charge? It is I who have been hounded, abused. It is *I* who have been pursued by what clearly appeared to me to be a lynch mob *led* by officers of the law. I shall sue for *two* million dollars.'

A small worried man appeared at Lieutenant Wymar's elbow. 'Now, just one moment, Lieutenant. Let's not get rash.

We're having enough trouble with the budget as it is.'

'Who are you?' I demanded.

He spoke almost apologetically. 'Mayor Pettibone.'

'Ah, ha!' I said. 'So finally you have come out of hiding. I've been trying to inform you that directly below my hotel window there is a series of holes in the street. When trucks rattle over them at night I find it *impossible* to sleep. I demand that the city do something about them immediately!'

I struck my walking stick sharply on the pavement, turned indignantly, and stalked away.

I rather expected to feel an authoritative hand on my shoulder, but apparently my abrupt departure had left them mired in indecision. A precipitous retreat often leaves the enemy in confusion.

I forced my way quickly through the crowd and within one hundred and fifty yards found a taxi. I entered it and directed the driver to a West Side address.

However, after half a mile, I ordered him to stop before a supermarket. 'I'll be out immediately,' I said. 'I have to make a small purchase.'

I entered the supermarket and exited immediately by a rear door. In the alley I tossed away my walking stick and hat. I pulled off my false beard, reversed my topcoat, making my attire brown rather than blue, and donned a cloth cap.

I walked down the alley and more than a block before I found another taxi. I settled in the back seat. 'The airport, please.'

I met Geoffrey the next day in St Louis.

He showed me the three Utrillos, the two Picassos and the two Modiglianis. 'Everything worked perfectly. I hid in the lavatory. After you cleared out the building I slipped into the gallery and shoved the pictures under my coat. When I ran out of the back of the building nobody paid much attention to me. They thought I was just someone you were chasing.'

I shrugged. 'They could have suspected anything they

wanted to, but they could have proved nothing. My lawyer would merely have to point out that while everyone hounded me, some dastardly thief took advantage of the situation to steal some paintings.'

He handed me my glass. 'Do you think we can pull this off again?'

I smiled. 'No. However, I am sure I shall think of something else next time.'

See and Tell

MARY LINN ROBY

Peter Douglas Morehead was on his way to school when he saw Miss Finch lying in the ditch, her head sticking out of the new tin culvert under Warren Road. Miss Finch's eyes were closed and she looked very peaceful with her long yellow hair spread out among the daisies and buttercups. Still, even Peter, who was only seven, knew that a ditch was a very strange place for a grown woman to go to sleep.

His first thought was to make his way down the slope and wake her up. On the other hand, he was late for school as it was, and if Miss Finch were anything like his father, it would take any amount of shaking to stir her. Besides, Peter did not particularly care for Miss Finch. Everyone in the village knew that she did not like children, and once, when Donald Allen's ball had been accidentally thrown over her hedge, she had pretended not to be able to find it.

Peter took another look at the white face among the flowers, and felt a vague sense of disquiet. If it had been mid-afternoon on a hot, sunny day, he could have understood anyone wanting to take a nap on the ground. He had done it often enough himself during the past summer. Peter smiled, remembering how the fat, white clouds had twisted themselves into the oddest shapes. But Miss Finch could not be particularly cosy on a cold morning like this. Besides, it had rained the night before, and the ground must be very damp. Peter wondered if she had been sleeping there all night.

He took a few steps towards the ditch, then came to an abrupt halt as he heard the school bell ring. Glancing down the hill he saw there were no children in the fenced yard. His heart began to pound. He had been late once this week already, and his father had told him that if it happened again he would have to be punished. Turning, he began to run down the road as fast as his fat legs would carry him.

The morning was so exciting that Peter completely forgot about what he had seen. After reading, there was clay modelling, and he was able to make a very successful elephant, which even Miss Simpson grudgingly admitted to being able to identify. Peter spent a long time adding a beautiful long trunk which curled about the elephant's front feet, and before he knew it, it was time to take out his red arithmetic book.

Adding was always difficult, and Peter's head was feeling a bit muzzy when Miss Simpson announced that it was time for 'See and Tell'.

'What have you got to tell us about today, Susan?' she said in her harsh voice. 'Come up front, and remember to speak clearly and distinctly.'

Susan's story was a long, rambling description of a trip she had taken recently to her grandmother's home in the next town, and Peter found his attention wandering. People didn't want to listen to dull stuff like that, he decided. People wanted to hear about something with a bit of excitement to it. He searched his mind for something to tell about in case Miss Simpson should call on him. He had stolen an apple from Mr Rheardon's store on Tuesday but, of course, one couldn't tell about things like that, no matter how superior a story it might make compared to that drivel that Susan was spouting. Then there was his frog, Sam. Sam had died last night, and Peter had found him in his box, stiff and cold. At first he had thought Sam was asleep, but then ...

An idea came to Peter just as Susan finally brought her tale to an end. Raising his hand high, he began to wave it wildly.

Miss Simpson's smile reflected the weary patience of the true professional.

'I'm sorry, Peter,' she said, 'but you know that we don't volunteer for "See and Tell". That wouldn't be fair, because some people find it a good deal easier to talk than others – and those people would be talking all the time.'

Her expression left Peter in no doubt as to the category into which he fell. His face grew hot. He hated Miss Simpson. She couldn't stop him from talking.

'But I saw something important this morning!' he blurted. 'I saw Miss Finch. She's lying dead in the ditch up at the top of Warren Hill!'

He looked around the room expectantly, only to find that his colleagues not otherwise engaged in such pursuits as tying their shoe lacings together, or breaking their pencils against the desk, did not seem particularly impressed. The cumulative effect was one of vague expectancy, as though they were waiting for him to go on.

'That's all there is,' Peter assured them angrily. 'My frog, Sam, died last night, and so I ought to know a dead person when I see one.'

He turned back to Miss Simpson and found that she was responding with all the intensity he could have desired. Her eyes were wide and staring, and her mouth hung open. Peter smiled at her.

'You nasty little boy!' she shrilled. 'To tell such a lie!'

Peter scowled. Miss Simpson was rather nasty herself when aroused. Still, he was no coward. 'I did not tell a lie!' he shouted defiantly. 'Miss Finch is dead in the ditch. I saw her on the way to school!'

Miss Simpson lost control altogether at that point. Despite his surface bravado, Peter turned cold inside.

'You march right down here!' she shrilled. 'Right down to the front of the room, Peter Morehead! We'll see ...'

Suddenly her voice dwindled into quiet. The children's heads turned as though operated on a single pivot. Mr Payson, the principal, was standing in the doorway. His smile was as toothsome as ever, but it had a certain set quality.

'Well, well,' he said in a friendly voice that deceived no one. 'What seems to be the problem here?'

'It's Peter Morehead, Mr Payson,' Miss Simpson said. She was breathless, as though she had been running, and her face was very white. Almost as white as Miss Finch's, Peter reflected. 'He's been trying to frighten the other children during "See and Tell".'

Mr Payson eyed her pensively for a moment, then turned to stare at Peter, who smiled hopefully, attempting to display a similar number of teeth. He was no longer cold inside. He knew the principal, both from personal contact and reputation. Mr Payson did not believe in losing his temper. Mr Payson was always reasonable. Most important of all, he seemed to be more interested in finding out why you did a thing than in punishing you for it. His own classes were the most disorderly in the building as a result.

'It seems strange that Peter would try to do a thing like that,' Mr Payson said. He sucked air through his teeth, making a strangely exotic sound. 'Why don't we get together and talk about it for a few minutes, Peter?'

He gestured invitingly towards the door, and Peter marched up the aisle and through it, smirking triumphantly at Miss Simpson as he passed her. Behind him he heard someone giggle.

'Now, what's all this about you running amok during "See and Tell"?' Mr Payson said when they were cosily settled in the tiny office that was musty with the smell of chemicals and littered with books.

Peter sat up very straight and pressed his knees together. 'I just told about something interesting that I saw on my way to school this morning,' he said, assuming his most innocent expression.

'Well, it couldn't have been anything so very dreadful then,' Mr Payson said jovially. 'Just what did you see?'

'A dead body,' Peter said succinctly. 'In the ditch.'

Mr Payson's smile faded. Peter noted with considerable interest that although his mouth was more or less closed, his teeth seemed still to protrude from odd corners. 'A body!' the principal exclaimed. 'Was it a dog? Or someone's dear pussycat? Poor Peter. I imagine it was a horrid shock.'

Peter stared at Mr Payson angrily. Why did everyone insist on treating him like a baby? Someone's dear pussycat! 'It was a woman,' he announced stiffly. 'It was Miss Finch who lives in the red brick house near the bridge. She was lying in the culvert with her head sticking out into the ditch. And she was dead. Just like Sam.'

If Peter had not known better, he would have thought Mr Payson was about to shout at him just as Miss Simpson had. The principal leaned forward in his chair until his forehead nearly touched Peter's. 'And who is Sam?' he demanded, not at all pleasantly.

Peter began to wonder if he had gone too far. Perhaps one death at a time was all these people could bear to hear about. 'My pet frog,' he said apologetically. 'Just an old bullfrog, sir.'

Mr Payson exhaled loudly and sat back in his chair. His eyes and nose and teeth seemed to pull into his thin face. His mouth curved in a weak smile. 'I'm beginning to understand,' he said, rubbing his hands. 'When did your pet die, Peter?'

'Last night, sir. I went to get him out of his box, and he was stiff and cold.'

'Frogs are cold-blooded creatures even when alive, of course,' Mr Payson said, unable to resist a touch of pedagogy. 'Still, I suppose that is beside the point. The important thing is that you lost your little pet. I expect you were very upset.'

Peter shook his head, puzzled. 'Not especially, sir,' he said. 'There's a pond behind our house. I can get another.'

Mr Payson nodded his head approvingly. 'Stout fellow,' he said. 'That's the spirit. There's no sense in showing how we feel these losses, is there? Now, the next thing I'm interested in is why you decided to say that Miss Finch is dead. Why not

Miss Simpson? Or, for that matter, me?'

'But you and Miss Simpson aren't dead,' Peter said plaintively. 'Miss Finch is. Dead in a ditch.'

Mr Payson assumed what was for him a most threatening expression. 'I think we've heard quite enough of that, Peter,' he said. 'Now, tell me, do you like Miss Finch?'

Peter decided to be honest. 'Not particularly,' he said. 'She kept a ball once when it happened to go over the hedge.'

'I see,' Mr Payson said. He sounded very satisfied. 'That will be all, I think, Peter. You may return to your room. I'll explain to Miss Simpson later.'

'Explain what, sir?'

The principal rose. 'Perhaps,' he said, 'your fault lies in carrying things just a bit further than they should go, Peter. It's very understandable that you would rather think of Miss Finch as being dead than your pet frog; a simple case of transference; no crime in itself. We all do it – attempt to avoid reality when we can't face up to the facts. Still, I don't expect you to understand all this mumbo jumbo. The point I'm trying to make is that now you should try to accept your pet's death. As you say, one can always get another frog. But one would be hard put to find another Miss Finch. Eh? Eh?'

Mr Payson broke into a high cackle of laughter, all the time urging Peter across the room and to the door. 'Now you trot along back to your class, my boy,' he said. 'We'll have a nice long talk again one of these days.'

Peter marched past him, down the corridor, around the corner and out the front door of the school. Once in the yard he broke into a run. Frustration burned inside him.

At the top of Warren Hill, he panted to a stop. At first, looking into the ditch, he could see nothing but grass and flowers. Then, moving to the right a bit and craning his neck, he saw her. Her eyes were still closed and she was very white. Still, Peter decided, before going on, it was best to make certain.

Picking up a small rock, he hurled it expertly, grinning with satisfaction as it struck the mark. No, Miss Finch was dead all right. If she had been sleeping, that would have awakened her, and no mistake.

The other side of the hill was taken at a trot. He had, he knew, discovered something of considerable general interest, and he expected to be given credit for it. Now the thing was to find someone who would believe him.

Miss Dewlap was standing in her front garden, wearing a pair of rubber waders which encased her legs, including her ample thighs, in glossy vermilion. Her torso was obscured by a man's red-and-black checked shirt, and her grey hair had been freshly cropped close to her scalp. A cigarette drooped from her lips as, balancing herself with one arm, she flung the other forward to cast a fly neatly into a pot of geraniums nearly thirty feet from where she was standing.

Peter watched her reel in her line with open admiration, Miss Finch temporarily forgotten.

A gruff baritone aroused him. 'Decided to give school a miss today?' Miss Dewlap inquired.

Peter nodded, instantly recalled to the immediacies of the moment. 'It's Miss Finch,' he gasped. This time he had decided not to be so casual in his presentation of the facts. Perhaps if he showed a touch of panic he might make himself more believable.

Miss Dewlap leaned her fishing rod against the side of the cottage and ambled over to the low hedge, her rubber waders making a pleasant swish-swish as her upper legs rubbed together. 'She lives next door,' she told Peter, removing what was left of her cigarette from the side of her mouth. 'What do you want her for?'

'I don't want her,' Peter said in a shrill voice. 'She's dead!'

Miss Dewlap said a word that Peter had never heard before with great emphasis.

'It's true,' he continued, being careful to maintain the mood. 'She's dead in the ditch at the top of the hill!' Gesturing dramatically with one hand, he rubbed his eyes with the other and made sobbing noises.

Miss Dewlap was undeceived. 'Cut out that nonsense,' she commanded, leaning over the hedge and tapping him sharply on the shoulder.

Peter recognized authority in a voice readily enough, even though he did not often hear it. Obediently he abandoned pretence. 'It's true,' he said. 'Honestly. I saw her on the way to school. I told Miss Simpson, but she called me a liar. Then I told Mr Payson, and he said I was upset because Sam is dead. But I'm not, and she is. Dead, that is.'

Miss Dewlap eyed him reflectively. 'Well,' she said, 'I'm not going to call you a liar, boy, although I've heard about some of the tricks you've been up to lately.'

'Aren't you going to call the police?' Peter suggested hopefully.

The stout woman laughed and lit another cigarette, striking the long wooden match on the back of her waders. 'Drat you, boy! Tell you what. You come in the house and have a piece of cake.'

This time Peter's tears were real enough. 'You don't believe me!' he bellowed. 'No one believes me!'

Miss Dewlap said nothing, propelling him grimly through the door and into the fond embrace of a small, excited dog. 'Down, Percy!' Miss Dewlap boomed, pushing the animal aside. 'Peter doesn't want you lapping his face.'

'But—' the boy began.

'You sit down here,' Miss Dewlap told him, pulling out a chair from the red kitchen table. 'Here's a knife and here's the cake plate. Cut yourself a big piece, and keep Percy company while I trot over next door and see if Miss Finch is home.'

'She's not,' Peter wailed. 'She's lying—'

'I know, I know,' Miss Dewlap growled. 'Dead in a ditch and all that. Still, I'll just make certain that you're not pulling my leg, if you please.'

For the first moments after the door slammed behind her, Peter amused himself trying to picture anyone pulling Miss Dewlap's leg. Then he took the cover off the cake plate and looked at the shocking-pink confectionery inside. Perhaps it was the memory of the white face among the flowers, or perhaps it was Miss Dewlap's reputation as the poorest cook in town; whatever the reason, Peter could not face any sort of gastronomical trauma. Cutting a large piece of the sticky substance, he put it on the floor, where Percy attacked it with gusto.

The dog was just lapping up the last pieces when Miss Dewlap returned, her face white and drawn. Taking a big brown bottle out of the cupboard, she spattered some liquid in the bottom of a glass. Peter watched while she emptied it in one gulp.

'You had me worried for a while there, boy,' she said. 'You lie like a trooper, don't you?'

'But I'm not lying!' Peter told her. For one incredible moment he thought she might have found Miss Finch in her kitchen next door, going about her usual chores. But he couldn't have been mistaken! He simply could not have been. He still remembered how the stone had bounced off that white face.

'Well, her best suitcase is gone, the brown leather that she paid too much for, and a good many of her better dresses are missing,' Miss Dewlap said. 'I expect she went to see her family. They live in Maine somewhere. Percy!'

Grabbing the dog from the floor, Miss Dewlap clutched him to her substantial bosom. Bits of pink clung to his whiskers.

'He's not supposed to have anything rich!' she announced in an outraged voice. 'Besides, that cake was meant to be a treat for you. Ordinary little boys like cake! Now, Peter Morehead, I think I should take steps. Little boys who lie can cause a good deal of trouble.'

Taking Peter by the collar, she marched him out of the house and down the street. Miss Dewlap had forgotten to remove her red waders, but the swishing sound was no longer comforting. Peter was all too familiar with the characteristics of adult anger.

'Now,' she said, depositing him in front of his house, 'there's your father coming home for lunch. I suggest you wait here while I tell him what you've been up to.'

Peter tried hard not to listen, but the words, 'truant', 'liar', and 'mischiefmaker' intruded themselves on his consciousness. Then Miss Dewlap was marching back up the street, and his father had him by the arm.

The licking was administered in the shed with an expertly applied shingle. Peter cried copiously, and shouted, too, since these reactions were all part of long-established custom. He was not, however, particularly hurt.

'You get inside and eat your lunch,' his father told him, 'and then back to school you go. We'll hear no more of this nonsense about Miss Finch. I know very well why you're saying what you are. You didn't like the woman, and you have some crazy notion that it would be nice if she were dead. But what you're spreading, my boy, is a malicious rumour, and that sort of thing can do a good deal of damage. First thing you know, my friend, Miss Finch will be starting slander proceedings against me.'

Peter nodded his head. He ate his lunch in downcast silence while his parents exchanged meaningful glances over his head, and then it was time to return to school.

It was a lonely walk since the children stayed for lunch at school. Peter was the only person walking up Warren Hill in the hot noonday sun. When he reached the top, he tried to force himself to stroll on, but his feet had minds of their own.

It was difficult to see Miss Finch now. Some of the grass which had been depressed by the dew that morning had sprung back, and if Peter had not known she was there, he doubted whether he could see her now. But then, she wasn't supposed to be there. Everyone had assured him that she was not. Peter felt a little tingle of self-satisfaction go up his spine. He knew he was right about one thing, at least. She was in the ditch. As to whether she were dead . . .

Gingerly, he let himself down over the bank, smelling the

sweetness of hog grass and buttercups. Miss Finch's eyes were closed. Peter knelt down and touched her skin. It was as cold as Sam's had been – dead or alive.

Now that he was close to the woman, Peter could see the little hole in the side of her head. There was blood around the hole. Peter knew blood when he saw it, and nothing would make a little hole like that besides a bullet.

Miss Finch had been shot to death in the ditch!

Peter felt a glow of satisfaction. He had been right then, all along. This morning it had seemed absolutely necessary that everyone acknowledge that he was right, but now he had learned a valuable lesson. It didn't matter whether anyone else knew the truth or not, as long as he was certain. As for the others, they had said that she was gone, and that, thought Peter happily, was the way it would be.

Disregarding the dirt he was accumulating on his clothes, Peter climbed the other side of the culvert. Glancing down at the school, he saw the children still playing in the yard. There would just be time for what he had to do.

The inside of the culvert was very dark and damp, and a little frightening. Peter crawled forward, groping with his hand for what he knew he must soon touch.

Suddenly there they were – Miss Finch's feet! The neat patent leather was smooth beneath his fingers. Her legs were like solid slabs of ice, and just as heavy. It was more difficult than Peter had thought, pulling absolutely dead weight. He inched her towards him – one, two, three pulls. Then, breathing heavily, he backed out of the culvert and into the sun.

The children had disappeared. The bell must have rung while he had been underground. But this was far more important. Now there was no sign of Miss Finch except for the nice leather suitcase that Miss Dewlap had mentioned, but it was easily pushed inside the culvert, too.

Peter felt a great sense of accomplishment. Now Mr Payson and Miss Simpson and Miss Dewlap and his father could all be right. They would never again hear anything else about

Miss Finch. In a few months, even the little that was left of her would not exist. Peter knew about such things. Once he had found a dead cat in the woods behind his house, and had made a point of going back to see it every week or two throughout a long summer. If Miss Finch were like that cat – and Peter expected that she was – there would not be much left of her by fall.

Patting the grass and flowers into place until it looked as though no one had ever been there, he clambered up the side of the bank. One final look and, with a grin, he started running down the hill.

The first class after lunch was always Reading. When Peter noisily threw open the door to the classroom, Miss Simpson was sitting at her desk with a copy of *Robinson Crusoe* propped up in front of her. Miss Simpson was always saying what a wonderful thing adventure was, but Peter knew now that she meant only the kind that came in books.

'Well, Mr Morehead,' she said in a voice that was so sweet that it made chills go up and down Peter's back, 'it's nice to see you again. We might as well not wait for "See and Tell". I imagine you can't wait to tell us what new, exciting thing has happened to you.'

Peter grinned at her so broadly it seemed as though his face might split. He was much too grown-up for silly children's games now. 'Nothing happened,' he lied happily. 'Not a single thing.'

Fair's Fair

JANE SPEED

I knew right away Mother had something besides breakfast on her mind when she set a bowl of oatmeal in front of me. I mean it was *Saturday*. She usually gives that 'Busy little engines need good fuel' stuff a rest on Saturdays and lets me have whatever I want.

I was still wondering if it would do me any good to point this out to her when Daddy came in and sat down at the table. So I decided to just put a lot of strawberry jam on the oatmeal to pep it up and not say anything. Maybe, if I kept quiet, Mother would halfway forget I was there and go ahead and talk to Daddy about whatever was bothering her. Of course, it might be just bills. You'd be surprised how worked up my parents can get on *that* subject sometimes.

Daddy drank his juice down in one gulp like he always does and picked up the morning paper. But I could tell by the way Mother was stirring and stirring her coffee that he wasn't going to get much read.

Sure enough, in about half a minute she said, 'Harry—'

He just said, 'Hm?' and kept his head behind the paper, although he must have known already that it was a lost cause.

'Herbert Wellman's mother died last week.'

'Did she, now?' Daddy folded the paper and put it aside then.

It actually took me a couple of seconds to figure out who Herbert Wellman was. That may sound funny because the

Wellmans live right next door to us. But I sometimes forget
their names because Jeddie Brubaker always calls Mrs Wellman the Cat Lady. That's because she likes cats so much. She
has a couple of her own and every night she puts bowls of
milk and scraps out for all the strays in the neighbourhood. I
know because my bedroom is over our kitchen and I watch her
sometimes from my window taking the stuff down their steep
old back-porch steps.

Some nights they get to howling and fighting out back – the
cats, I mean – and Daddy wanted to complain about it once
but Mother wouldn't let him. She said cats were all poor
Isobel Wellman had. She had no children and she hardly even
had a husband. And it does seem that way because Mr Wellman is almost never there.

He comes home late every night, sometimes not till after
I'm in bed, and he's never there on weekends at all. On weekends he always goes to look after his mother's place. It's in a
little town called Penn Oaks about fifty miles from here. Only
I suppose now she's dead he won't be doing that any more.

'Well, it's about time—' Daddy began, then the way he
stopped all of a sudden I knew without looking that Mother
must have given him the old 'Little pitchers have big ears'
signal.

'Amy, dear,' she said to me in that phony bright kind of
voice she always uses when she's going to try to talk me into
something I don't particularly want to do. 'It's such a lovely
morning, why don't you go outside and play.'

Wouldn't you know? Just when things were getting interesting. Still – she didn't seem to notice that I hadn't finished
my oatmeal (frankly, that strawberry jam didn't work out too
well), so I just slid off my chair and went out the screen door.

I made as much noise as possible going down the back
steps, then I tiptoed around and hoisted myself up on to the
garbage can under the open breakfast-room window. I'd hardly
missed a thing.

'– what it's going to be like for Isobel now,' Mother was saying, 'having him home on weekends.'

'Well – fine, I should think. I mean, isn't that what you've been complaining about all these years? – his spending every spare minute at his mother's and leaving poor Isobel with nothing but those damn cats. Oh, I agree, I agree.' Daddy said this last part kind of fast as though Mother had started to interrupt him. 'That's no way to treat a wife. But Herb had his problems, too, with that mother of his. She must have been a real Tartar – wouldn't budge out of the old house and yet she refused to hire anyone to look after things for her. So – now she's gone. Maybe Herb and Isobel can finally settle down and lead a normal life.'

'I just hope,' Mother said, kind of gloomy and mysterious, 'it isn't too late.'

'Now what the devil do you mean by that?'

'Oh, Harry! They've been living that way for fifteen *years*. People can't just snap back and forth like – like puppets.'

For a minute neither of them said anything, then Mother started again and her voice sounded different, sort of quiet. 'Have you forgotten what Isobel Wellman was like when they first moved here? How pretty she was?'

I nearly fell off the garbage can when she said that. You should *see* Mrs Wellman. For one thing, her fingernails are always a lot dirtier than my mother'd ever let me get away with. That's because next to cats she likes gardening best of all, and she doesn't wear garden gloves because she says she likes the feel of the soil.

This year she's got a lot of sweet peas that she's really crazy about. They *are* sort of pretty – kind of a pinkish lavender. But not Mrs Wellman. I mean she's okay to talk to and all that, but she's not *pretty*. She's all caved-in looking and beaky-nosed and her hair goes every which way as though she never combed it.

Jeddie Brubaker says she's a witch. And you know something? I used to halfway believe it was true. That's when I was a lot younger, of course. But Mrs Wellman used to do all kinds of cooking and baking and I guess she had more than she needed because she was always handing stuff out to the neighbourhood kids. For a long time I was afraid to take anything from her for fear it would cast a spell on me or something.

Then one time Jeddie dared me to take a cookie and eat it right there. And I did and it was pretty good. Not as good as my mother's, but at least I didn't fall down in a fit or anything. You just can't believe half of what that klunky kid says.

'And how hard she tried' – Mother was really going strong now – 'to make a nice home for that man. The meals she used to cook – and then he never came home for them. After a while she just gave up and made the best life she could out of those cats and her garden. What I'm trying to say is, I think she's come to *count* on Herb's not being there.'

'Oh, Madge.' I heard Daddy's chair scrape back. 'I really think you're making too much out of this. They'll work things out. People do, you know.'

Mother gave a big sigh and said, 'I hope you're right.' Then she got up, too, and started clearing off the table, so I slid down off the garbage can in a hurry and ran back and got myself going in the old rope swing in case Daddy looked out back to see what I was doing.

After a while he and Mother both came out and he said he was going to drive her over to the shopping centre to get some groceries and did I want to come along. But I'd already spent my allowance and it's kind of boring just hanging around over there if you can't buy anything, so I decided to stay home. I pumped myself up good and high so I could wave to them all the way out the driveway, then I just let the swing glide almost to a stop.

All of a sudden out of nowhere Marmy jumped into my lap. She's one of Mrs Wellman's cats, my favourite. I used to think Mrs Wellman got the name out of *Little Women*. It would fit, too, because Marmy's always being a mother. Almost every time you turn around she's got another litter of kittens.

But Mrs Wellman said she named her that because she's what's called a marmalade cat, kind of splotchy yellow all over. She's not much to look at – Marmy, I mean. She's small, for one thing, and she stays skinny even though Mrs Wellman feeds her a lot, and she kind of sags in the middle.

But I like her because she's so smart. She really knows who's her friend and who isn't. Right now, if my father was home and came out the back door she'd be off like a streak. Daddy wouldn't *do* anything mean to her, you understand, but she just knows somehow that he doesn't really care for cats.

Not like that dumb Beau. That's Mrs Wellman's other cat. Beau Brummell. He's Marmy's son, but he's about three times as big as she is. He's tiger except for a patch of white on his chest, really a big handsome tom. But he's all looks and no brains. Or else he's just so conceited he's sure everyone is going to admire him.

Honestly, that cat never learns. Like with Jeddie Brubaker. Jeddie's always tormenting Beau; he actually tied a can to his tail once, but Beau still comes right up and rubs against his legs. You wouldn't catch Marmy within a mile of that pest – Jeddie, I mean.

Marmy was licking my hand with her scratchy tongue and purring away like an engine. Then suddenly she stopped and arched her back, and in one leap she took off up the trunk of the tree and disappeared in the branches. I couldn't figure out at first what had scared her, then I looked over next door and I saw that Mr Wellman had come out on their back porch.

I'd never got a really good look at him in the daytime before. I saw him from my window last night, though, and I know why Marmy ran. Mr Wellman doesn't like cats. Last night he came out on the porch in his pyjamas and bathrobe, smoking a cigar. Then he looked down and saw the stuff Mrs Wellman had put out for the strays.

He stomped down the steps like he was real mad and dumped out the milk and put the scraps in the garbage can. And as he went back inside I heard him yelling to Mrs Wellman that she wasn't to do that any more; he'd had enough of those yowling cats cluttering up the back yard.

He just stood there now, looking around and frowning as though he didn't much like anything he saw. I guess he was still unhappy because his mother died.

Then I saw Beau. He was walking along the porch railing towards Mr Wellman, slow and fancy like a tightrope walker. And I knew just what he had in mind. I wanted to call out and warn Beau, but it wouldn't have done any good with that stupid cat.

Sure enough, Beau jumped down right in front of Mr Wellman and started rubbing against his legs. Mr Wellman jerked away and said a really bad word. Then, before I knew what was happening, he pulled his leg back and brought it forward hard. The toe of his shoe caught Beau right smack in the stomach.

Beau let out an awful howl and went sailing out over the steps like he was flying. He landed on his feet all right, but not for long. He kind of staggered around and then fell over on his side, and all the time he kept up such a terrible howling I wanted to put my hands over my ears. Only I didn't dare move even an inch for fear Mr Wellman would look over and see me there. If he could do a thing like that to Beau—

All at once Beau stopped howling. A sort of big shiver ran all through him, and then he just lay still. Mr Wellman started down a couple of steps, and just then Mrs Wellman came out the back door. Before she could say anything he turned around to her and said, 'Isobel, I'm sorry. But that damned cat cut right across my feet as I was walking down the steps. I couldn't help tripping over him. It's a miracle we're not both down there.'

That – just – wasn't – so. Mr Wellman had been standing on the porch. I saw him. He wasn't going down the steps at all. I don't know whether Mrs Wellman believed him or not. She didn't say anything. She just went down the steps past him and knelt beside Beau and stroked him for a minute. I think she was crying, but she didn't make any noise.

Then she got up and went back under the steps and brought out a spade, and very gently she lifted up that big old cat in her arms.

For some reason that made Mr Wellman mad. He stomped down the steps and said, 'Oh, for God's sake, stop making such a tragedy of it.' And he grabbed Beau and the spade out of her hands and started to the back of the yard.

I was scared he was going to stop near where I was, but he kept right on going. And then I saw where he was headed. He could have buried Beau anywhere in that whole *yard*, but instead he got down right in front of Mrs Wellman's sweet pea bed and started chopping at it, digging fast. When he had a hole big enough, he just threw Beau in like a sack of garbage, then he covered him over with dirt and that tangle of pulled-up sweet peas.

All the time Mrs Wellman just stood there watching him. She never said a word. Once, though, she rubbed her hands down the sides of her skirt as though her legs hurt her.

Mr Wellman got up and went back without even looking at her. He threw the spade in the tool basket, then he went up the steps and in the door, letting it slam behind him. And after a couple of minutes Mrs Wellman went inside, too.

As soon as they'd gone I got off the swing and ran into our house as fast as I could. It surely did seem empty. I wondered what was taking my parents so long. I began to think maybe they'd had an accident and been killed and I'd have to live in this house all alone next door to Mr Wellman for the rest of my life.

I was never so glad to hear anything as our car driving in. As soon as my parents came into the kitchen Daddy asked me, the way he always does, 'Anything exciting happen while we were gone?' It's a kind of game and I always make up a lot of stuff, just silly, you know – he isn't supposed to believe it.

Only today, when something really did happen, I couldn't think of a thing to say. Daddy looked at me kind of funny for a minute, then he shrugged and went on helping Mother put away the groceries. I guess he thought I was just tired of the game.

I hung around inside the rest of the day. To tell the truth, I was afraid if I went out I might run into Mr Wellman and I was sure if he took one look at me he'd know I knew what he did to Beau and how he'd lied about it.

Mother noticed after a while and she began to worry that I was coming down with something. She felt my forehead and took my temperature, and pretty soon after supper she said I'd better go up to bed and get a good night's sleep. When I didn't put up a fight, Daddy said I really *must* be sick.

Mother kissed me goodnight and said I could read a little while if I wanted to, so I finished my library book. But even after I'd turned off the light I didn't feel really sleepy.

I got out of bed and went over to the window to see if anything was happening next door. There was a light on in the Wellmans' kitchen, but everything seemed quiet. Then I looked down at the bottom of the steps, and there, just like always, was a big bowl of milk and a plate of scraps. Mrs Wellman must have forgotten about what Mr Wellman told her last night. Boy, if he saw that, he was really going to be mad!

I was just hoping and hoping he'd go right up to bed and not come out on the porch. But just then a puff of smoke came through the screen door and Mr Wellman pushed it open and came out. He stood there smoking for a while just like last night. Then he must have looked down and seen the food because he let out a roar and started for the steps. But before he even got down to the first one he sort of pitched forward.

He didn't go flying like Beau because he was so big and heavy. He just fell straight down and his head knocked over the bowl of milk. I waited to see if he was going to get up and stagger around, but he didn't. So I decided I'd better go tell somebody what happened because he must be pretty badly hurt. His neck looked all bent around, the wrong way sort of.

But I didn't have to after all because just then Mrs Wellman came out the back door. She must have heard him call out. She stood there and looked at him for a minute and then she did the funniest thing. She stooped down by the railing at one side of the steps and untied something – string, I guess – and very carefully, like she wanted to save it, she wrapped it around her fingers all the way across the steps and untied it at the other side. Then she stood up and tucked it into her pocket.

I thought maybe then she'd go down to see about Mr Wellman, but she didn't. She just went back inside the house.

Almost right away our telephone started ringing. And after about a minute I heard my father running down our back steps. He went across the driveway and knelt down beside Mr Wellman. And when Mrs Wellman came out again he talked to her for a couple of minutes, then he went with her inside their house.

Pretty soon a police car came up and then an ambulance, and everybody poked around at Mr Wellman and they talked some more. And then finally they put Mr Wellman on a stretcher and covered him all up and took him away.

For a long time after I got back into bed I lay there wondering if I ought to tell Daddy what I saw. I know Mr Wellman didn't fall down the steps by accident. But then – what happened to Beau wasn't an accident either. So if I didn't tell on Mr Wellman, why should I tell on Mrs Wellman? After all, fair's fair.

The Doe and the Gantlet

PAT STADLEY

I knew Ward was watching the place every time we rode our motorcycles up the small canyon in back of the house. It was one we had on our list – big and rich-looking, but no servants and lots of shrubbery around the fence.

There was a little hill that moved right up to the fence, and today Ward gunned his motor and I saw the woman sit up on the pad by the swimming pool and look at us.

She was really something to see. Little in the right places and full where she ought to be and with a sunsuit that wouldn't interfere with her tanning. I was looking so hard I nearly ran up on Ward, who'd stopped his motor and was watching her, keeping his back straight and flexing his muscles under his T-shirt.

Ward's proud of his build and he's always ragging us to work out and we usually do what he says because there's nobody I know that's going to cross Ward. Not in our gang, the Ghost Riders, nor in any others we tangle with, even counting the Night Hawks.

I gave our gang its name because we ride at night with no lights, picking the main highways and helling it down between the traffic. You ought to see people's eyes when we come roaring up on them, shagging in and out of the cars. And suppose the cops pick us up – what's a five-buck traffic ticket to us?

You see, we've got dough. Real dough. And we keep the gang down to six, though other guys are always hinting about joining up. But Ward says too many guys and somebody'd be talking.

We got the coolest set-up you ever seen. We ride our cycles up the canyons just outside the little towns and right on up to the top of the hills. Then we cut the motors and take out the glasses and we can look clear around and down on all the houses on the little hills.

And Ward takes out our list and we sit and watch the owners come and go and how many people there are and what kind of dogs. Everything. Hell, I bet we know more about who lives in the Oaks and the Woods and all the other fancy name places and what they do and how much dough they got – more than even the coppers know.

Sometimes we sit up there and pretty soon we know to the second when Mr Money Bags is going to leave and go to his smoker and where the prowl cars are – and when we've got them figured good we pick out one and then one night we visit the place and load up.

We hide the loot, then climb back on the cycles, drop over the hills, and come out in the next town over. And if anybody asks questions – well, we're just riding the fire trails.

It beats holding up nervous service-station managers for two bits or trigger-happy liquor owners on the off chance you might get a haul.

So you can see why Ward stopped. Even though the house was on our list, we hadn't pinpointed it yet and so we hadn't spotted the doll. We all stopped and stared until she turned her back on us and lay down again. I could hear Neil breathing behind me but it was Ward I was watching. There aren't many women that'd turn their backs to him.

When he kicked that motor, he really laid to it and he took off spinning, his rear wheel spitting dirt in my face. But on the other side of the hill he'd cooled down and we eased our way between the trees and turned north into a long, narrow canyon. There was a little waterfall at the end and a pool big enough to get wet in.

We were almost there when we spotted the doe. She'd evidently come down for water, and our motors had kept driving her back into the canyon until now she was trapped, with cliffs on both sides and no place to go except between us.

She stood looking at us, ears pricked forward, her head lifted, her coat kind of red-gold in the sunlight. Bob looked at me, his face flushed and excited, and then he drove his motorcycle straight at her. Of course he couldn't touch her – she sprung away from him, but we fell in right behind him and formed a little circle. When we saw he'd missed, I went next.

I popped the clutch and shot forward and when she jumped, I leaned away from her so that the rear wheel spun, flipping the sand, and I was so close I could see the fear in her eyes.

Ward sat back and watched us and we drove that doe near crazy, here and there, around in circles. She broke through Milo once and it was all we could do to turn her, and Ward just sat and laughed like crazy. Then, suddenly, she stood still in the middle of the circle and I could see the white of her eyes and her smooth, brown hide getting all wet with sweat. Then Ward waved us back, stood up and kicked over on his starter.

He rode straight for her. And she stood there like she was waiting for him, her sides heaving, and when he was on her, she reared back on her hind legs and struck out like lightning with her front hoofs, and I thought, 'There goes Ward's face which he's so proud of.'

But like I said, Ward is all muscle and his reflexes are really fast. He ducked just in time and her hoofs caught him in the shoulder and he went down in a tangled heap under his motor. Then she was over him in one big leap, between Tim and me, and down the canyon.

Milo and Bob ran for Ward, pulling the cycle off him and I thought he'd clip somebody, he was so mad. Nobody laughed and I wouldn't have crossed him at that moment for all the loot we got stashed away. His face and shirt were dirtied from where he'd landed, and blood was coming from the scratch on his shoulder.

We weren't sure just what was coming off, so we just sat on our motorcycles and looked at him. Suddenly he laughed, although I could see his eyes were still wild-looking, and then we all laughed too. We laughed so hard we fell off the cycles, and we pounded one another and then we opened the beer we'd brought and the fifth I'd swiped from my old man, and we sat down and drank and it was the most exciting thing that had ever happened to us.

And pretty soon it got dark. I lit the lantern and the shadows came out kind of red on the ground and the whisky was warm in our stomachs, and then I saw Ward was getting real quiet and I figured maybe we were going to knock over another house, although we'd hit one already that week.

He got on his cycle and we followed him, and when he got to the top of the hill he took out the glasses and he sat looking down at the house by the little hill, and even without the glasses we could see the lights winking in the pool.

Then he kicked his starter. 'Come on,' he said, 'let's take a house.'

We came down the canyon quiet and we cut the motors about a block away. We came the rest of the way on foot. When we got to the little hill, we wriggled forward till we could see over it and into the yard and it was plenty peaceful-looking. There was just the lights from the pool, and Ward held us pinned down to the earth a full fifteen minutes, and then he crawled to the fence and we went right behind him.

We were over it quick and half of us slipped through the shrubbery to one side and the other three down the other, and then we'd reached the patio and Ward was about to step on it when we saw the woman move inside. We dropped to the ground in a hurry and she came out on the patio and stood there in her bare feet looking over the pool towards the mountains.

She had on one of those short nightgowns and her legs were

slim and brown and she raised an arm upward and stretched, and it was then Ward stepped out on the cement.

She froze right there. I watched her and I don't think she even breathed, and then all the rest of us came out and I was so close I could smell the perfume she was wearing.

She took one look over her shoulder at me and I could see her brown eyes widen and then the same thing hit all of us. She was just like the doe, brown and quivering, and I could see Ward reach up and rub his shoulder lightly and smile, and I'd never seen him look like that before.

And then she was past him just as he reached for her and his fingers touched the softness of her gown and she was running for the pool. Tim stepped towards her and Neil closed in from the other side, but she slipped between them and cut the water cleanly in the prettiest dive I've ever seen.

I don't know which of us was more surprised – Ward, I guess, though he was still smiling a little. Then we all moved around the pool and we stood there and watched her come to the surface.

She came up in the deep end and treaded water for a moment, that shortie gown floating around her. She turned in a little circle looking up at us and I could see that she was more frightened than even the doe had been. I could hear the other guys sucking in their breath and I felt the same way – kind of icy cold inside and my heart pounding so hard I couldn't hardly hear anything.

Then I looked at Ward. He was hunched down by the edge, his fingers trailing in the water, and he nodded. I threw off my jacket, knelt down and took off my boots. She kept her eyes on me, her hands moving in the green water.

I'm a pretty good swimmer and I dived to the side of her, figuring I'd have a little fun before I grabbed her, but when I'd surfaced she was behind me and before I could turn, she'd clipped me right across the neck muscles and in under the ear. I yelped, then she was on me and shoved my head under the water, and when I took that quick breath, I breathed water instead and came up sputtering and gagging. Milo had to reach down and haul me up on the cement and they all stood there and laughed at me.

Then Tim went in the water after her and I pushed myself up to watch. Tim's pretty good in the water and he's got long arms. He paddled around her, flicking a hand at her once or twice. But she stayed just out of reach, not wasting any energy and watching him. And when he made a rush for her, she dropped to the bottom, and when she'd surfaced she was a good five feet away from him. He turned over and swam lazily for the edge of the pool and climbed out. But his face was a little red.

Milo had stretched out on a pad and he'd plugged the little portable radio in and I could hear the music coming, soft but solid. Music really sends Milo and you could see his face light up when Ward nodded at him. But Milo's built something like an ape. He's slow on the ground and slower in the water and it was duck soup for her to stay out of his way. It was just like she was teasing him the way she'd twist or just roll away. But it really wasn't that – she was just conserving her strength, using it only when she really had to. And you could see it was getting through to the guys.

Bob didn't do any better than the rest of us but he kept after her longer and I could see she was beginning to tire now.

Then I looked at Neil. He'd been sitting beside me, snapping his fingers to the music and breathing kind of heavy. He'd already got out of his boots and when Ward looked at him he hit the water fast. For the first few times she stayed away from him but her turns were slower and it took her longer to dive. Then he got an arm around her and I could see her go limp against him and I thought for a minute the fun was all over. And so did Neil, because he turned her so he could look down at her, and she came to life like a wild thing, her fingernails raking his face, and in a flash she was loose from him.

Neil just seemed to hang there. Then he raised a wet hand, wiped his face, looked at the blood on his fingers, and you could see the anger coming up in him and he turned towards her again. That was when Ward snapped his fingers. Neil came out of the water slow-like.

And now it was Ward's turn. He took off his boots, then his T-shirt and you could see the long, red streak where the doe had ripped him.

He slid into the water easily, the muscles cording under his skin. Nobody said anything this time. We watched him swim lazily around her, his hand washing every now and then towards her so that the water would slap into her face. Then he dived for her, bumping her and knocking her to one side and just as quick he was around and back down the other side, so that he could clip her again.

The third time, though, she was all set for him. As he went by, she waited until his face was close and then she hit him as hard as she could, her fist slamming into his face. But she was tired by now and besides, the blow missed slightly, just catching his cheek. He rolled to one side, came up a foot away, and you could see the red mark her fist had made. And as he paddled water and blew the air out, I could see the excitement boiling in him.

And then he was at her again, and no matter which way she turned or dived, he stayed right behind her, but not touching her. Finally she came to the surface slowly, close to the edge where I was sitting, and her eyes were so wide I could see the terror inside her. And then Ward reached across to her, grabbed a piece of her gown, gave a quick yank and it ripped away.

She gave a little shudder and one hand reached out of the water towards me and she grabbed a boot and smashed it into Ward's face. I saw him slip under the water, the red streaming out from him and his body rolling slowly round and round.

I shouted at Tim and Bob and they hit the water together. In no time they had Ward and were pulling him over to Milo and Neil. I reached down in the pool and grabbed her and pulled her up and she came, unresisting, like all the fight had gone out of her.

And then I could see Ward beginning to move in the water and I knew he wasn't really hurt. I felt her stiffen and before I knew it, she had broken loose from me and was running to where they stood. I hollered at them, but Tim and Bob were down in the water shoving upward and Neil and Milo had their arms around him, pulling. They didn't hear me and didn't see her. And then she was right beside them and she picked up the plugged-in radio by its leather handle and stood there just a second looking down at Ward before she dropped it on him.

Not a peep came out of any of them. It was over that quick.

And I didn't wait around none. I went past her and she kind of turned a little, watching me. I had to go real close to her but I didn't stop. I went straight back to the fence. I'd seen her eyes and it wasn't anything to forget. Have you ever seen a woman's eyes just after she's killed five men?

The Last Day of All

FAY GRISSOM STANLEY

Sari wakened, as she always wakened now, to the faint, interminable buzz of the air conditioner droning on the roof, to the far-off, interminable whirring of the cicadas in the sage, to the hoarse, asthmatic breathing of her husband sleeping in the room beyond. Today there was a new note: Carmen was singing downstairs, banging about the kitchen with the pots and pans, systematically destroying the crockery in her haste to be off for Santa Fe and the fiesta. Sari pulled the light covers up around her shoulders, feeling suddenly weary and resentful and refrigerated beyond endurance.

'That damned air conditioner!' she thought savagely. That merciless, damned air conditioner sitting up there buzzing in the fresh air and buzzing out the stale, forever filtering and purifying and regulating the moisture of every breath they took, faultlessly and forever buzzing about its business of screening out pollens and keeping Al alive one day longer, of keeping her hanging about in its static climate like her own fur coat in summer storage. Oh, God, if she could only flip the switch and shut the thing off and never again hear that sound! If she could only walk out of here and board a train and never again see this hateful land of desert and desolation and respiratory invalids who lingered and lingered and lingered ... !

Sari shut her eyes fiercely, hugged her pillow up around her ears, but it did not help. The cooler buzzed on as it always had, and sleep did not return. She tried a moment longer and then she felt under the pillow for the flask she kept there, screwed off the top and tilted it to her mouth. After the second drink it was better, she was really awake for the first time, and she suddenly remembered.

For, after all, today *was* the day. The last day of all. The day Al had set for her decision. Well, she'd made her decision, she'd laid her plans, and she was ready.

And, really, it was Al who had helped her most, choosing this final Saturday of the fiesta almost as if he were aiding her in the thing which, she knew now, she would have to do: almost as if he were making her a present of the thing she needed most – a whole afternoon without the servants. Even more, it had been Al who told Juan he could take the car into town, who, in the last minute, had solved the problem of the telephone by shooting the damned thing while cleaning his gun. Now it was done, they would be isolated for the period that was necessary, and all that was left was the matter of preparing the cigars.

At first, of course, she'd planned to use aconite. Such a pretty name: aconite. She'd thought so the moment she came across it in the book. In fact, it seemed to leap out of context to meet her eye almost as if the letters were raised from the page. She'd read it again, feeling a sudden lift of excitement.

'Aconite,' she'd murmured aloud. 'Isn't that what the doctor gave me for my throat that time, Al?'

Al looked up then from his own book, wearing that expression of strained courtesy which meant that he'd been interrupted, that it irritated him to be interrupted, that he was firmly mastering his irritation. 'I believe so, my dear. It is a medicine commonly prescribed for laryngitis.' He pronounced it meds'n. He'd been pronouncing it meds'n for two months now, ever since he met his precious Margaret Langley.

'All right, meds'n,' she'd agreed. 'But it says here it's a poison, too. Did you know it was a poison, Al?'

Still that expression of patient exasperation. 'Yes, my dear,

I was aware that it is a poison. Quite a deadly one, I believe. But why, Sari? Are you by any chance planning on doing away with yourself again?'

Sari had felt the slow, scorching rise of the flush that swept her face, that tight knot of rage hardening in her stomach again. Would he never, never, never, shut up about that, never, never, never, let her forget that stupid night in the spring when she'd tried to frighten him into more allowance with a note and an empty bottle of sleeping pills?

Desperately, Sari had hung on to her anger, making her mind a black void, counting to a thousand slowly by tens. Then, on the page beneath her hand, she'd felt that cool word, aconite, and she'd been in control again. Yes, he'd shut up about it, he'd shut up about it, now, Sari had thought, and, thinking it, she'd almost smiled.

'Don't be a fool, Al; it was just something here in my mystery,' she told the polite face across the desk and turned again to her place in the book. But now the story seemed to have been blotted off the page, leaving only that word scattered here and there across its face. That word and all that word could do. Aconite and the way that aconite worked. That was pretty, too.

Sari liked to think of Al sitting there in his chair, feeling that first warning tingling in his throat, in his stomach, feeling that first numbing wash of paralysis along his nerves, and then, finding himself powerless to move, to alter this thing that was happening to him. She liked thinking of Al sitting there, trapped in his chair, conscious, clear-minded, to the last, watching, counting, waiting, as his pulse and respiration slowed, slowed, slowed, and finally stopped.

Sari had closed her eyes then, firmly imprisoning the scene beneath her eyelids. But it would not stay fixed, it wavered and dimmed, was replaced by another that left her suddenly sick with panic. It was only a little adobe police station, but, queerly, there were the two traditional lamp posts in front. Then that scene faded and still others crowded in. The interior of the police station, the courtroom scene, and last, the prison. Someone had told Sari once that there they cut your hair.

Sari had reached up trembling to feel the heavy golden knot at her neck and then she'd suddenly risen and gone upstairs. In her own bathroom she locked the door, found the bottle of sherry in the clothes hamper, took one long, merciful drink. It was better then. It was always better then, but there was still the question: Did she really have to do it?

It was the sight of her own face in the mirror above the washstand that finally decided her. Except for the hair there just wasn't much left – she'd waited too long as it was. Waited until she couldn't possibly go back on the stage, until no one could possibly want her – no, not even Tony – not without the money. Not with only a thousand a month.

For that was what Al had told her she could have. A thousand a month. No more. No less. Speaking of it in that dry voice as if he were discussing an oil well, a section of land, speaking of it almost as if he were doing her a favour, as if a thousand a month could pay her for that wrecked career, for that faintly sagging body, for that desert- and drink-ruined face, for all those patient years of waiting.

But it's not fair, it's not fair, she'd raged at the face in the mirror, just as she screamed out at Al that morning a week before.

Al, she remembered, had simply sat back in his chair, folded his arms across his chest and wearily shut his eyes. 'Look, my dear, let's not toss a scene. I've a headache and I'm not in the mood for it and there's nothing you could say that would possibly alter my decision. I've made my offer and I'd strongly advise you to accept it.'

He'd advise her to accept it, to bow her head and trot meekly off to Reno, to stand away and watch Margaret Langley step into her place and in a year, a month, a week, maybe, stretch out her elegant hand for her long-awaited prize. 'And if I don't?' she'd asked.

'Well, then, my dear, I should simply have to get the divorce myself. Without the alimony, of course. I *do* have evidence, you know.'

It had all suddenly been too much. 'Evidence!' she shrieked. 'Evidence! And don't you think I've got evidence, too! Do you think you're the only one who can send around detectives and open letters and listen at doors? Do you think I haven't evidence like the evidence you're talking about, Al, and evidence that will interest the income-tax people, as well, and evidence that will make that upstage Beacon Hill chippy of yours so sick she'll never want to see you again? And do you think I won't use that evidence if it comes to that ... ?'

She stopped abruptly. She'd said too much already. He was standing then and she'd been suddenly terrified of what she saw in his face.

'No,' he'd said softly, coming towards her. 'No, Sari, you won't use that evidence. You think you will now, but when you've considered it more carefully you'll see that it wouldn't do you any good. You'll see that even if you contested me, even if you won the suit, you'd scarcely get more than I'm offering now, and in return you'd simply be torn to bits by my lawyers. I mean that, Sari – I'm too big to fight in court. I'm too big and I like to have my own way too much. I get my way at whatever cost, you know that about me, don't you, my dear? You know I always have my way, don't you, Sari?'

Sari had nodded mutely. She knew. How well she knew.

'All right then – so now I want a divorce and I want to marry Miss Langley and it would seem logical from the record that I will get my way. Not only that, but I'm desperate this time, Sari. I'm a sick man – the doctor tells me my heart won't stand another attack of asthma like that last one – and I haven't much time. I advise you not to stand in my way. I advise you to accept my terms and do as I say – no, don't answer now – think about it quietly and sensibly for a while and I'll ask you again in a week ...'

It had ended there, and Sari had thought about it quietly

and sensibly until she knew he was right, knew there was only one thing she could do.

The aconite? She'd considered it again, sitting on the edge of the bathtub, feeling its cold edges beneath her hands. Perhaps after all, it was too risky, it would be crowding things too far to expect even the little local doctor to diagnose that as he should. She didn't know, but perhaps if she got something that would bring on a genuine attack, something like – well, cat fur or mink, which was even worse. She hadn't gone back downstairs that night; she'd just sat on the edge of the tub and had got beautifully, hilariously stewed.

And, even later, even now, Sari thought there was something wonderfully funny about the idea that it was Margaret Langley's mink that would do it, the tiny pinch of fur she'd pulled from Margaret's scarf that day at the La Fonda. Now all she had to do was to insert it into the single contraband cigar that Al smoked after meals, and then sit back and let him do the rest.

'But I've got to do that now – while he's still asleep,' she told herself urgently, getting out of bed, hastily flinging on her clothes. Last of all she got the purse which held the cigars, tiptoed down the stairs, and let herself out at the terrace door.

Once safely in the greenhouse, she took out the three cigars, the long, needle-thin crochet hook, and the little twist of tissue paper bound around a tiny ball of fur. She spoiled the first cigar, as she'd been afraid she might, but on the second it worked perfectly. That only left the third – she shuddered a little – to be smoked. Later, after it was all over, she would substitute it for the other, the one she'd remove from Al's inert fingers.

This was almost the worst part of all, she thought, but it had to be done and she had already struck a match when she saw the shadow which fell across the glass of the greenhouse door. Wild with panic, she ducked under a plant shelf and lay there trembling and panting on the damp, hard-packed floor. 'Like Peter Rabbit in the flower pot,' she thought a little hysterically. 'Just like Peter Rabbit and Mr McGregor.' But then the shadow moved and she saw that it was only Juan who was slowly, meticulously putting away the tools.

She didn't know how long she was trapped in the plant room, but by the time she got to the house Al was already up and breakfasting.

He glanced up at the door. 'Well, well, out so early, my dear? You know, you surprise me sometimes, Sari – I had no idea you went in for morning walks. At any rate, come have a cup of coffee and let me get that smudge off your nose.'

He stood up and was coming towards her with a cup in his hand. If he came nearer, a foot closer, he was sure to smell that awful reek of cigar that enveloped her. Muttering some excuse, she ducked, almost ran, for the stairs.

After she'd washed up and changed and brushed her teeth she came down, and, seeing that Carmen had laid the table for their lunch, she exchanged the cigar she'd prepared for the one at Al's plate. 'All right, that's done,' she told herself firmly and went out to pay Juan and Carmen and let them off for the day.

Coming back, she stopped, suddenly rigid – there was a murmur of voices from the study. Who in God's name was it, and what were they doing here, and would they stay for lunch, Sari wondered in a hasty jumble. And should she go back and retrieve the cigar now or take a chance on their not staying ... ?

Slowly, deliberately, she forced herself forward along the hall, to the door of the study and inside. It was Marcy Hunt, Santa Fe's worst painter, its most accomplished gossip. She greeted Sari gaily, made a place for her on the sofa and plunged into the latest scandal. Marcy, clearly, was in no hurry to go.

How long *was* it altogether? An hour? Two? Sari could no longer tell. She was conscious only of the sun slowly fingering its way across the floor, of the clock ticking away in the corner, of Marcy's steady voice beating, beating, beating, her back to the moment when she would be trapped and lost. Hammering her into a dull submissiveness where she could neither move nor think.

In the end, it was Al who saved her. 'Aren't you going to miss the fiesta, Marcy?' he asked her rather pointedly. 'Of course, we'd be delighted to have you for lunch, but I'm sure it will be gayer in town and our cook's off and I imagine we're in for one of those heated-up casserole affairs . . .'

Even Marcy couldn't have stayed after that. She gathered up her bag, stopped at the door for a final flash, and, at last, was gone. 'Great God!' Al breathed heavily, turning back to the study. 'Great God!' Sari agreed, hurrying off to the kitchen to take out the casserole Carmen had put on for their lunch.

She'd intended to have a drink, too, before they sat down, but then when she brought in the salad she saw that Al was already in the dining-room, mixing a cocktail at the sideboard. He'd never done that before, he didn't like her to drink before lunch. She stopped short, her eyebrows raised in a questioning arc.

'For you, my dear,' he told her, placing the glass beside her plate, holding her chair for her to be seated. 'After all, it is a rather special occasion, don't you think?'

Sari served the plates and waited for him to sit down, waited for him to go on.

'Don't you remember, Sari, it's our last day together, or what I presume is our last day – for you *are* going to give me my divorce, aren't you, my dear?'

Sari looked across the table at that cold, bullying face, so very sure of itself, and drained off her cocktail at a single draught. 'No, Al, I'm not.'

Al said nothing for a long moment, only rose and took Sari's glass to the sideboard to fill it again and then placed it at her plate. She looked at it longingly, knowing she shouldn't have it, knowing he only wanted to make her tight, but in the end she gave way and tossed it off. She shuddered slightly and then asked, 'Well?'

'Well, what, Sari? You've given your answer, but you don't think that will change my plans, do you? You should have listened to me before, my dear – I told you I always got what I wanted. You remember that, don't you, Sari?'

Sari remembered, but she remembered through a queer sort of lethargic haze and she scarcely cared. There was a curious, numb feeling of well-being creeping along her shoulders, down her arms, and a half-familiar tickling in her throat. She looked across the table with eyes gone suddenly out of focus, saw his blurred face, and then she knew.

She wanted to get up, to run, to shriek for help, but she could not move. Even if she'd had the strength, it wouldn't have mattered for she – or had it been Al all the time? – had set the trap too well. Not, curiously, that it mattered now, it was only that Al had won again.

'But they will catch you, Al. They will catch you and hang you and then you'll have lost,' she whispered, forcing the words through her constricted throat, struggling to sit up to where she could see his face.

There was a smile on it. Sure of itself. 'No, my dear, I don't believe they will, for, you see, you have simply done me the service of killing yourself – if you will remember – tried once before – conveniently left a note . . .'

Sari couldn't, somehow, hear the rest, but she saw the cigar. Saw how Al clipped off the end, settled back expansively, and raised it to his lips. She slumped in her chair, content. It had almost been worth it.

The Nail and the Oracle

THEODORE STURGEON

Despite the improvements, the Pentagon in 1970 was still the Pentagon, with more places to walk than places to sit. Not that Jones had a legitimate gripe. The cubical cave they had assigned to him as an office would have been more than adequate for the two or three days he himself had estimated. But by the end of the third week it fit him like a size-6 hat and choked him like a size-12 collar. Annie's phone calls expressed eagerness to have him back, but there was an edge to the eagerness now which made him anxious. His hotel manager had wanted to shift his room after the first week and he had been stubborn about it; now he was marooned like a rock in a mushroom patch, surrounded by a back-to-rhythm convention of the Anti-Anti-Population Explosion League. He'd had to buy shirts, he'd had to buy shoes, he'd needed a type-four common-cold shot, and most of all, he couldn't find what was wrong with ORACLE.

Jones and his crew had stripped ORACLE down to its mounting bolts, checked a thousand miles of wiring and a million solid-state elements, everything but its priceless and untouchable memory banks. Then they'd rebuilt the monster, meticulously cross-checking all the way. For the past four days they had been running the recompleted computer, performance-matching with crash-priority time on other machines, while half the science boys and a third of the military wailed in anguish. He had reported to three men that the machine had nothing wrong with it, that it never had had anything wrong with it, and that there was no reason to believe there ever would be anything wrong with it. One by one these three had gone (again) into ORACLE's chamber, and bolted the door, and energized the privacy field, and then one by one they had emerged stern and disappointed, to tell Jones that it would not give an answer to them: an old admiral, an ageless colonel and a piece of walking legend whom Jones called to himself the civilian.

Having sent his crew home – for thus he burned his bridges – having deprived himself of Jacquard the design genius and the twenty-three others, the wiring team, all the mathematicians, everyone, Jones sighed in his little office, picked up the phone again and called the three for a conference. When he put the instrument down again he felt a little pleased. Consistencies pleased Jones, even unpleasant ones, and the instant response of all three was right in line with everything they had done from the time they had first complained about ORACLE's inability to answer their questions, all through their fiddling and diddling during every second of the long diagnostic operation. The admiral had had an open line installed to Jones's office; the colonel had devised a special code word for his switchboard; the civilian had hung around personally, ignoring all firm, polite hints until he had turned his ankle on a cable, giving Jones a reason to get him out of there. In other words, these three didn't just want an answer, they *needed* it.

They came – the admiral with his old brows and brand-new steel-blue eyes; the colonel with starch in his spine and skin like post-manoeuvre proving grounds; the civilian limping a bit, with his head tilted a bit, turned a bit, a captivating mannerism which always gave his audiences the feeling that history cared to listen to them. Jones let them get settled: this admiral whose whole career had consisted of greater and greater commands until his strong old hand was a twitch away from the spokes of the helm of the ship of state; this colonel who had retained his lowly rank as a mark of scorn for the academy men who scurried to obey him, whose luxurious quarters were equipped with an iron barracks bed; and this civilian with the scholarly air, with both Houses and a Cabinet rank behind him, whose political skills were as strong, and as deft, and as spiked as a logroller's feet.

'Gentlemen,' said Jones, 'this may well be our last meeting. There will, of course, be a written report, but I understand the – uh – practicalities of such a situation quite well, and I do not feel it necessary to go into the kind of detail in the report that is possible to us in an informal discussion.' He looked at each face in turn and congratulated himself. That was just right. This is just between us boys. Nobody's going to squeal on you.

'You've dismissed your crew,' said the civilian, causing a slight start in the admiral and a narrowing of the colonel's eyes and, in Jones, a flash of admiration. This one had snoopers the services hadn't even dreamed up yet. 'I hope this is good news.'

'Depends,' said Jones. 'What it means primarily is that they have done all they can. In other words, there is nothing wrong with ORACLE in any of their specialities. Their specialities include everything the computer is and does. In still other words, there's nothing wrong with the machine.'

'So you told us yesterday,' gritted the colonel, 'but I got no results. And – I want results.' This last was added as an old ritual which, apparently, had always got results just by being recited.

'I followed the procedures,' said the admiral, intoning this as a cardinal virtue, 'and also got no results.' He held up a finger and suspended operations in the room while he performed some sort of internal countdown. 'Had I not done so, ORACLE would have responded with an "insufficient data" signal. Correct?'

'Quite correct,' said Jones.

'And it didn't.'

'That was my experience,' said the civilian, and the colonel nodded.

'Gentlemen,' said Jones, 'neither I nor my crew – and there just is not a better one – have been able to devise a question that produced that result.'

'It was not a result,' snapped the colonel.

Jones ignored him. 'Given the truth of my conclusion – that there is nothing wrong with the machine – and your reports, which I can have no reason to doubt, there is no area left to investigate but one, and that is in your hands, not mine. It's the one thing you have withheld from me.' He paused. Two of them shifted their feet. The colonel tightened his jaw.

The admiral said softly, but with utter finality, 'I can*not* divulge my question.'

The colonel and the civilian spoke together: 'Security—' and 'This is a matter—' and then both fell silent.

'Security.' Jones spread his hands. To keep from an enemy, real or potential, matters vital to the safety of the nation, that was security. And how easy it was to wrap the same blanket about the use of a helicopter to a certain haven, the presence of a surprising little package in a Congressional desk, the exact relations between a certain officer and his – *argh!* This, thought Jones, has all the earmarks of, not *our* security, but of three cases of *my* security . . . I'll try just once more.

'Thirty years ago, a writer named William Tenn wrote a brilliant story in which an Air Force moon landing was made, and the expedition found an inhabited pressure dome nearby. They sent out a scout, who was prepared to die at the hands of Russians or even Martians. He returned to the ship in a paroxysm, gentlemen, of laughter. The other dome belonged to the US Navy.'

The admiral projected two loud syllables of a guffaw and said, 'Of course.' The colonel looked pained. The civilian, bright-eyed, made a small nod which clearly said, One up for you, boy.

Jones put on his used-car-salesman face. 'Honestly, gentlemen, it embarrasses me to draw a parallel like that. I believe with all my heart that each of you has the best interests of our nation foremost in his thoughts. As for myself – security? Why, I wouldn't be here if I hadn't been cleared all the way back to *Pithecanthropus erectus*.

'So much for you, so much for me. Now, as for ORACLE, you know as well as I do that it is no ordinary computer. It is designed for computations, not of maths, specifically, nor of strictly physical problems, though it can perform them, but for the distillation of human thought. For over a decade the contents of the Library of Congress and other sources have poured into that machine – everything: novels, philosophy, magazines, poetry, textbooks, religious tracts, comic books, even millions of personal records. There's every shade of opinion, every quality of writing – anything and everything that an army of over a thousand microfilming technicians have been able to cram into it. As long as it's printed and in English, German, Russian, French or Japanese, ORACLE can absorb it. Esperanto is the funnel for a hundred Oriental and African languages. It's the greatest repository of human thought and thought-directed action the world has ever known, and its one most powerful barrier against error in human affairs is the sheer mass of its memory and the wide spectrum of opinion that has poured into it.

'Add to this its ability to extrapolate – to project the results of hypothetical acts – and the purposely designed privacy structure – for it's incapable of recording or reporting who asked it what question – and you have ORACLE, the one place in the world where you can get a straight answer based, not in terms of the problem itself, but on every ideological computation and cross-comparison that can be packed into it.'

'The one place I couldn't get a straight answer,' said the civilian gently.

'To your particular question. Sir, if you want that answer, you have got to give me that question.' He checked a hopeful stir in the other two by adding quickly, 'and yours. And yours. You see, gentlemen, though I am concerned for your needs in this matter, my prime concern is ORACLE. To find a way to get one of the answers isn't enough. If I had all three, I might be able to deduce a common denominator. I already have, of course, though it isn't enough: you are all high up in national affairs, and very close to the centre of things. You are all of the same generation' (translation: near the end of the road) 'and, I'm sure, equally determined to do the best you can for your country' (to get to the top of the heap before you cash in). 'Consider *me*,' he said, and smiled disarmingly. 'To let me get this close to the answer *I* want, namely, what's wrong with ORACLE, and then to withhold it – isn't that sort of cruel and unusual punishment?'

'I feel for you,' said the civilian, not without a twinkle. Then, sober with a coldness that would freeze helium into a block, he said, 'But you ask too much.'

Jones looked at him, and then at the others, sensing their unshakable agreement. 'OK,' he said, with all the explosive harshness he could muster, 'I'm done here. I'm sick of this place and my girl's sick of being by herself, and I'm going home. You can't call in anyone else, because there isn't any-one else: my company built ORACLE and my men were trained for it.'

This kind of thing was obviously in the colonel's idiom. From far back in his throat, he issued a grinding sound that came out in words: 'You'll finish the job you were ordered to do, mister, or you'll take the consequences.'

Jones shouted at him, 'Consequences? What consequences? You couldn't even have me fired, because I can make a damn good case that you prevented me from finishing the job. I'm not under your orders either. This seems a good time to re-mind you of the forgotten tradition that with this' – he took hold of the narrow lapel of his own sports jacket – 'I outrank any uniform in this whole entire Pentagon.' He caught the swift smile of the civilian, and therefore trained his next blast on him. 'Consequences? The only consequence you can get now is to deny yourself and your country the answer to your question. The only conclusion I can come to is that something else is more important to you than that. What else?' He stood up. So did the officers.

From his chair, the civilian said sonorously, 'Now, now ... gentlemen. Surely we can resolve this problem without raising our voices. Mr Jones, would the possession of two of these questions help you in your diagnosis? Or even one?'

Breathing hard, Jones said, 'It might.'

The civilian opened his long white hands. 'Then there's no problem after all. If one of you gentlemen—'

'Absolutely not,' said the admiral instantly.

'Not me,' growled the colonel. 'You want compromise, don't you? Well, go ahead – you compromise.'

'In this area,' said the civilian smoothly, 'I possess all the facts, and it is my considered judgement that the disclosure of my question would not further Mr Jones's endeavours.' (Jones thought, the admiral said the same thing in two words.) 'Admiral, would you submit to my judgement the question of whether or not security would be endangered by your showing Mr Jones your question?'

'I would not.'

The civilian turned to the colonel. One look at that rock-bound countenance was sufficient to make him turn away again, which, thought Jones, puts the colonel two points ahead of the admiral in the word-economy business.

Jones said to the civilian, 'No use, sir, and by my lights, that's the end of it. The simplest possible way to say it is that you gentlemen have the only tools in existence that would make it possible for me to repair this gadget, and you won't let me have them. So fix it yourself, or leave it the way it is. I'd see you out,' he added, scanning the walls of the tiny room, 'but I have to go to the john.' He stalked out, his mind having vividly and permanently photographed the astonishment on the admiral's usually composed features, the colonel's face fury-twisted into something like the knot that binds the lashes of a whip, and the civilian grinning broadly.

Grinning broadly?

Ah, well, he thought, slamming the men's-room door behind him – and infuriatingly, it wouldn't slam— Ah, well, we all have our way of showing frustration. Maybe I could've been just as mad more gently.

The door moved, and someone ranged alongside at the next vertical bathtub. Jones glanced, and then said aloud, 'Maybe I could've been just as mad more gently.'

'Perhaps we all could have,' said the civilian, and then with his free hand he did four surprising things in extremely rapid succession. He put his finger to his lips, then his hand to the wall and then to his ear. Finally he whisked a small folded paper out of his breast pocket and handed it to Jones. He then finished what he was doing and went to wash up.

Shh. The walls have ears. Take this.

'All through history,' said the civilian from the sink, his big old voice booming in the tiled room, 'we read about the impasse, and practically every time it's mentioned, it's a sort of preface to an explanation of how it was solved. Yet I'll bet history's full of impasses that just couldn't be solved. They don't get mentioned because when it happens, everything stops. There just isn't anything to write down in the book any more. I think we've just seen such an occasion, and I'm sorry for each of us.'

The old son of a gun! 'Thanks for that much, anyway, sir,' Jones said, tucking the paper carefully away out of sight. The old man, wiping his hands, winked once and went out.

Back in his office, which seemed three times larger than it had been before the conference, Jones slumped behind his desk and teased himself with the small folded paper, not reading it, turning it over and over. It had to be the old man's question. Granted that it was, why had he been so willing to hand it over now, when three minutes earlier his refusal had been just about as adamant as – adamant? So, Jones, quit looking at the detail and get on the big picture. What was different in those three minutes?

Well, they were out of the one room and into another. Out of one room that was damn well not bugged and into one which, the old man's pantomime had informed him, may well be. Nope – that didn't make sense. Then – how about this? In the one room there had been witnesses. In the second, none – not after the finger on the lips. So if a man concluded that the civilian probably never had had an objection to Jones's seeing and using the question, but wanted it concealed from anyone else – maybe specifically from those other two ... why, the man had the big picture.

What else? That the civilian had not said this, therefore would not bring himself to say it in so many words, and would not appreciate any conversation that might force him to talk it over. Finally, no matter how reluctant he might be to let Jones see the paper, the slim chance Jones offered him of getting an answer outweighed every other consideration – except the chance of the other two finding out. So another part of the message was: I'm sitting on dynamite, Mr Jones, and I'm handing you the detonator. Or: I trust you, Mr Jones.

So be it, old man. I've got the message.

He closed his eyes and squeezed the whole situation to see if anything else would drip out of it. Nothing ... except the faint conjecture that what worked on one might work on the other two. And as if on cue, the door opened and a bland-faced major came in a pace, stopped, said, 'Beg pardon, sir. I'm in the wrong room,' and before Jones could finish saying, 'That's all right,' he was gone. Jones gazed thoughtfully at the door. That major was one of the colonel's boys. That 'wrong room' bit had a most unlikely flavour to it. So if the man hadn't come in for nothing, he'd come in for something. He hadn't taken anything and he hadn't left anything, so he'd come in to find something out. The only thing he could find out was whether Jones was or was not here. Oh: and whether he was or was not alone.

All Jones had to do to check that out was to sit tight. You can find out if a man is alone in a room for now, but not for ten minutes from now, or five.

In two minutes the colonel came in.

He wore his 'I don't like you, mister' expression. He placed his scarred brown hands flat on Jones's desk and rocked forward over him like a tidal wave about to break.

'It's your word against mine, and I'm prepared to call you a liar,' grated the colonel. 'I want you to report to me and no one else.'

'All right,' said Jones, and put out his hand. The colonel locked gazes with him for a fair slice of for ever, which made Jones believe that the Medusa legend wasn't necessarily a legend after all. Then the officer put a small folded paper into Jones's outstretched palm. 'You get the idea pretty quick, I'll say that, mister'; he straightened, about-faced and marched out.

Jones looked at the two scraps of folded paper on the desk and thought, I will be damned.

And one to go.

He picked up the papers and dropped them again, feeling like a kid who forces himself to eat all the cake before he attacks the icing. He thought, maybe the old boy wants to but just doesn't know how.

He reached for the phone and dialled for the open line, wondering if the admiral had had it cancelled yet.

He had not, and he wasn't waiting for the first ring to finish itself. He knew who was calling and he knew Jones knew, so he said nothing, just picked up the phone.

Jones said, 'It was kind of crowded in here.'

'Precisely the point,' said the admiral, with the same grudging approval the colonel had shown. There was a short pause, and then the admiral said, 'Have you called anyone else?'

Into four syllables Jones put all the outraged innocence of a male soprano accused of rape. 'Certainly not.'

'Good man.'

The Britishism amused Jones, and he almost said Gung ho, what?; but instead he concentrated on what to say next. It was easy to converse with the admiral if you supplied both sides of the conversation. Suddenly it came to him that the admiral wouldn't want to come here – he had somewhat further to travel than the colonel had – nor would he like the looks of Jones's visiting him at this particular moment. He said, I wouldn't mention this, but as you know, I'm leaving soon and may not see you. And I think you picked up my cigarette lighter.'

'Oh,' said the admiral.

'And me out of matches,' said Jones ruefully. 'Well – I'm going down to ORACLE now. Nice to have known you, sir.' He hung up, stuck an unlit cigarette in his mouth, put the two folded papers in his left pants pocket, and began an easy stroll down the catacombs called corridors in the Pentagon.

Just this side of ORACLE's dead-end corridor, and not quite in visual range of its security post, a smiling young ensign, who otherwise gave every evidence of being about his own business, said, 'Light, sir?'

'Why, thanks.'

The ensign handed him a lighter. He didn't light it and proffer the flame; he handed the thing over. Jones lit his cigarette and dropped the lighter into his pocket. 'Thanks.'

'That's all right,' smiled the ensign, and walked on.

At the security post, Jones said to the guard, 'Whoppen?'

'Nothing and nobody, Mr Jones.'

'Best news I've had all day.' He signed the book and accompanied the guard down the dead end. They each produced a key and together opened the door. 'I shouldn't be too long.'

'All the same to me,' said the guard, and Jones realized he'd been wishfully thinking out loud. He shut the door, hit the inner lock switch, and walked through the little foyer and the swinging door which unveiled what the crew called ORACLE's 'temple'.

He looked at the computer, and it looked back at him. 'Like I told you before,' he said conversationally, 'for something that causes so much trouble, you're awful little and awful homely.'

ORACLE did not answer, because it was not aware of him. ORACLE could read and do a number of more complex and subtle things, but it had no ears. It was indeed homely as a wall, which is what the front end mostly resembled, and the immense size of its translators, receptors and the memory banks was not evident here. The temple – other people called it Suburbia Delphi – contained nothing but the animated wall, with its one everblooming amber 'on' light (for the machine never ceased gulping its oceans of thought), a small desk and chair, and the mechanical typewriter with the modified Bodoni type face which was used for the reader. The reader itself was nothing more than a clipboard (though with machined guides to hold the paper exactly in place) with a large push button above it, placed on a strut which extended from the front of the computer, and lined up with a lens set flush into it. It was an eerie experience to push that button after placing your query, for ORACLE scanned so quickly and 'thought' so fast that it was rapping away on its writer before you could get your thumb off the button.

Usually.

Jones sat at the desk, switched on the light and took out the admiral's lighter. It was a square one, with two parts which telescoped apart to get to the tank. The tight little roll of paper was there, sure enough, with the typescript not seriously blurred by lighter fluid. He smoothed it out, retrieved the other two, unfolded them, stacked them all neatly; and then, feeling very like Christmas morning, said gaily to the unresponsive ORACLE: 'Now!'

Seconds later, he was breathing hard. A flood of profanity welled upwards within him – and dissipated itself as totally inadequate.

Wagging his head helplessly, he brought the three papers to the typewriter and wrote them out on fresh paper, staying within the guidelines printed there, and adding the correct code symbols for the admiral, the colonel and the civilian. These symbols had been assigned by ORACLE itself, and were cross-checked against the personnel records it carried in its memory banks. It was the only way in which it was possible to ask a question including that towering monosyllable 'I'.

Jones clipped the first paper in place, held his breath and pushed the button.

There was a small flare of light from the hood surrounding the lens as the computer automatically brought the available light to optimum. A relay clicked softly as the writer was activated. A white tongue of paper protruded. Jones tore it off. It was blank.

He grunted, then replaced the paper with the second, then the third. It seemed that on one of them there was a half-second delay in the writer relay, but it was insignificant: the paper remained blank.

'Stick your tongue out at me, will you?' he muttered at the computer, which silently gazed back at him with its blank single eye. He went back to the typewriter and copied one of the questions, but with his own code identification symbols. It read:

THE ELIMINATION OF WHAT SINGLE MAN
COULD RESULT IN MY PRESIDENCY?

He clipped the paper in place and pushed the button. The relay clicked, the writer rattled and the paper protruded. He tore it off. It read (complete with quotes):

'JOHN DOE'

'A wise guy,' Jones growled. He returned to the typewriter and again copied one of the queries with his own code:

> IF I ELIMINATE THE PRESIDENT, HOW
> CAN I ASSURE PERSONAL CONTROL?

Wryly, ORACLE answered:

> DON'T EAT A BITE UNTIL YOUR EXECUTION.

It actually took Jones a couple of seconds to absorb that one, and then he uttered an almost hysterical bray of laughter.

The third question he asked, under his own identification, was:

> CAN MY SUPPORT OF HENNY BRING PEACE?

The answer was a flat NO, and Jones did not laugh one bit. 'And you don't find anything funny about it either,' he congratulated the computer, and actually, physically shuddered.

For Henny – the Honourable Oswaldus Deeming Henny – was an automatic nightmare to the likes of Jones. His weather-beaten saint's face, his shoulder-length white hair (oh, what genius of a public-relations man put him on to that?), his diapason voice, but most of all, his 'Plan for Peace' had more than once brought Jones up out of a sound sleep into a cold sweat. Now, there was once a man who entranced a certain segment of the population with a slogan about the royalty in every man, but he could not have taken over the country, because a slogan is not a political philosophy. And there was another who was capable of turning vast numbers of his countrymen – for a while – against one another and towards him for protection: and he could not have taken over the country, because the manipulation of fear is not an economic philosophy. This Henny, however, was the man who had both, and more besides. His appearance alone gave him more non-thinking, vote-bearing adherents than Rudolph Valentino plus Albert Schweitzer. His advocacy of absolute isolation brought in the right wing, his demand for unilateral disarmament brought in the left wing, his credo that science could, with a third of munitions-size budgets, replace foreign trade through research, invention and ersatz, brought in the tech segment, and his dead certainty of lowering taxes had a thick hook in everyone else. Even the most battlestruck of the war wanters found themselves shoulder to shoulder with the peace-at-any-price extremists, because of the high moral tone of his disarmament plan, which was to turn our weapons on ourselves and present any aggressor with nothing but slag and cinders – the ultimate deterrent. It was the most marvellous blend of big bang and beneficence, able to cut chance and challenge together with open-handed Gandhiism, with an answer for everyone and a better life for all.

'All of which,' complained Jones to the featureless face of the computer, 'doesn't help me find out why you wouldn't answer those three guys, though I must say, I'm glad you didn't.' He went and got the desk chair and put it down front and centre before the computer. He sat down and folded his arms and they stared silently at each other.

At length he said, 'If you were a people instead of a thing, how would I handle you? A miserable, stubborn, intelligent snob of a people?'

Just how do I handle people? he wondered. I do – I know I do. I always seem to think of the right thing to say, or to ask. I've already asked ORACLE what's wrong, and ORACLE says nothing is wrong. The way any miserable, stubborn, intelligent snob would.

What I do, he told himself, is to empathize. Crawl into their skins, feel with their fingertips, look out through their eyes.

Look out through their eyes.

He rose and got the admiral's query – the one with the admiral's own identification on it – clipped it to the board, then hunkered down on the floor with his back to the computer and his head blocking the lens.

He was seeing exactly what the computer saw.

Clipboard. Query. The small bare chamber, the far wall. The ...

He stopped breathing. After a long astonished moment he said, when he could say anything, and because it was all he could think of to say: 'Well, I'll ... be ... damned ...'

The admiral was the first in. Jones had had a busy time of it for the ninety minutes following his great discovery, and he felt a little out of breath, but at the same time a little louder and quicker than the other guy, as if he had walked into the reading room after a rubdown and a needle-shower.

'Sit down, Admiral.'

'Jones, did you—'

'Please, sir – sit down.'

'But surely—'

'I've got your answer, Admiral. But there's something we have to do first.' He made waving gestures. 'Bear with me.'

He wouldn't have made it, thought Jones, except for the colonel's well-timed entrance. Boy, oh boy, thought Jones, look at 'em, stiff as tongs. You come on the battlefield looking just like a target. On the other hand, that's how you made your combat reputation, isn't it? The colonel was two strides into the room before he saw the admiral. He stopped, began an about-face and said over his left epaulet, 'I didn't think—'

'Sit down, Colonel,' said Jones in a pretty fair imitation of the man's own brass gullet. It reached the officer's muscles before it reached his brain and he sat. He turned angrily on the admiral, who said instantly, 'This wasn't my idea,' in a completely insulting way.

Again the door opened and old living history walked in, his head a little to one side, his eyes ready to see and understand and his famous mouth to smile, but when he saw the tableau, the eyes frosted over and the mouth also said: 'I didn't think—'

'Sit down, sir,' said Jones, and began spieling as the civilian was about to refuse, and kept on spieling while he changed his mind, lowered himself guardedly on to the edge of a chair and perched his old bones on its front edge as if he intended not to stay.

'Gentlemen,' Jones began, 'I'm happy to tell you that I have succeeded in finding out why ORACLE was unable to perform for you – thanks to certain unexpected cooperation I received.' Nice touch, Jones. Each of 'em will think he turned the trick, single-handedly. But not for long. 'Now I have a plane to catch, and you all have things to do, and I would appreciate it if you would hear me out with as little interruption as possible.' Looking at these bright eager, angry, sullen faces, Jones let himself realize for the first time why detectives in whodunits assemble all the suspects and make speeches. Why they *personally* do it – why the author has them do it. It's because it's fun.

'In this package' – he lifted from beside his desk a brown paper parcel a yard long and 15 inches wide – 'is the cause of all the trouble. My company was founded over a half century ago, and one of these has been an appurtenance of every one of the company's operations, each of its major devices and installations, all of its larger utility equipment – cranes, trucks, bulldozers, everything. You'll find them in every company office and in most company cafeterias.' He put the package down flat on his desk and fondled it while he talked. 'Now, gentlemen, I'm not going to go into any part of the long argument about whether or not a computer can be conscious of what it's doing, because we haven't time and we're not here to discuss metaphysics. I will, however, remind you of a childhood chant. Remember the one that runs: "For want of a nail the shoe was lost; for want of a shoe the horse was lost; for want of a horse the message was lost; for want of the message the battle was lost; for want of the battle the kingdom was lost – and all for the want of a horseshoe nail." '

'Mr Jones,' said the admiral, 'I – we – didn't come here to—'

'I just said that,' Jones said smoothly, and went right on talking until the admiral just stopped trying. 'This' – he rapped the package – 'is ORACLE's horseshoe nail. If it's no ordinary nail, that's because ORACLE's no ordinary computer. It isn't designed to solve problems in their own context; there are other machines that do that. ORACLE solves problems the way an educated man solves them – by bringing everything he is and has to bear on them. Lacking this one part' – he thumped the package again – 'it can then answer your questions, and it accordingly did.' He smiled suddenly. 'I don't think ORACLE was designed this way,' he added musingly. 'I think it ... became ... this way ...' He shook himself. 'Anyway, I have your answers.'

Now he could afford to pause, because he had them. At that moment, the only way any of them could have been removed was by dissection and haulage.

Jones lined up his sights on the colonel and said, 'In a way, your question was the most interesting, Colonel. To me professionally, I mean. It shows to what detail ORACLE can go in answering a wide theoretical question. One might even make a case for original creative thinking, though that's always arguable. Could a totally obedient robot think if you flatly ordered it to think? When does a perfect imitation of a thing become the thing itself?'

'You're not going to discuss my question here,' said the colonel as a matter of absolute, incontrovertible fact.

'Yes I am,' said Jones, and raised his voice. 'You listen to me, before you stick that trigger finger of yours inside that tunic, Colonel. I'm in a corny mood right now and so I've done a corny thing. Two copies of a detailed report of this whole affair are now in the mail, and, I might add, in a mailbox outside this building. One goes to my boss, who is a very big wheel and a loyal friend, with as many contacts in business and government as there are company machines operating, and that puts him on the damn moon as well as all over the world. The other goes to someone else, and when you find out who that is it'll be too late, because in two hours he can reach every paper, every wire service, every newscasting organization on earth. Naturally, consistent with the corn, I've sent these out sealed with orders to open them if I don't phone by a certain time – and I assure you it won't be from here. In other words, you can't do anything to me and you'd better not delay me. *Sit down, Admiral*,' he roared.

'I'm certainly not going to sit here and—'

'I'm going to finish what I started out to do whether you're here or not.' Jones waved at the other two. 'They'll be here. You want that?'

The admiral sat down. The civilian said, in a tolling of mighty sorrow, 'Mr Jones, I had what seemed to be your faithful promise—'

'There were overriding considerations,' said Jones. 'You know what an overriding consideration is, don't you, sir?' and he held up the unmistakable ORACLE query form. The civilian subsided.

'Let him finish,' gritted the colonel. 'We can – well, let him finish.'

Jones instantly, like ORACLE, translated: *We can take care of him later*. He said to the colonel, 'Cheer up. You can always deny everything, like you said.' He fanned through the papers before him and dealt out the colonel's query. He read it aloud:

'IF I ELIMINATE THE PRESIDENT, HOW CAN I ASSURE PERSONAL CONTROL?'

The colonel's face could have been shipped out, untreated, and installed on Mount Rushmore. The civilian gasped and put his knuckles in his mouth. The admiral's slitted eyes went round.

'The answer,' said Jones, 'makes that case for creative thinking I was talking about. ORACLE said: "DETONATE ONE BOMB WITHIN UNDERGROUND HQ. SPEND YOUR SUBSEQUENT TENURE LOOKING FOR OTHERS."'

Jones put down the paper and spoke past the colonel to the other two. 'Get the big picture, gentlemen? "UNDERGROUND HQ" could only mean the centralized control for government in the mountains. Whether or not the President – or anyone else – was there at the time is beside the point. If not, he'd find another way easily enough. After that happened, our hero here would take the posture of the national saviour, the only man competent to track down a second bomb, which could be anywhere. Imagine the fear, the witch-hunts, the cordons, the suspicion, the "Emergency" and "For the Duration" orders and regulations.' Suddenly savage, Jones snarled, 'I've got just one more thing to say about this warrior and his plans. All his own strength, and the entire muscle behind everything he plans for himself, derives from the finest *esprit de corps* the world has ever known. I told you I'm in a corny mood, so I'm going to say it just the way it strikes me. The kind of *esprit* is a bigger thing than obedience or devotion or even faith, it's a species of love. And there's not a hell of a lot of that to go around in this world. Butchering the President to make himself a little tin god is a minor crime compared to his willingness to take a quality like that and turn it into a perversion.'

The civilian, as if unconsciously, hitched his chair a half inch away from the colonel. The admiral trained a firing-squad kind of look at him.

'Admiral,' said Jones, and the man twitched, 'I'd like to call your attention to the colonel's use of the word "eliminate" in his query. You don't, you know, you just *don't* eliminate a live President.' He let that sink in, and then said, 'I mention it because you, too, used it, and it's a fair conjecture that it means the same thing. Listen: WHAT SINGLE MAN CAN I ELIMINATE TO BECOME PRESIDENT?'

'There could hardly be any *one* man,' said the civilian thoughtfully, gaining Jones's great respect for his composure.

Jones said, 'ORACLE thinks so. It wrote your name, sir.'

Slowly the civilian turned to the admiral. 'Why, you sleek

old son of a bitch,' he enunciated carefully, 'I do believe you could have made it.'

'Purely a hypothetical question,' explained the admiral, but no one paid the least attention.

'As for you,' said Jones, rather surprised that his voice expressed so much of the regret he felt, 'I do believe that you asked your question with a genuine desire to see a world at peace before you passed on. But, sir – it's like you said when you walked in here just now – and the colonel said it, too: "I didn't think ..." You are sitting next to two certifiable first-degree murderers; no matter what their overriding considerations, that's what they are. But what you planned is infinitely worse.'

He read, 'CAN MY SUPPORT OF HENNY BRING PEACE? You'll be pleased to know – oh, you already know; you were just checking, right? – that the answer is Yes. Henny's position is such right now that your support would bring him in. But – you didn't *think*. That demagogue can't do what he wants to do without a species of thought policing the like of which the antheap experts in China never even dreamed of. Unilateral disarmament and high morality – scorched earth! Why, as a nation we couldn't do that unless we meant it, and we couldn't mean it unless every man, woman and child thought alike – and with Henny running things, they would. Peace? Sure we'd have peace! I'd rather take on a Kodiak bear with boxing gloves than take my chances in that kind of a world. These guys,' he said carelessly, 'are prepared to murder one or two or a few thousand. You,' said Jones, his voice suddenly shaking with scorn, 'are prepared to murder every decent free thing this country ever stood for.'

Jones rose. 'I'm going now. All your answers are in the package there. Up to now it's been an integral part of ORACLE – it was placed exactly in line with the reader, and has therefore been a part of everything the machine has ever done. My recommendation is that you replace it, or ORACLE will be just another computer, answering questions in terms of themselves. I suggest that you make similar installations in your own environment ... and quit asking questions that must be answered in terms of *your*selves. Questions which in the larger sense would be unthinkable.'

The civilian rose, and did something that Jones would always remember as a decent thing. He put out his hand and said, 'You are right. I needed this, and you've stopped me. What will stop *them*?'

Jones took the hand. 'They're stopped. I know, because I asked ORACLE and ORACLE said this was the way to do it.' He smiled briefly and went out. His last glimpse of the office was the rigid backs of the two officers, and the civilian behind his desk, slowly unwrapping the package. He walked down the endless Pentagon corridors, the skin between his shoulder blades tight all the way: ORACLE or no, there might be over-riding considerations. But he made it, and got to the first outside phone booth still alive. Marvellously, wonderfully alive.

He heard Ann's voice and said, 'It's a real wonderful world, you know that?'

'Jones, darling! ... you certainly have changed your tune. Last time I talked to you it was a horrible place full of evil intentions and smelling like feet.'

'I just found out for sure three lousy kinds of world it's not going to be,' Jones said. Ann would not have been what she was to him if she had not been able to divine which questions not to ask. She said, 'Well, good,' and he said he was coming home.

'Oh, darling! You fix that gadget?'

'Nothing to it,' Jones said. 'I just took down the THINK sign.'

She said, 'I never know when you're kidding.'

Doctor's Orders

JOHN F. SUTER

The pain. The pain is everywhere. No, not everywhere, but I throb in the places where there is no real pain. And now it is only an ache and an exhaustion, but it seems as if there is no time, no space, nothing but this. But I am a little stronger than I was. So little. But I am stronger. I have to get well. I intend to get well. I will get well.

'Mr Shaw, I think she'll come out of it all right. As you know, it was either your wife or the baby, for a while. But she's improved, I assure you. Of course, there will always be that weakness which we can't correct.'

'I understand. Just to have her well again is all I care about.'

I had better open my eyes. Jeff isn't here. I can't sense him. But I can stand the white room now. I no longer have a wish to die. Even though he didn't live. I could grieve and grieve and grieve, and I wanted to when Jeff first told me. But there is no strength in that sort of grief. I will get well.

'You did tell her that the baby died?'

'Yes, Doctor. It was hard for her to take at first. Very hard. Then I told her that it had been a boy. That pleased her, in spite of – of what happened.'

There. The world is back. So much sunshine in the room. So

many flowers. I wonder if Jeff—

'Did you tell her that the child is already buried?'

'Not yet. If you're sure that she's stronger, I'll tell her to-day.'

'You don't think she'll hold it against you for going ahead with the funeral, Mr Shaw?'

'Jessie is very level-headed, Doctor. She'll understand that we couldn't wait. And – if you don't think it's out of style to say so – we love each other.'

I'm sure Jeff has done whatever is best. If only it – he – had lived until I could have seen him ... How long have I been here? Where is Jeff? Is he being sensible, as I begged him to be? Is he at work, so that he won't endanger his job, the job that's so important to him? Oh, I do love him, and I do so want to give him fine children.

'Perhaps, then, Mr Shaw, it would be better for you to tell her the rest of it than for me to do it. It might be easier for her to believe someone who loves her. Sometimes the patient thinks the doctor doesn't know as much as she herself does.'

'That part won't be easy.'

I hope the children will look like Jeff. I'm not ugly, but I'm so – plain. Jeff has the looks for both of us. That's one of the reasons they all said he was only after my money. But he's refused to let me help him. He's independent. He keeps working hard managing the sporting-goods department, when neither of us would ever have to work again, if we didn't want to. I must get well, for his sake. I will get well.

'Easy or hard, Mr Shaw, it has to be done. Someone has to tell her. It will come best from you. She must never try to have a child again. Never. It will kill her. Make no mistake about it – having another child will kill her.'

'I'll take the responsibility, Doctor. You needn't say a thing to her. I think I can convince her. Perhaps I can even persuade her to move away for a while, so that old associations won't keep haunting her.'

I'm glad that I made my will in Jeff's favour before I came to the hospital. He doesn't know about it, and it wasn't necessary, as it turned out. But I'm glad. He's been so good to me that now I'm sure of him ...

The door swung inwards, silently. She turned her head, slowly, and a tired smile crept across her white face. A tall young man with crinkled blond hair was in the doorway.
   'Jeff.'
   He was at her bedside, kissing her palm. 'Jessie.'
   When they both could speak, she gripped his fingers. 'Jeff, I've been lying here thinking. Everybody has troubles of some kind or other. We can overcome this. I'm going to get strong, fast. Then we're going to have another baby, just as quickly as we can. Aren't we?'
   He smiled proudly. The truth was exactly the right answer.
   'We certainly are, sweetheart. We certainly are.'

The Man Who Laughs at Lions

BRYCE WALTON

Something happened in Manhattan that should have been included in my autobiography of a white hunter, *The Last Safari*, for in its oddly delicate way it was fully as predatory and rapacious as anything that ever happened in the African jungle. But my book had just been accepted by the Norman Press and my agent was still discussing terms with the publishers – the only bait that could have tempted me into Manhattan or any other city. All those millions of strange people swarming in and out of their burrows frightened me, so after a few days I holed up in a rather humble hotel on East 34th Street and hardly ventured out except for rations and Scotch whisky. Otherwise I probably wouldn't have been so convincingly on hand when the phone rang. I picked it up, and the clerk downstairs said, 'You've got a lady visitor, Mr Vanderveer.'

I looked into the bureau mirror and wished I were younger, or anyway a bit better-looking. Then I wondered who the lady could be, for I hadn't been in town long enough to have any lady friends. My agent, however, had expressed concern over my detachment and I thought he might have taken direct unsolicited action against it. 'Please ask for her name,' I said.

The clerk said, 'Mrs Frank McClinton.'

After a moment in which nothing registered, I felt a deadly, sort of oyster-like twitch in my stomach. I hadn't turned on a light, and a charcoal greyness filtered through dirty windows from the rainy concrete valley outside.

The incident was one I had deliberately forgotten, and now I suddenly felt it in the room as a ghostlike and intrusive element hard to get hold of and hard to remember. The familiar queer chitters and whistles came faintly out of a misty green tangle. Then in the distance, out on the burning Rhodesian plain, I saw the yellow dust rising and whirling among the giant ant hills. The big guns began booming again. There was the wet rust odour of blood. Then that terrifying sound that I had heard only once before and had no desire to hear again, even in my imagination – that awful bell-toned baying that came at me with the speed of a poisonous wind . . .

'Tell her I'll be right down,' I said, and started to hang up, but the clerk said, 'She's on her way up, Mr Vanderveer.' And I just had time to put on a robe and down a double Scotch before she buzzed my door.

A pale, slim, frightened girl stood in the dim hallway. She stood poised as if prepared to take flight in an instant. Disordered wisps of hair hung over her face and if she wore make-up it was subtle or lost. Dark sleepless marks showed under eyes that were very wide and black and tense with confused fears. I felt an immediate flood of sympathy for her – the way she stood watching me, an awkward defensive way that made me think of a lost homeless child, with one shoulder slightly raised as if she expected to be scolded and struck.

She never quite looked at me, and often looked at the floor or the walls. Her voice was low. 'I should have called first. I'm sorry for just barging in like this. I don't really want to bother you—'

She started backing towards the elevator. 'Just a minute,' I said, and she stopped. 'It's no bother. By the way, Mrs McClinton, you do represent the big-game-hunting Frank?'

She raised her chin as if looking up at some imagined image of him. (He was, as I remembered him, a huge man about six four.) 'There's only one Frank, you know. He's strictly one of a kind, isn't he?'

'A genuine collector's item,' I said.

'But he doesn't hunt much any more, I mean, anything big. He stopped that a short time after we were married.'

'That's fortunate,' I said, 'for the animals, I mean. What do you want to see me about, Mrs McClinton?'

'About Frank. But this is just silly being here. I've got to be at my analyst's office at three.'

'You have nearly an hour,' I said. 'Come in.'

She walked in past me at once, without another word. She might have been responding by reflex action as if obeying a military command.

I took her coat and she retreated timidly into the shadows near the window. She stood and watched me nervously like a wet, scared bird hunkering under a leaf. I went to the bureau that I had converted into a bar and poured liberal doses of Scotch into two glasses.

'Hope you like Scotch,' I said. 'I don't like anything else. I didn't anticipate guests, so Scotch is all there is – with or without soda.'

'Oh, I can't drink anything like that,' she said with an odd rapid shyness. 'They say that's the most irresponsible thing I can do – as bad as going out alone or without permission. They just started letting me go alone to my analyst – it's sort of an experiment.'

'They?' I said.

'Frank and Dr Rosner. Frank has a terrible temper, you know. And – well – I don't like to be punished any more than anyone else does.'

I managed some sort of smile. 'Made to sit in a corner, I suppose. Or sent to bed without your supper?'

'The worst thing is when Frank makes me stay in the apartment and never go out, except to see Dr Rosner. Sometimes for months.'

I put one glass on her side of the coffee table, the other on mine. I took my time when getting another cigar from the box and lighting it – one of those connoisseur's pleasures I have sent over regularly from Gibraltar, firmly rolled, slim, with streaks of green in delicate brown leaf that smoked dry and cool with a strong and incomparable flavour.

But this time I hardly tasted it. The girl interested me and aroused more and more of a rare kind of sympathy in me – the kind I feel when seeing an animal struggling with futility and courage in a steel trap.

'Sit down,' I said.

She sat down quickly, again as if obeying a military order. Her knees were locked together and she tried to pull her skirt further down than its design allowed for. Her hand almost knocked over the glass of Scotch. She kept glancing at the glass and jerking her eyes away.

I sat down and raised my glass. 'So how is our gun-happy old Frank?'

'This is just silly,' she said and clenched her small pale hands. 'I mean, thinking I might be able to help Frank. It's so ridiculous. But Dr Rosner's office is only a few blocks away, on Lex, and I was walking along and the first thing I know, here I am—'

I asked how she knew I was even in the country, and it seemed she had noticed a brief mention in Earl Wilson's column of my arrival on the *Queen Mary*. She assumed I was the same Jon Vanderveer who had been Frank's guide on a hunt. He had mentioned my name, and had bought my first book.

'You want to help Frank? *Frank?*'

She sat in that strange adolescent way and looked up at the window and the sliding rain. 'Frank doesn't need help,' she said finally in a tired slow way. 'It's a silly stupid idea of mine, that's all. Frank doesn't need anybody or anything but himself. He never has and he never will. He's steel – you know, hard as steel—'

'You thought he needed help?' I asked. 'What sort of help?'

She turned towards me and blinked very slowly three times. Then she said very solemnly, 'It's so silly, Mr Vanderveer.

Don't laugh, but I had the feeling that Frank might be afraid of something.'

I stared at her, and realized that my cigar had gone out.

Her hands passed vaguely over her hair as she looked away from me. 'Imagine that?' she whispered. 'Frank being afraid of *anything*!'

I was relighting my cigar and could only shake my head, but our eyes met for an embarrassed moment.

Her voice was lower now, more hesitant and extremely cautious. 'A silly stupid thing to have imagined and I'd better leave now, Mr Vanderveer.'

'But what makes you think he might be afraid of something?' I insisted.

'He's never been afraid, he couldn't be, not Frank. Why, we had a house on Long Island, twenty-five rooms, and every room, every wall, covered with heads. Most dangerous game on earth, he told me, and Frank got them all. The things he's done – and the way he laughs at anything and everything that everyone else is afraid of! He just laughs—'

She stared at me shyly a moment and gave a tight little smile. 'When he comes into a room, Mr Vanderveer, he dominates everyone, and people feel about this high. He's not like other men – he's way up there, and it's such a rare wonderful privilege even to know a man like that. That terrible but wonderful strength of his, and all that power. He's there, always there, and you know you're safe. No more feeling lost or helpless so long as he's there. No more responsibility or struggle. I know I'll always be supported and protected and there'll never be anything to worry about—'

She still sat in that strange adolescent way, in awkward, nearly hopeless defensiveness. I watched her draw her underlip in and break its tremble with even white teeth.

'But assuming that Frank might be afraid, just a little afraid of something,' I said, 'how does that involve me?'

'Well, if he was afraid of something – I mean, just a little bit afraid – then you must know what he's afraid of.'

'Why should I?'

'He has bad dreams. That's what made me have the crazy idea that he might be afraid. Dr Rosner says that nightmares usually are caused by repressed fears of some kind.'

'But why did you come to me about it?'

'I thought I could help him find out what he was afraid of and let him know – I mean, consciously know – and then he would get rid of the repression, whatever it is, and stop having these nightmares. Dr Rosner says that consciously facing a real fear is one thing, but that a repressed fear can keep getting worse. It festers, he says, and can make even very strong healthy people sick. And Frank doesn't know he dreams. I mentioned it and he got very mad at me, said he never dreams at all. He wouldn't, he couldn't admit it, even to himself, and that's why he has the bad dreams.'

'And you want to help him find out what his real fear is?' I said.

'He mustn't get sick too,' she whispered faintly. 'Then what would become of me? About the only people who care about me now are Frank and Dr Rosner, and I'm afraid Dr Rosner wouldn't care a bit if Frank didn't pay him – pay him an awful lot, you know.'

'So why should I know what he's – what he might be – afraid of, Mrs McClinton?'

'Because you're in his nightmares – in almost every one of them.'

'Are you sure?'

'He calls your name. Sometimes he almost screams it.' She leaned towards me across the coffee table. 'He's yelled it many times. "Help me, Vanderveer, for God's sake, get them off me," he says.' She gave me a quick, nervous, ingratiating smile. 'What does that mean, Mr Vanderveer?'

This time I skipped the soda. I was perspiring heavily. The room was darker.

'Yes,' I heard myself saying. 'There was something . . .'

*   *   *

He was, indeed, an absolutely fearless man. Our boys had a Masai name for him – *Marsimba*, meaning 'the man who laughs at lions'.

He never played it safe the way most hunters do. He never shot from the security of an armour-plated truck or from a tree shed. He never shot backed up by a dozen black boys with big guns. He took all the straight odds and he often hunted alone. He never backed off from anything, not even a charging rogue hippo. He's the only hunter I ever knew to stand up alone to a rogue hippo.

Unfortunately, his lack of concern for his own life involved the lives of others. He never gave a damn for anything but himself, his own power, his own glory. But there was nothing unique about him as a type. There are true sportsmen, and I refer to those who practise honourable hunting, but Frank McClinton wasn't one of them. He was one of a minority who kill for the pure love of killing. Nothing unique about killing for the love of killing, of course. But McClinton was, individually speaking, one of a kind – a rare collector's item.

McClinton was the most kill-crazy, gun-happy client I ever knew or heard about, and I've known and heard about some prize specimens.

When I met McClinton I had decided to give up the guide and white-hunter business. I was fed up with hunting and with the characters who can afford to do it for pleasure. I had just returned to the Congo from four months in the Kivu district with a German gorilla hunter and was resting up at the big hunting lodge of John Kreiger, Provost Marshal, where I was angling for an assistant marshal's job. Then I got a wire from Kreiger, who at that time was tracking down poachers near Stanleyville, asking me to hire out to an old friend of his with whom he had served on some Allied Commission in Germany after the war. This friend was on a long hunt, needed a guide; and Kreiger asked me to take the job as a personal favour. I couldn't very well refuse – at least, that was how I felt at the time.

McClinton was a sullen, powerful brute who never said much. He had his own boys, guns and trucks. He moved thoroughly equipped, but he did need a guide, he said, to cross the Zambezi into lion country. He knew that lions hunt the richest territory and he didn't intend to be outdone. So I tied up with him on the Lunga River in Northern Rhodesia.

Our safari hardly stopped for breath from that time until the disastrous finale. McClinton had incredible endurance fortified by a mad obsession for killing. He kept going, and asked nothing of me but that I keep showing him the way. His purpose: to slaughter as much as possible in the shortest time.

My boy, Gombi, a thin, wiry half-Masai youth with sad sensitive eyes, was with me as he had been for years. We were inseparable, like father and son – more so, perhaps, for we had shared hundreds of hunts and knew that rare wordless sort of understanding that comes only from breathing the same air of death many times.

And in McClinton we both smelled death. McClinton pushed too hard, and when I told him that it was dangerous to hunt when tired, he laughed. He sneered at any hint of weakness or fear. And he kept pushing, driving, without mercy or reprieve. Inevitably, accidents resulted. Injuries, even deaths, meant nothing to McClinton – except perhaps that more unworthy organisms had gone under.

Day and night he kept pushing, turning everyone out before dawn every morning and often not returning to camp until the next day. He killed steadily – everything that moved. He bagged zebra, buffalo, sassaby, koodoo, wildbeest, rhino, hippos, crocodiles, antelopes, leopards. He slaughtered wart hogs and ostriches and even long-tailed songsters. He hardly looked back or paused to pose for a picture. He kept pushing and killing and leaving the carcasses black and fly-blown in the sun.

He had got everything but what he had to have – a bull elephant. He said he wanted nothing less than the biggest damn tusker in Africa, and he wouldn't stop until he got it. All of us began to run down, to give out under the scorching sun. With the deadening fatigue grew a kind of perpetual fear that lay with us every night and followed our weary marches and soured our stomachs. I saw it in Gombi's eyes and he in mine – the fear that comes from killing without hunting.

When I insisted that our boys were exhausted and had to rest up, McClinton simply kept striding on alone, never looking back – contemptuous, implacable, striding off with his .475 or the .256 Mannlichers – and I followed, and Gombi followed me, because McClinton's safety was my reputation and good name.

We had crossed the Zambezi into lion country and had camped on the plain where only a few trees grew from scattered elevations. A low line of hills was strung to the left – a hunter's paradise and killer's pigpen, with small herds everywhere, watching us without fear – for in those days you could go within forty yards of any animal in Africa and often it wouldn't move away.

The Wagandas started a fire and were laying out the traps and tents. Gombi sat sharpening his skinning knife. I had put a spare rifle and some ammo inside a hollow tree in case of an emergency and we had tramped the grass flat several yards around to prevent snakes from creeping in too close. Herds of antelope appeared within fifty yards of camp, though the springbok stayed at a safer distance, and a number of gazelles sported like jackrabbits in the twelve-inch, dung-coloured grass. And, of course, there were the millions of tiny flies biting, bringing blood all the time, swarming into the nose and mouth.

Then Gombi called to me and I saw that McClinton and two of his Kaffirs were gone from camp. Gombi pointed them out half a mile distant, and we followed at once, although Gombi kept shaking his head and muttering that McClinton was a baas with maggots in his skull. When we overtook McClinton he commanded Gombi to run ahead because he was a superior tracker. This time we were going to get a tusker.

We slogged under the blazing sun and had to tear our way through thickening brush of thorn and brambles, and finally through high yellow grass between the giant ant hills and stretches of yellow dust. McClinton kept the boys moving without rest, kept Gombi out ahead, kept him circling, coming back, tracking, smelling and retracking.

Finally Gombi came back to me and said sadly, '*Mingi tembo*,' and that meant 'big elephants very close'. McClinton knew what it meant. He was already moving. We had talked about the correct shots. McClinton knew that the shoulder shot was the best, shattering the thick concentration of blood vessels and killing in seconds. He knew that the head shot was usually dangerously inadequate because bullets lose their power in spongy airsacs of the skull unless one gets in a straight shot in the soft spot above the eyes. McClinton knew more about shooting than most hunters, but no hunter knows everything. No hunter who had hunted in Africa all his life knows everything about hunting in Africa.

Gombi signalled and we followed him as he trotted into the bush where thickets alternated with open plain and high grassland. I broke my rifle at the breech and inserted two shells. Vegetation grew denser, bushes became thick and high. Trees, massive with vines, appeared, and the sun blazed white and hot. There was no breeze as Gombi led us through the slashing grass, then moved faster, pointing.

To the right the Kaffirs were heading for the safety of the trees. We stayed low and moved with Gombi, and I told McClinton that there were young with cows out there and that if he killed them he would have to take the responsibility when Kreiger got back; but McClinton didn't seem to hear me, hardly knew I was there. He plodded ahead, huge and hunched against the sun. I reminded him that shooting a cow carrying a calf was bad, and that, worse, when you killed cows with young the entire herd might go rogue and it would be necessary to kill all of them. McClinton smiled a little, as if the idea was an interesting one.

Tickbirds flew up from the elephants as we dropped and crawled ahead on our hands and knees. Less than fifty yards away, in thick brush to our right, I could see clearly their walls of ancient wrinkled hides almost blending with the brush and towering above the grass.

Gombi crawled up ahead, and McClinton moved in close behind him. I yelled suddenly for McClinton to turn back, but the sudden shrill trumpeting sounds came and I doubt if he heard me. He was like a man under a hypnotic spell plunging through the thickening grass, and as the brush got higher I lost my sense of direction.

The sun was a fuzzy blur. I saw McClinton turn vague and shadowy in whirling yellow dust. Then the big guns roared ahead of me. Trumpet calls shrilled. The beasts screamed and the ground shook. A bull's fan ears were almost on me in the dust. The bull came for me in that massive swaying run. Its trunk wobbled, then curled in a high bitter scream. It came straight in, so it had to be a head shot.

I fired up from the ground, from my knees. The bull seemed to turn flabby and old; it sagged as slobbers flew over me from the gaping mouth. It gave a last sick trumpeting call, and as it came down, its trunk slammed me flat in the dust where I lay stunned, with part of its leg weight over me.

Gombi was yelling. He kept saying, 'Come back, *baas*, come back!' He was running after McClinton like a wet smear of mud, calling, yelling for him to come back.

But McClinton was confused, half blinded in the dust. He ran around weaving, shouting, still looking for his tusker, the biggest damn tusker in Africa.

But the elephants were gone now – all of them. McClinton ran off into the dust against a cloud of dead grass and the wavering silhouette of giant ant hills.

Gombi was yelling again – and I heard him quite clearly.

'Hell-dogs,' he said. 'The hell-dogs . . .'

That deadening smell hit me full out of the rising wind. I managed to get to my hands and knees and saw the devil's pack streaking over the hill half a mile away. It rolled towards us across the plain with a terrifying speed and its stench came ahead in a gagging mist.

I was coughing and yelling at McClinton. I screamed to him to come back into the bush. There we could stand them off because of the thorn and brambles, but he didn't hear me. Either that or he was laughing at me, laughing at the idea of running from a bunch of mangy dogs. But Gombi kept after McClinton, getting carried further and further from safety. He was doing it for me, I knew.

And the dogs came on down the hill.

Then McClinton saw them more closely and lifted his rifle. A pack of lousy dogs, I imagine he thought, and that was why he laughed. By then over fifty of them were cutting in, beginning to circle, as their bell-like sounds, a kind of *Ooooooing*, filled the air.

The African hunting dog is the most deadly vicious animal on earth – of this I have not the slightest doubt. Its life is one long dedication to the joy of killing – the only other animal to share this propensity with man. Perhaps the most rapacious predator on earth is two-legged man, but the African wild dog has qualities uniquely its own.

But neither man nor dog serves nature's purpose. Man kills indiscriminately, taking his kills off the top, usually slaying prime animals. In contrast, the four-legged predator takes off the bottom. The wolf takes the weakling and stray. The killer whale does the same in the sea. But only man and the wild dog kill for the pure joy of killing.

The African dogs hunt with feverish and inexhaustible pleasure. They run and slay both night and day and never tire of ripping flesh and smelling fresh hot blood. They run in giant packs, numbering over a hundred, and they never tire, for they run in never-ending relays. They don't hunt for food but for joy. Indiscriminately they kill anything that lives, not omitting one another. They are the most fearless beasts in Africa, where all other animals except the hippo and rhino fly from them in terror.

I have seen hell-dogs chase a lion to earth, ripping it to pieces as it runs. The hell-dog never attacks an animal's throat, but runs beside and behind the panicked prey, cutting it down with razor fangs, slashing the tendons, hamstringing, ripping open the bellies, spilling out an animal's insides while it runs on in blind terror.

All the time one hears that horrible *Ooooooing* call – like hundreds of delicate, high-toned bells.

At least fifty of them were circling McClinton as he fired into them. He had stopped laughing now. He killed as the dogs ran, but then he had an empty breech and no time for reloading. Yellow and black streaks of light shot up and McClinton yelled. He ran then, but it was too late for him to select his own course. Blood seeped out of his ripped trousers. He dropped the gun. His arms swung and the muscles of his neck strained as he ran.

I dropped several dogs with my Savage. Others immediately fell upon those I had shot, tore them apart, and ate them. I kept yelling at McClinton to circle back into the bush. I had eight cartridges left, seven in the magazine and one in the breech. I'd left my .45 sidearm in camp as well as a bandolier of ammo.

I kept shooting, and then I had nothing to shoot with while the hell-dogs split into four packs and began circling McClinton. Another pack broke off and came for me. I clubbed two and retreated deeper into the brambles. The others stopped to eat their dead.

McClinton was really running now. The dogs had him going, and the dogs always enjoy enthusiastic effort. The more enthusiastic it is, the more they encourage and prolong it. The *Ooooooing* devils grinned and ran him. They ran and goaded him. They slashed and darted in. They wanted him to run, run faster, keep on running. They wanted sport. And when McClinton slowed down, they leaped in again. His khakis, bush jacket, shirt, all were in flapping shreds.

He ran in a circle. He ran back past the bush where I was hiding. Gombi appeared, but on his knees. He looked more like a smear of some sort, an oily clot that screamed. Then the dogs rolled over him.

McClinton circled past me again. He ran. He ran past where I stood behind the brambles and watched him running.

He yelled for me to help him. But there was nothing I could do – not a blessed thing.

His gait was one of fused terror and flight. Wounds impeded the flow of movement, making it a series of shuddering paroxysms rather than a gait. But his speed was not impeded much, not for a while.

He ran past me again, around, past me again. The dogs enjoyed it and encouraged it. They knew how to keep him running, but he was weakening just the same. He began to wobble a bit. But he kept on running.

The dogs were skilled beyond belief, and they weren't ready for the kill. When McClinton slowed down again, the pack leader leaped in and ripped with finely controlled fangs – not too much, just enough – very delicate, you understand, like the controlled clicking of a meat slicer.

McClinton ran past me again. I didn't count how many times, but now he was moving quite slowly. His clothes flew behind him in tatters. His body was a smear of mud formed of dust, sweat and blood. As he went away from me again, he seemed to float or drift like part of a mirage. He didn't really resemble a man any more, only some miserable mad thing, the muscles of his neck pulled back and his legs jerking up and down, in one final prolonged spasm of effort.

The pack split in half then, and followed him half on each side. When his speed faltered, the hell-dogs also slowed to a trot. They even let him go a bit ahead of them, taunting him. They knew all the tricks for keeping the game going a while longer.

They ran McClinton for over an hour, I should say. At the end he was shuffling, but still moving as best he could. He knew he didn't dare fall, didn't dare stop, so he kept shuffling around until the Wagandas who had followed us from camp in a truck arrived, and five rifles opened up on the dogs from the safety of the armoured truck.

While the boys gave McClinton their best first-aid, I buried Gombi and put a marker over his grave. By then the plane we had radioed for came in and took McClinton to a trading-post hospital on the river . . .

When I finished, the hotel room was dark, or would have been but for a neon sign flashing outside the window. After a while Mrs McClinton gave a low soft laugh.

'Dogs,' she said. 'Who would have believed it?'

I looked at my watch. 'I'm afraid you're late for that appointment with Dr Rosner.'

'Dogs,' she said again. 'So that's what it was. You know, he got rid of all his hunting dogs. He stays away from dogs, but I never thought – and there was that funny business in Mexico. We were in a little café. Some dogs came in and went among the tables feeding on bits of shrimp and fish. Frank moved back. He turned pale. He backed clear to the door and ran out and kept running. He said he just felt like running.'

'I'm sure he did,' I said.

'And those awful scars on his body. He said he got them during the war.'

'No,' I said. I got up and turned on the lamp. Her cheeks were flushed and there was something darker now in her sad eyes, and she gave me a quick secret smile.

Months later, in Australia, I received a letter from her addressed originally to my publishers and forwarded to me by my agent.

Inside was a picture from a newspaper and clipped to it was a note from Mrs McClinton. The picture was of Mrs McClinton smiling and waving at me. I hardly recognized her at first glance – she was very chic-looking.

The newspaper caption read: *Divorce Settlement of Five Million.*

The note said:

Dear Mr Vanderveer: Thanks – a million if you want it – for helping me out. It was so easy and I wasn't really afraid – at least, not for long.

I never saw Dr Rosner again. On my way home that day I stopped off at a place downtown and purchased a couple of dogs.

Gratefully yours,
Myra

The Unsuspected

JAY WILSON

A thing about murder is that you go for broke – alone. There are no rehearsals, no retakes, no changes in bits of business to make them fit – no changes in the cast. When the victim gurgles his last, the curtain goes up. The killer is at centre stage, alone with a cast that has not read his script.

Mr Piper was thoroughly aware of this. He had considered it most carefully. Because murder seemed to be the quickest, easiest, and, really, the safest solution to a problem which had become more urgent in the past few years.

At fifty-five, Mr Piper was nearing retirement. On the surface he was an affable, pink-cheeked, slightly plump little man who looked some years younger than his age. He appeared so because he had lived a pleasant life. A bachelor, he bought good Scotch, enjoyed the theatre, played weekend golf on public courses, and maintained a better-than-average little apartment. A man who had only himself to consider could afford these little pleasures and luxuries on even a bank teller's salary. But, of course, they took most of that salary. What little he could save additionally, even as senior teller in the uptown branch of the New Amsterdam Trust Company, went for little extras such as hopeful long shots at the track or the more consoling ministrations of *demoiselles* of the evening.

Such indulgences are habit-forming. Mr Piper had come to regard them as no more than a reasonable compensation for the monotony of a banking career which had reached its zenith at a considerably lower altitude than he had once anticipated. His problem was the continuance of his pleasures on funds supplemental to the meagre pension which would shortly be his sole means of support.

Mr Piper had often considered using money out of his cash trays to make quick little profits on the stock market, with no harm done as long as he returned the bank's money before it was missed. If he made enough quick profits, he would accumulate some capital which, in turn, could be speculated into further capital until there was enough to spread out over the years, over and above his pension, to make the difference between survival and a life worth living. The thought of bank examiners had always deterred Mr Piper.

Murder, as a safer solution, occurred to Mr Piper after George Manetti became a depositor and began making his deposits and withdrawals at Mr Piper's station. Manetti's mistake was in taking a liking to Mr Piper and talking too much. This was because the calculating meanness of Mr Piper's inner being did not show through his affable exterior, and because during business hours Manetti could not afford to like anyone, and the less he said the better. It would have shaken what little trust Manetti had in mankind to have known that Mr Piper came to view him with cold objectivity as no more than the means for Mr Piper's old-age comfort.

Manetti was carried on the bank's books as a green-goods broker. Mr Piper became quickly aware of the pattern of Manetti's withdrawals and deposits. The withdrawals were usually just before bank-closing time Friday afternoons when Manetti would present a cheque to cash for five, ten or fifteen thousand dollars. The deposits were usually Monday mornings, and averaged more than the withdrawals.

'You gave me all new bills Friday,' Manetti said one Monday morning. 'They kept sticking together and I was tossing more than I wanted in the pot. Always give me used fifties.'

Mr Piper looked across the counter at the burly, olive-hued young man. 'You are a gambler?' he inquired.

Manetti's bland features became animated in a genial grin. 'Only technically, Mr Piper. Gamblers are guys who think money talks. Poker players listen to the cards. I'm a poker player. I make a living playing poker with gamblers.'

It had been the protective instinct of kind for kind that had made Mr Piper glance sideways to see if the next teller had heard. Apparently he had not. He said, 'If you want to keep your account in this bank, Mr Manetti, you'd best not discuss your – uh – profession quite so loudly.'

Manetti was in Mr Piper's hands from that moment. Manetti's grin spread. 'Yeah. I forgot. Thanks, Mr Piper. You're a right guy. I picked this place to bank because nobody would figure I would. I like privacy when I put and take.'

Manetti, unfortunately for Manetti, continued to think of Mr Piper as a right guy – and to talk. Successful, he needed to brag a little. 'One of my secrets, Mr Piper, is training. Most of these guys I do business with drink. I don't. From here I always go to my place and get some sleep before I meet them. By the time they can't tell treys from aces I'm still alive in there and sandbagging them.'

The thought of killing Manetti was born and fed by envy. Mr Piper watched Manetti's account grow. Here was a young man who was easily and steadily building a small fortune, while he, Mr Piper, after more than thirty years of exemplary service, protecting more money than Manetti would ever dream of, would soon be retired on a pittance pension. He would be expected to retire gracefully and gratefully after the customary office banquet, at which they would present him with the customary engraved watch with the customary jocular remark that it would measure out all the good time he had to loaf in while his old friends would still be watching the clock in the bank.

Mr Piper began to wonder how long Manetti's luck would hold out. How long would it be before someone who had been sandbagged once too often decided to break it off and do a little sandbagging of his own on a dark street? Gone would be Manetti, and his money with him – doing Manetti not one bit of good. Not anywhere near what it could do for Mr Piper.

Once born, it was a thought that would not die. Nor did Mr Piper want it to. Rather, he nourished it as he sat in his chair, evenings, sipping Scotch and soda. With ten or fifteen thousand dollars he could, on retirement, become a silent partner in some promising little business that needed a shot in the arm. It would return him the income he would need to supplement his pension. That was all Mr Piper asked – the means to continue his pleasant way of living. Mr Piper knew a thing or two about contracts. He would see to it that the contract under which he bought into the promising little business would provide a way to freeze out the other owner if it began really to prosper – or if a quick sale of assets should be indicated.

To get the money in the first place, of course, he would have to get rid of Manetti. A prime consideration was whether or not he could safely do this. Could he, for instance, gain access to Manetti in his apartment while he was resting before a game?

Mr Piper found himself casing the joint. He stood across the street from the apartment house in which Manetti lived. It was a middle-class building. There was no doorman. The people who went in either used a key or pressed a buzzer button in the foyer. Between five-thirty and six-thirty scarcely anyone went in or out. The white-collar folk who lived there were reading their newspapers, watching TV or eating dinner.

Mr Piper crossed the street and entered the foyer. George Manetti was listed as occupying a second-floor apartment. A man emerged, opening the foyer door, as Mr Piper stood there. He hurried out into the street, not looking at Mr Piper. The tenants in that building took little or no notice of one another. They preferred to remain invisible to one another. Entrance and exit could be safely made.

The script developed as Mr Piper sat in his rooms and

sipped his good Scotch. Certain things were in his favour. Highly important, Manetti trusted him. Manetti would believe any plausible excuse Mr Piper might make to come up and see him. Mr Piper would know when to strike. It would be after Manetti had made one of his larger withdrawals. Mr Piper possessed a small pistol which could never be traced to him by ballistics experts. He had bought it several years ago in another state while on a vacation. Fired while thrust hard against Manetti, it would make very little noise. Later it could be dropped from a ferryboat into the middle of the river. There would be any number of far more logical suspects in the gambling fraternity than a respectable senior teller with over thirty years of impeccable service in the New Amsterdam Trust Company. A reflection against Mr Piper would be a reflection against the New Amsterdam Trust Company. The police would think several times before they risked the wrath of that mighty institution over the demise of a small-time gambler. Because Manetti was far from really big time, there would be no stir if the police simply wrote the case off – as they very likely would, Mr Piper decided, if they did not quickly find a shady character who could not clear himself.

The other side of the coin appeared to offer few risks. There was a minimum chance of being seen entering or leaving or, if seen, of being later identified. A killer not associated with the bank would not bother to remove any chequebooks or statements connecting Manetti with the bank. Therefore Mr Piper had better leave any such records to be found. It meant the police would quickly find out that Mr Piper knew about the cash Manetti had withdrawn but which was missing when Manetti was found. But, after all, how could he help knowing as he had known about Manetti's many previous withdrawals? It would be best to play this straight. The bank would learn about Manetti's death anyway, check the account, and report the withdrawal to the police. It could tend to point to a bank employee trying to cover his trail if no evidence of Manetti's association with the bank was found on the scene. It would tend to indicate innocence if such normal evidence was found. Nor could Mr Piper afford the risks of a manufactured alibi. If questioned he would simply claim to have been at home reading a book. Without strain he stood an innocent man against whom nothing could be proved. The weakness or two in his position would actually turn into strengths.

That was the important thing – to be able to weather any routine questioning without strain. To be able to answer truthfully to everything except for one simple lie – that he had been at home.

Then there was the matter of what to do with the money. Mr Piper pondered this carefully. A safe-deposit box in a suburban bank seemed the best bet. It should be rented in advance, of course. He could open a small savings account under an assumed name and, under those cordial conditions, rent a box without being questioned or thought about. He would have to remember only to go there and pay the annual box rental before a bill was mailed to a non-existent person. He would not touch the money until after retirement.

That left only the problem of what to do with the money until he could get it to the safe-deposit box. If the big event took place on a Friday evening he would be unable to get the money to its hiding place until Monday morning. But it would be highly important that he be at his station promptly Monday morning as he had been for years. Any deviation could be suspect when related to other factors. He would have to wait to get to his suburban bank. In fact, there was the possibility he might have to wait several days. If that was the way the ball happened to bounce, it would also be dangerous to hide a packet of bills unguarded in his apartment. Mr Piper chuckled and had another drink when he thought of the solution to this final problem. Placed with the other bills in his cash trays at the bank the money would become utterly invisible. Immediately that it was safe he would get it off to the waiting safe-deposit box.

Mr Piper was fascinated by his plan: the script of the play he had written for himself. The action was simple, the lines few and easy. Manetti had become less than human. He was no more than a stage prop necessary for Mr Piper's star role. It was too bad, Mr Piper thought, that there would be no audience to applaud.

Two weeks later Mr Manetti made his largest withdrawal. The cheque he pushed across the counter towards Mr Piper was for twenty-five thousand. Mr Piper stared at the cheque.

George Manetti laughed. 'That still leaves a couple of hundred in the account, Mr Piper. Make it the usual fifties in a package.'

'I – I'll have to get some from the vault, Mr Manetti.'

Manetti grinned. 'Rub it for luck, Mr Piper. One of those Wall Street tycoons is sitting in tonight. A real big shot. I'll double my lettuce before I quit and let the gamblers fight it out.'

Maybe he would and maybe he wouldn't double it, Mr Piper thought in the vault. If he did, maybe fifty thousand would be enough to get Manetti followed home. Manetti could be dead or broke – or both – before morning. But before either happened, Manetti would be at home with ten thousand more in cash than Mr Piper had planned to go into action for.

Mr Piper knew that if his play was to go on stage at all, this was curtain time.

At precisely six o'clock that evening Mr Piper's cotton-gloved finger pressed the buzzer button to Manetti's apartment.

Presently Manetti's voice spoke sleepily from the foyer speaker. 'Yeah? Whossit?'

'Piper. You know. Piper at the bank. I hate to bother you, but I've got to see you for a moment.'

'Huh? Piper? Bank? Oh, yeah! Hey, what's up?'

'I think I overpaid you this afternoon. Can I please come up and verify? I mean, I'm short in my cash tally and the examiners are just about due. They could be in first thing Monday morning.'

'Oh. Sure, Mr Piper. Come on up. I'll push the door button.'

Mr Piper removed the cotton gloves as he walked along the corridor from the self-operated elevator. TV sounds came from the doors he passed – shots, shouts and loud voices. The Western programmes were on the air. It was an assistance Mr Piper had not counted on.

Manetti was waiting at the door to his apartment. He was in pyjama trousers and a T-shirt. For a moment Mr Piper knew dismay. Would a tiny bullet destroy that powerful body? Quickly enough, that is, so there would be no final struggle?

'Come on in, Mr Piper!' Manetti said cordially and loudly.

'Please, Mr Manetti!' Mr Piper pleaded, moving quickly into the apartment. 'Not so loud! I mean, you know how it is with the bank. I shouldn't be here at all.'

'Huh? Oh, yeah.' Manetti laughed as he closed the door. 'You got this Mrs Grumpy watching all the time. You know, Mr Piper, you got a dog's life.'

Mr Piper smiled. 'It has its advantages, Mr Manetti. A dog is allowed one bite.'

Manetti placed a powerful arm around Mr Piper's soft shoulders. 'Well, don't waste that bite on me, Mr Piper,' he said genially. 'I didn't mean anything. Now, what's this about you being short?'

'Well, I must have put one too many thousand-dollar packets in the package I gave you. I counted it out very quickly. I mean, that's what I'm short in my cash tally.'

'Well, now, that's easy, Mr Piper. We'll just count the packets and see.'

No one saw Mr Piper leave. He left Manetti dead with two bullets through his upper spine. There had been hardly any sound; only a grunt of surprise when Mr Piper had pressed the little pistol hard into Manetti's back, then two muffled reports that blended in with the TV sounds. Mr Piper had put on the cotton gloves and left no fingerprints.

Back in his apartment Mr Piper put the pistol and the brown-paper package of money in his dresser drawer. He didn't bother to count the money. He knew it was all there. He needed a drink. A stiff one. He poured it and collapsed in his favourite chair. It had been something of an ordeal. His nerves needed steadying. He needed for the while not to think. He needed to drink himself quietly into oblivion – to forget the horribly quiet way Manetti had sagged to the floor.

Mr Piper awakened the next morning sprawled across his bed, still fully dressed. His head ached horribly and he had no recollection of when he had come to bed. He remained perfectly still, combating a raw, inner emptiness and a nightmarish apprehension of having passed some sort of a point of no return. Then memory flooded back.

For a while longer Mr Piper remained motionless on the bed, intuitively shrinking from facing both physical distress and an assessment of his situation at the same time. Finally, having rerun the film of memory several times, Mr Piper stumbled to his feet. He went to his dresser. The money and the pistol were there in the drawer. The ball had indeed bounced.

A shower. He needed a shower – and a shave. He needed food. He needed a drink. Mr Piper shuddered. No, not a drink! He needed to clear his head. Until he could do that he needed once more not to think.

Restored once more to a state of convalescence, Mr Piper sat down in his favourite chair and endeavoured to estimate his situation calmly. Nowhere could he recall anything going in the least amiss. Manetti had died quite easily when he had turned his back to Mr Piper; so easily that Mr Piper knew he would soon be able to put the scene quite out of mind. He had only to take a ferryboat ride to New Jersey and drop the pistol in a paper bag off the stern into the middle of the river. Monday morning he would put the money in his cash tray. He was in! In with a twenty-five-thousand-dollar nest egg to keep life beautiful!

Mr Piper got up and made himself a Bloody Mary. He drank a silent toast to the success of his plan and the manner in which he had carried it out.

Manetti's death was reported in the Sunday paper. It was only a short item on an inner page. George Manetti, a known card player, had been found shot in his apartment the previous evening. A cocker spaniel, being taken out for a walk, had sniffed and fussed at the door to Manetti's apartment. The spaniel's owner had called the superintendent, who had opened the apartment. The police said there was evidence of murder for robbery.

Mr Piper read the item carefully. So they had found a chequebook showing Friday's withdrawal and, of course, not the money. Mr Piper shrugged. This he had anticipated. All it meant was that the police would come to the bank to verify the withdrawal. He, Mr Piper, had nothing to hide. That was the beauty of it all. He could tell the truth, almost the whole truth, and scarcely anything but the truth.

Mr Piper turned to the sporting section of the paper. The thing to do was to get back into his normal routine. There was a double-header that afternoon. A very good double-header too. And that evening, he mused, perhaps Fern would be free. Mr Piper chuckled. He was indeed a man of many parts.

No one at the bank, it seemed, had noted the item about Manetti in the Sunday paper. Mr Piper had not the slightest difficulty in cashing the money with the rest that was in his cash trays Monday morning.

Detective Sergeant Henderson arrived as the doors opened for the day's business. A few minutes later Mr Piper was summoned to the branch manager's office. The manager, Mr Farnsworth, was young, Ivy League, and hoping for an early vice-presidency. In college he had been known as Duke – a title bestowed in recognition of suave competence. He did not rise from behind his desk when Mr Piper entered. He had the slightly dazed look of a sea captain whose first command had just stove in her bow on a submerged derelict. He waved to a burly man seated in the chair beside his desk.

'Piper, this is Sergeant Henderson. Police. It – it seems that one of our depositors has been murdered!'

Sergeant Henderson did not rise. He acknowledged Mr Piper with a nod. If there was a crucial moment, Mr Piper thought, this would be it. He could tell nothing from Henderson's expressionless features. He felt the palms of his hands become slightly moist. He forced himself to return the policeman's steady gaze for a moment, then turned to Mr Farnsworth. The truth, he reminded himself, only one small lie, and he was safe.

'Yes, sir. I read it in the paper yesterday. The name stood out because Manetti always came to my station. I was just about to come in and tell you about it when you sent for me.'

'What we found,' Sergeant Henderson said, 'was a chequebook of this bank. The last stub showed a cheque to cash for twenty-five thousand. The money wasn't in the apartment.'

Mr Piper nodded. 'Yes, sir. He cashed a cheque for that amount Friday afternoon. I gave it to him in fifties. There is only a hundred or so left in the account.'

'Do you have the serial numbers?'

'No, sir. I mean, Mr Manetti made frequent deposits and withdrawals. Besides, he preferred used bills. We put those up in packets of five hundred and a thousand dollars, but we don't note serial numbers ordinarily.'

Sergeant Henderson sighed. 'Well, at least we can establish that he left here Friday afternoon with twenty-five thousand on him.' He looked at Mr Piper. 'And right now you're the only one we know who knew he had it.'

This was it! Mr Piper stiffened with a show of indignation. 'Well! I could hardly be expected not to know, could I? I also knew of several other depositors who left the bank with considerable amounts of cash!'

Sergeant Henderson raised a large, placating hand. 'OK,

OK. Don't get sore. A cop has to collect facts. For instance, where were you Friday night, say, between five p.m. and ten?'

'In my apartment, reading a book!' Mr Piper snapped.

'Now, just a minute!' Farnsworth cut in. 'Piper here has been with this bank for more than thirty years! He has an impeccable record! He'll retire on a good pension. Of course he knew this man had that money. And why shouldn't he be home reading a book? And if you are, by the slightest chance, suggesting Piper might have done this, would he have left that chequebook there to lead you here? Besides, you said Manetti was a gambler. You have a world of more likely suspects!'

Mr Piper exulted inwardly that Mr Farnsworth should point out all these things to Henderson.

Sergeant Henderson grinned. 'Don't get excited, Mr Farnsworth. Nobody over at Manetti's place saw anything, nobody heard anything, and nobody left any fingerprints that hadn't ought to be there. Ballistics probably won't be able to trace the weapon. On the face of it, Mr Piper could have done it as easy as anyone else. Only he didn't. Nobody that's been a bank teller over thirty years has got it left in him to leave himself so wide open. We'll just go about it the usual way – pass the word around and wait until somebody begins flashing fifty-dollar bills.' Henderson stood up. He nodded to Mr Piper. 'Well, thanks for the information – and I didn't mean to get you shook up.'

'Don't mention it!' Mr Piper said. 'After this I'll be sure to have a witness to testify that I'm behaving myself.'

'That's when I'll be looking twice at you, Mr Piper.'

Mr Farnsworth said, 'Uh – would it be possible not to publicize the bank in this? I'm sure there will be some way we can show our appreciation.'

'There wouldn't be any way you could do that, Mr Farnsworth,' Henderson replied coolly. 'If we could keep the bank's name out of it we would. But when we catch the guy, we'll have to establish that Manetti had the money – and that brings you people into it. So long.'

And that was that, Mr Piper thought jubilantly. The police would putter around among Manetti's associates until they got tired of it and wrote the case off as not important enough to waste any more money or effort on.

Mr Piper turned to find Mr Farnsworth glaring at him across the wide desk. 'This is bad, Piper,' he said. 'Very bad. It is going to be bad for us to have accepted an account from such a fellow.'

Mr Piper couldn't have cared less. He said, 'But it was a good account, Mr Farnsworth.'

'Not that good, Piper! Not that good at all! And suppose that detective reports that I tried to bribe him?'

'He won't,' Mr Piper said reassuringly. Mr Piper was inwardly amused. Mr Farnsworth was more perturbed over the superficialities than he, Mr Piper, was concerned over the deed itself. He went on, 'They may never catch anyone. In that case if we just keep quiet no one need know anything about it.'

'Don't be an ass, Piper! You know perfectly well I've got to report this downtown – and then try to explain why we accepted this account!' Mr Farnsworth groaned. 'This will fix my chances but good!'

'Oh, come, Mr Farnsworth. I'm sure you're making a mountain out of a molehill.'

Mr Farnsworth glowered. 'You think so? You think they select vice-presidents from among branch managers whose depositors get murdered? Even the way we carried him will make it worse – green-goods broker!'

Mr Piper felt it was time to soothe Mr Farnsworth and get back to a normal routine. 'But you could hardly be expected to know what kind of green goods, Mr Farnsworth. They'll understand.'

'They'll understand nothing!' Mr Farnsworth rasped. 'They'll understand only that I didn't know who I was doing business with!' Mr Farnsworth's eyes narrowed. 'You said he always came to your station. Do you mean to tell me that there was nothing about this account to give you an inkling about

Manetti? To support the suspicion you should have had when he preferred used fifties?'

Mr Piper thought rapidly. The branch manager could check records and learn the pattern of Manetti's withdrawals and deposits. In his present frame of mind he would leap to the conclusion that only an utter fool would not have identified Manetti as an unusual type of depositor, one whose account should at least have been brought to the attention of the branch manager. For over thirty years Mr Piper had a record of astuteness and meticulous regard for the bank's interests.

'Piper! I asked you a question! I want an answer!'

Mr Piper assumed a slightly hurt expression. 'Perhaps I did have intimations, Mr Farnsworth. Perhaps Manetti did say things now and then that may have made me slightly suspicious. But it was a good and growing account on the books. It was helping the branch standing. That was good for you, Mr Farnsworth. Naturally you would have had to close it out if you had personally suspected anything. If I did wrong in keeping my suspicions to myself I did so with the best of intentions.'

Mr Farnsworth was not impressed. He snapped, 'You know what the road to hell is paved with, don't you?'

Mr Piper was becoming annoyed. There wasn't a thing this whippersnapper could do to him. It was time he was told. 'I think, Mr Farnsworth,' he said quietly, 'that you are exceeding good taste and your authority. I have had over thirty years' service with the New Amsterdam Trust Company. You just stated it was an impeccable record. I have never been reprimanded. If a reprimand is called for in this case I will be ready to accept it from those who have known me much longer than you have.'

Let young Farnsworth chew on that! Mr Piper thought.

Young Farnsworth regarded Mr Piper with fury in his eyes. 'What it boils down to,' he said, 'is that you did not report an account about which you were suspicious. Now you're standing on your record and claiming the right to one mistake, eh?'

Mr Farnsworth leaned across his desk and waggled a long finger at Mr Piper. 'Well, I've got news for you! I've got absolutely nothing to lose and perhaps a great deal to gain by taking decisive action, now that I've found out about the Manetti account! You, Piper, are fired!'

'You can't make it stick!' Mr Piper retorted, not fully understanding yet what being fired could mean to him. 'My record—'

'Blast your record!' Mr Farnsworth raged. 'Maybe you didn't blast Manetti, but you've certainly blasted me! Can't make it stick, eh? Well, we'll see!' He reached for the telephone on his desk. He glared coldly at Mr Piper as he said, 'Give me Martinson . . . Hello? Martinson? As of this minute you are head teller. Go tally out Piper's cash!'

A Gazetteer of British Ghosts 50p
Peter Underwood

In the British Isles there are more ghosts seen, reported and believed in than anywhere else in the world . . .

In his thirty years' study of the subject, Peter Underwood has come across hundreds of fascinating, gruesome and chilling apparitions, both famous and obscure, which he here records.

From Abbots Langley to Woodstock, from the racing ghost in cap and goggles to the ghastly headless horses dragging a headless man, this gazetteer gives you the history, appearance and powers of the ghosts of Britain – and the nearest inns and hotels at which to stay, for those brave enough to investigate . . .

'Guaranteed to set the reader running his finger down the index, fearing the worst about some of the buildings he knows and frequents' SPECTATOR

You can buy this and other Pan books from booksellers and newsagents; or direct from the following address:
Pan Books, Cavaye Place, London SW10 9PG
Send purchase price plus 15p for the first book and 5p for each additional book, to allow for postage and packing

While every effort is made to keep prices low, it is sometimes necessary to increase prices at short notice. Pan Books reserve the right to show on covers new retail prices which may differ from those advertised in the text or elsewhere